A Scent of Lilac

Frances G. McCoy

Dedication

To all the women on whose shoulders
I have stood and for all the women
who stand on mine.

Chapter 1 - 1973

"Mabel, wake up." Nurse Duncan shook a sleepy Mabel. Dragging herself from her dreams, Mabel rubbed the sleep out of her eyes. Seeing Nurse Duncan drove some of the weariness from her body, but she was still tired nonetheless. Her limbs were slow to respond.

"I'm awake," she said, trying to stifle a yawn.

Her friend Sammie hopped back and forth in agitation, holding onto two suitcases. "It's about time," she said. "We've gotta get outta here."

The clock above the gray door of Mabel's room showed it was 4:30 in the morning. Through her fogginess, she tried to comprehend what was going on. Shouting voices echoed from the hall as the Pleasant Meadows hospital staff rushed past her door.

"Hurry up and get dressed." Nurse Duncan tossed Mabel her clothes. "We don't have much time."

Mabel threw off her covers and dressed in her usual black wool skirt and white Oxford shirt. She slipped into her flats, briefly regarding Sammie who wore a similar outfit. 'How strange.' Mabel was used to seeing her friend in terribly mismatched, brightly colored clothing. Why was Sammie dressed this way?

Sticking her head out the door, Nurse Duncan waited a beat for the hallway to clear, then raced in the opposite direction of the commotion. The two girls followed with equal haste to the service elevator near the activity room. Once inside, Sammie frantically pushed the descend button as if it would speed up the slow-moving car.

'Where the heck are we going . . . and why are we in such a hurry?'

"Go to the basement and wait for me," Nurse Duncan said. "If you don't see me in fifteen minutes, Sammie, take Mabel to the loading dock like I showed you last week. And whatever you do, don't get caught."

"Got it," Sammie said as the elevator doors closed.

When the elevator came to a bumpy stop in the basement, Sammie thrust a suitcase to Mabel. Steam hissed from the overhead pipes as they swiftly made their way through the maze of hallways. Sammie's familiarity with the darkened hallways surprised Mabel, never hesitating as she led them to the pitch-black room where they were to wait for Nurse Duncan.

"Ready for your adventure?" Sammie said.

"Where are we going?"

Sammie put a finger on her lips, silencing her, then pulled Mabel into the darkness of the room. Mabel held her breath as they heard work boots running by their location. Warm adrenaline pumped through her veins, burning off the lethargy in her muscles. She was ready to fight off any potential attacker.

"Did you see them?"

"No, but I swear I saw them get on the elevator."

Mabel recognized the voices of the security guards from her floor.

"I bet they're hiding in the soldiers' ward. You know how much Sammie loved sneaking up there."

"I'll radio the nurses' station and tell them the basement is clear."

The ding of the elevator interrupted the men's conversation. Hoping it would be Nurse Duncan coming to get them, the girls gripped each other's hands tightly when they heard Dr. Gilbert's voice.

"Where are they?"

"We checked down here and they ain't here."

"Check again."

"Boss . . ."

"Check again. Do you have a problem with that?"

Heavy boots stomped in the opposite direction. Holding as still as they could to not give away their hiding spot, the girls listened for an indication of which direction Dr. Gilbert might have gone. Mabel nearly screamed when she heard the men yelling they found someone. Shoes echoed on the concrete floor as the guards dragged whomever they found back in their direction. Mabel was certain her heart was beating loud enough for everyone to hear. Surely this nervous, involuntary beating in her chest would give away their location to Dr. Gilbert.

"Get your hands off me."

"Nurse Duncan, what are you doing down here?" Dr. Gilbert asked.

"Looking for the girls," she said.

"Looking for them or helping them to escape?"

"What are you implying, Dr. Gilbert?"

"I'm saying I know what you've been doing. This is the last time you will be interfering with my research."

"I don't know a thing about your research. I was told to look for two missing patients, and that's exactly what I'm doing."

"But I told Stephanie to assign you to the soldiers' ward on the ninth floor. What are you doing in the basement?"

"I thought I saw them heading down here."

"Tie her up so she cannot interfere. Keep looking for the girls. Do not let them escape. I don't want to explain to Robert Flanigan how I lost his daughter before her conversion therapy was completed. Especially after he paid such a handsome price for a compliant child."

Mabel couldn't have heard that correctly. *'No.'* Her father was the reason she was stuck in this hellhole? How could he do this to her? Sammie wrapped her arms firmly around Mabel, effectively keeping her from charging at Dr. Gilbert in a blind rage.

The girls heard duct tape being torn from a roll. The muffled sounds told them the men had put a piece over Nurse Duncan's mouth.

"Grab her feet," one of the security guards said.

They heard a scuffle, then silence. The girls stayed huddled together for several more tense moments until Sammie whispered in her ear, "Let's go."

Mabel did her best to keep up, but her sluggish muscles made it a challenge. The adrenaline she felt earlier had disappeared. Now it took a great effort to stay on her feet. After running into dead ends twice, Sammie finally found the way to the loading dock. She opened the squeaky door as quietly as she could and they tiptoed out onto the dock. Mabel saw a white van covered with dozens of stickers on the backdoor panels parked at the end of the loading dock.

The girls broke into a sprint with their suitcases bouncing against their legs. They were almost to the van when the squeak of the door signaled someone was following them.

"There they are!" Dr. Gilbert said.

Sammie and Mabel opened the side panel of the van with a jerk, tossed their suitcases in, and scrambled inside. Mabel did not recognize the two strangers sitting in the front seats in the van. The girls crashed against the back seat as the driver smashed the accelerator to the floor. Tires squealing, they fishtailed out of the loading dock area and raced toward the delivery exit. Police cars with flashing lights sped through the entrance of Pleasant Meadows, paying no attention to the van leaving the facility. Mabel looked out a side window and saw a red-faced Dr. Gilbert placed in handcuffs and shoved into the back seat of one of the cars.

"Mabel, these are my cousins, Mack and Claire," Sammie said. "Well, second cousins actually. My mom grew up with them."

"Hello," Mabel managed, struggling to find her voice after that ordeal. "What's going on?"

"We escaped PMS and hopefully that quack Dr. Gilbert will be rotting in jail."

"Sammie, watch your language."

"Sorry, Mack. You don't know what it was like in there."

Mabel studied the driver. She was glad he didn't have facial hair like most of the staff at the hospital. She caught his blue eyes looking at her in the mirror and thought he looked vaguely familiar, but with her memory loss, it was hard to tell if she would have known him at some earlier time. His fingernails were spotted with grease and he wore some type of uniform that strained against the muscles in his arms. He looked to be as tall as her younger brother, Bobby, but it was hard to tell from where she was sitting in the back seat.

"I'm sorry we're meeting under such stressful circumstances," Claire said. She was a beautiful woman with a long neck and a round face. Her dark brunette hair was pulled back into a loose bun with several wisps of hair falling out of it. She was on the thin side with a tailored tan pantsuit fitting perfectly against her body, but it was her eyes that captivated Mabel. She'd only seen green eyes like Claire's once before.

It was those eyes that had landed her in a mental hospital.

Chapter 2 - 1973

Mabel and Sammie sat in the back of the white van, driving away from the institution.

"Can we get out of these disgusting clothes soon?" Sammie asked.

"That's our first stop," Mack said.

Mabel was glad she was finally away from that awful place. The recent snow covering the fields and trees in a fluffy white blanket was impossible to see in the dark hours of the morning, but she felt the chill in the air even with the heater going full blast. She sat with hunched shoulders and hung her head as she thought of Nurse Duncan and how she wasn't able to escape with them. She'd been the one staff member who made the mental institution bearable and Mabel couldn't help feeling guilty. Nurse Duncan had created the distraction so she and Sammie could leave. Her heart tore at the inevitability that those men had hurt her when she confronted Dr. Gilbert.

Mabel's eyes began to close as she listened to the steady hum of the tires on the paved road. Fighting the tiredness in her body, she tried to concentrate on the conversation between Sammie and her cousins. She had several questions but couldn't will her mouth to ask them.

As she leaned her head against the window, a sign indicated Wheatonville ahead. They were heading towards home, back to her family, only she couldn't go back there. Her dad would just send her back to Pleasant Meadows to finish her conversion therapy.

"What's wrong?" Claire asked.

"I can't go back to Wheatonville."

"We're not taking you there," Mack said.

"Then where are we going?"

Sammie grabbed Mabel's hand and tenderly told her, "Someplace the likes of Dr. Gillfish and your dad will never find us."

Mabel tried to fight off the beginning of a migraine by steadying her breathing. It had been weeks since her last one. The debilitating headaches were a constant reminder of her father's betrayal.

"Mack, pull into the next truck stop," Claire said.

"Are you sure? I wanted to put more distance between us and the hospital."

"I'm sure," Claire said, looking back at Mabel.

Ten minutes later, Mack pulled the van behind two semi-trailers hiding it from the view of the road. Mabel thought it was silly to be so cautious because Dr. Gilbert had been arrested. Who cared about them now besides her father, who didn't even know she'd escaped?

"Girls, you can change here."

"Come on," Sammie said, grabbing her suitcase.

Mabel followed her to the bathroom on the outside of the building. They squeezed into the cramped space where Sammie threw her bag on the sink and told Mabel to stand by the toilet. In under five minutes, Sammie had transformed. She wore dungarees, a flannel shirt, and leather work boots. Gone was the colorful outfit Mabel was used to seeing, but this outfit seemed more like the real Sammie. These clothes looked more natural on her; the normally guarded look Sammie wore on her face disappeared when she saw herself in the small, rusted mirror over the tiny sink.

"Wow, you look different," Mabel said.

"Yeah, this is the real me." Sammie stuffed her discarded outfit in the overflowing trash can. "I figured the more outrageous outfits I wore at PMS, the less Dr. Gillfish would bother me. Okay, your turn."

The girls switched places and Mabel opened her bag, unsure what she'd find inside. A knock on the door startled them as Mabel pulled a pair of jeans out of the suitcase.

"Girls, are you ready? We have to leave now."

She heard the urgency in Claire's voice and wondered what had happened. She quickly dressed and stuffed her clothes into the suitcase, nodding to Sammie that she was ready to go. Sammie opened the door a tiny crack, looking to see if it was safe to leave. Mabel ran after Sammie back to the van.

"What's wrong, Mack?" Sammie asked.

"You two have been reported missing and in about ten minutes there will be cops all over this area."

Mack sped out of the parking lot and turned right at the next stoplight. From the opposite direction, a highway patrol car hurtled past. Everyone held their breath to see if the car would turn around and come after them.

Mabel tore her attention away from the sun appearing on the horizon. They pulled into an abandoned gas station with only a station wagon and another vehicle sitting with its engine running.

"I thought you would need to say goodbye before we left," Claire said.

A tall, muscular figure stepped out of the driver's side of the running car. In the faint gray light, Mabel watched as he put a baseball cap on backward and strutted towards them. Her heart jumped to her throat when she realized the shadowy figure belonged to her brother. She jumped out of the van and crashed into him.

"Well, Mayflower, it looks like you're going to have your California adventure after all."

"What are you talking about?"

"Mack and Claire are taking you to California. Far away from the clutches of our father."

"I can't go with these strangers, Bobby. What will I do without you? What about Bonnie?"

"You have to go because we know when Dad finds out you've escaped, he'll just throw you back in there. You can trust Mack and Claire. They're good people. Mack was my boss."

"I don't understand why your boss would be helping me," Mabel said. Folding her arms across her chest, she waited for further explanation from her brother.

"We don't have time for me to explain," Bobby said. "You need to leave. Now!"

Mabel dropped her arms in frustration. Bobby was right about their dad, but Mabel still struggled with why Bobby wouldn't give her any explanation. This couldn't be the only solution. Bobby handed her a package telling her it was something to help her start her new life. The honk of the horn let them know their time was up. They hugged in a tight embrace; neither wanted to be the first to let go.

"I love you, sis. If I thought there was another way to keep you safe, I'd do it in a heartbeat."

"I love you. little brother. Thanks for protecting me."

"Come on, Mabel," Sammie said impatiently out the window.

"I need a favor, Bobby. If Bonnie comes looking for me, tell her where I am."

"Are you sure?"

"I love her. Even though I can't remember what happened between us, that's the one thing I do remember. I left something for her in the cabin. Make sure she gets it. Promise me."

"I will."

Mabel turned to head back to the van, but it had been moved while she was talking to Bobby. She spun around in confusion until she saw Sammie waving to her from the back of the station wagon. Mabel gave Bobby one more hug. She wasn't sure if she'd ever see him again. He'd been her rock and now it felt like it had been smashed into gravel. She waved goodbye as she got in the car, staring out the back window until she could no longer see him standing there.

"Ladies, we're going to put as much distance between us and Pleasant Meadows as we can. I think for tonight, Oklahoma will be a good place to stop."

"Sounds good to me," Sammie said. "We can drive all night long if you want."

Mabel should've been excited about going to California, but this wasn't the way she pictured it. She thought this would be a trip she'd make with

Bonnie as they set out to create a life together.

"You're quiet, Mabel," Sammie said.

"I was thinking about Nurse Duncan."

"I'm sure the police have everything under control."

"I hope so. She was the only one who didn't think we were sexual deviants."

"That's because we're not."

"Dr. Gilbert said we were."

"Dr. Gillfish is a quack and you should forget everything he ever said to you."

"Sammie's right, Mabel. There's nothing wrong with you," Claire said.

* * *

"Where is your sister, Bobby?"

"I don't know, Dad. Last I knew, she was in that hellhole you threw her in. Don't tell me you lost her," he said, goading his father.

Bobby could tell his dad thought he was behind Mabel's disappearance from the hospital since he'd kept the vital information from him for months that Mabel was no longer in a coma. Bobby was unaware of the relationship between his father and Dr. Gilbert.

"Your sister is not well and needs help."

Bobby slammed down the hood of the car he was working on, almost smashing his dad's fingers. The fact his dad knew Mabel escaped was not good news. How had he found out so quickly?

Bobby struggled to control his rising temper. The last thing he wanted was to lash out in anger or say something he would regret. His sister needed him to keep his cool.

"You will not act that way toward your father."

"*My father* wouldn't try to cut out my sister's brain just because he disagreed with her sexuality. Now get the hell out of my garage so I can go back to work. And leave me the hell alone. If you come in here again, I'll have you arrested for trespassing." Bobby spun on his heel and stomped into his office. He braced himself against the door praying his sister would make it safely to California without their father's knowledge.

Chapter 3 - 1970

The red, orange and yellow streamers limply hung from the ceiling dragged down by the stuffiness of the gym, long ago losing the decorative fashion. The decorations on the wall clung desperately to the last stickiness of the tape that held them in place. Corrine and Mabel waited in line at the refreshment table to get a glass of lukewarm punch.

"Who's that?" asked Mabel's best friend Corrine, "He's gorgeous."

It took Mabel a moment to pull her attention away from the beautiful brown-haired girl being escorted through the gymnasium doors by a tall boy in a letterman's jacket to focus on what Corrine had said.

"I guess so."

Her attention was drawn back to the girl. All Mabel could see was her eyes. It didn't matter that the music was blaring from the worn-out speakers and her friends were trying to get her attention from the dance floor. Those eyes held Mabel's entire gaze. She had never seen such beauty—not in a magazine and certainly not in this town where most of the women had faces like worn shoe leather.

The athletic boy and the beauty made their way to the refreshment line where Mabel and Corrine were standing. Mabel became aware of her palms, sticky with the overly sweetened punch. She almost dropped her cup as a pair of jade-green eyes regarded her through the longest lashes she'd ever seen.

"How's the punch?" asked the boy. Mabel could only stare at him. She knew he was saying something because his lips were moving, but his words made no sense. Corrine gave her a nudge on the arm.

"Ex . . . Ex . . . Excuse me?"

"I asked about the punch. Judging by your reaction it's so good it leaves you speechless, or so bad you're trying to find a polite way to tell me not to drink it." The group started laughing. Nothing had ever sounded as sweet as this beautiful girl's laugh.

"Hi. I'm Charles and this is my girlfriend, Bonnie."

It was a lovely name for the curvy, wavy-haired brunette returning her stare. Mabel's cheeks warmed when Bonnie smiled at her.

"I'm Corrine and the one who's forgotten how to speak is Mabel. Welcome to Wheatonville's Fall Harvest Dance. Are you new students?"

"We just transferred from Kingsville this week. Haven't made it to any classes yet," Charles said. "Our dads work together and decided to move their business to Wheatonville. We heard about the dance tonight and thought it would be a good place to meet people without those first-day-of-class jitters."

"Wel . . . welcome," Mabel finally sputtered.

"Would you care to dance?" Charles asked Bonnie.

Mabel watched as Bonnie slipped her hand so easily into Charles's outstretched palm. She admired the girl's long, thin fingers, imagining how they might feel wrapped around her own. The swaying of Bonnie's hips as she let Charles lead her to the dance floor reminded Mabel of the perfect rhythm of the metronome on the piano at home. After wiping her sticky hands on a napkin, she carefully refilled her punch cup and went to sit on an empty folding chair. *Just look away.'* But she couldn't. Bonnie moved to the music with mesmerizing grace. The other girls looked like dancing tree stumps as Bonnie twirled effortlessly around the floor in a fast dance.

Her reverie was broken by Jay, one of her best friends since third grade. She was supposed to be his date for the dance, but Mabel had no interest in dating. She'd only agreed to go with him because she liked to dance, and he was a good dancer. As he plopped down beside her, she tried not to gag from the woodsy menthol smell of his aftershave.

"Girl, what on earth are you doing sitting here? I can't remember the last time you weren't out there in the middle of the dance floor. Come on."

He grabbed Mabel by the arm and dragged her to an open space on the floor. She lost herself in the music, letting it swirl inside her body. When the musical notes reached her muscles, they responded in the most coordinated and complicated movements. She was a favorite partner at school dances, but her usual coordination disappeared as Bonnie and Charles came back into view, twirling together on the floor. Now Mabel danced in molasses. Her dexterity evaporated, causing her to stumble when Bonnie brushed by her in the middle of a spin. When the band switched to a slower song, Mabel begged to get off the dance floor with Jay.

"Mabe, what's wrong?" he asked, following her out of the building into the cool autumn night.

"Nothing. I just needed some fresh air. It's pretty stuffy in there." She inhaled deeply, catching a whiff of burning leaves in a neighbor's yard.

"Uh-huh. I don't believe you. You never needed fresh air at a dance before tonight. What's going on?"

"Well, tonight I need it. Do you have a problem with that?"

"Don't get all huffy with me. I was just checking to make sure you're okay because you're acting a little strange tonight."

"I'm fine, Jay. Go back inside. You shouldn't miss the dance because of me. I heard Becky Lewis asking about you earlier."

"Ah, Mabe, you don't have to be jealous. Becky's just a friend." He bumped his shoulder into her and quirked his lips in a teasing grin.

"I'm not jealous, and anyone can see she wants to be more than your friend. Go back inside. I'll come back as soon as I get some air."

"You sure? I can hang out here with you for a couple more minutes."

"I'm sure. Don't keep Becky waiting."

"Mabe, she isn't the one I came to the dance with tonight, and she's not the one I want to date." He gently kissed Mabel's cheek and went back inside, leaving her to her thoughts.

I have no interest in going out with you or anyone else in this town.' Foolishly, Jay held out hope one day Mabel would return his feelings, but she had big plans for her future. She was going to college to become an astronomer. Allowing Jay or anyone else to trap her in Wheatonville wasn't an option.

Mabel walked along the dirt path in the back of the old red-brick gymnasium where the dance was being held. She reached over the fence that led to the darkened cinder track and football field. She unlatched the gate and slowly climbed to the top of the old, rickety aluminum bleachers that sat at the edge of the field. Stretching out carefully against the cold metal seat, she stared up into the starlit night. Mabel loved watching the radiance of the stars brighten the darkened canvas of the nighttime sky. As she found the Big Dipper, she felt her stomach somersault as she thought of green eyes staring at her across the refreshment table. She remembered the excitement she felt when Bonnie had almost touched her on the dance floor and how her feet almost got tangled with Jay's.

She could still smell Bonnie's enchanting spicy citrus perfume enveloping her and still hear the sound of her laughter. Images of Bonnie continued to fill Mabel's mind: the seductive quality of her dancing, the fullness of her lips, and the roundness of her breasts. What would it be like to French-kiss this exotic beauty?

The physical excitement the images induced was quickly dashed by guilt. *'I can't be having these thoughts about another girl. If anyone found out I was thinking about a girl like this, I would be locked away. My parents would think I was possessed and try to have the demon driven from me. My dad would be more than happy to drive the devil away himself with his favorite leather belt. I can't give him another excuse to punish me.'* Mabel tried to wish away the mental images of the beautiful brunette, but they became more vivid as she continued staring at the stars.

"What am I going to do?"

"About what?"

Mabel screamed and barely stopped herself from rolling off the bleacher seat. She had been daydreaming about Bonnie, and now the girl stood before her in the flesh. Heat assaulted Mabel's cheeks despite the cool autumn night. She tried not to squirm from the scrutiny of Bonnie's eyes.

"Sorry about that," Bonnie said. "I called your name a couple of times, but I guess you didn't hear me."

"Uh . . . yeah, I guess I didn't."

"Do I make you nervous?"

Mabel looked at Bonnie. Was this new girl aware of all the sinful thoughts running through her mind? Even now, she couldn't stop thinking about kissing the lips that were twisted into a teasing smile.

"Sorry, I'm being a total idiot."

"Well, not a total idiot. I think it's cute listening to you try to put together a coherent sentence." Bonnie smiled up at Mabel as she moved to sit down beside her on the bleachers. "Actually, I came looking for you."

"You did? Why?" She couldn't rationalize why she felt so nervous around Bonnie, but she was fully aware of the butterfly convention gathering in her stomach and beyond as Bonnie moved closer to her on the bleacher seat. Mabel's body betrayed her as she leaned into the empty space between them.

"Bonnie, do you ever feel different?"

"What do you mean?"

"I mean, do you ever get the feeling like you're not like everyone else? That there might be something . . . wrong with you?"

Heat flamed from her cheeks as Bonnie closed the distance between them. Mabel stared at her teasing red lips. She closed her eyes to stop her runaway thoughts, but her mind could only focus on the fire in her leg where Bonnie sat pressed against her on the bleachers. The smell of Bonnie's citrusy perfume spun her mind in a dizzying circle. Looking at her did not help her addled brain, either. The next thing Mabel knew, her insides exploded in tiny electrical shocks when Bonnie grabbed her hand, wrapping surprisingly strong fingers around her sticky and sweaty palm.

"Mabel? Is something wrong? You don't look so good." The back of Bonnie's hand swiped across her forehead. "You're a little warm. Are you feeling ill?"

"I'm . . . I'm . . . I'm fine," Mabel managed to choke out from the sluggishness of her brain and the thickness of her tongue. Everywhere Bonnie touched sent her senses into fiery overload. Bonnie's hand moved from her forehead to her cheek. As she brushed the pad of her thumb over Mabel's bottom lip, Mabel held her breath. Then slowly, Bonnie dipped her head closer to her face.

"There you two are! We wondered where you'd disappeared to."

Mabel sucked in a breath at the interruption from Jay and the others. She moved away from Bonnie and a sudden chill went through her as her connection to Bonnie was severed.

"Mabel was just telling me about the stars," Bonnie said as the group got comfortable on the bleachers.

"Oh, Bonnie, please don't think we're all like Mabel. I hope she didn't get too crazy pointing out all the constellations. She's probably excited to have a new audience," Corrine said.

"I didn't mind at all," Bonnie said, giving Mabel a lopsided grin.

Charles bent down to kiss her. "Well, I have to say that's something different for you to talk about."

Mabel had to turn away from the scene, desperate for anything else to focus on. Charles was doing the very thing she had nearly done with Bonnie moments before everyone showed up. It wasn't fair. She could still feel where Bonnie's breath had tickled her cheek and her thumb had moved over her lip.

Jay scooted closer to Mabel and draped his arm—possessively—around her shoulder. He tried to kiss her, but she turned her head so his lips only found her hair. It was all Mabel could do not to push him away in disgust.

"You guys wanna get out of here?" Corrine said. "The dance is almost over anyway."

"We can go to Daisy's Diner," Corrine's boyfriend, Oscar, said.

"Bonnie, do you and Charles want to join us?" Corrine gave them an expectant look.

"Will you be coming?" Bonnie asked Mabel.

"Mabel?" Jay asked in a louder voice.

Ten eyes stared at her, waiting for a response. "Sure, if everyone else is going. Just remember I have to be home by eleven. I can't be late again, Jay. You know how my dad is when I miss curfew." Mabel didn't want to think about how her dad would react if she was late tonight.

"Great. Charles, do you mind? I really would love to hang out with our new friends."

"Anything for my baby." Charles swept Bonnie up from the bleacher seat and pulled her into another kiss. This one was longer and more passionate than the first.

As Mabel watched Bonnie close her eyes and wrap her arms around his neck, she fought to keep the contents of her stomach from coming up. She had no right to feel jealous over a girl she'd just met—over *any* girl—but she did.

She jumped up and ran down the steps before she could do something really stupid and start crying in front of all of them. The group yelled at her to wait for them, but Mabel kept walking.

Chapter 4 - 1970

After Charles dropped her off, Bonnie walked into her house and heard her parents waiting for her in the living room. She wasn't surprised they'd waited up, but she wasn't in the mood to share the details of her first social event in her new school. Still, she knew it would be rude not to talk with them before heading to bed. With a sigh of resignation, she plastered a smile on her face and walked into the living room.

"How was the dance, sweetie?" her father asked as he got up to turn off the television.

"It was groovy."

"Did you make any new friends?" her mother asked hopefully. Of course, the new friends her mother wanted her to make were totally different than the ones she'd made tonight. Her mother was a world-class snob, having been born into money, and she expected her daughter to follow in her footsteps by making friends with the *right* people. She even picked out the boys for Bonnie to date.

"I met a few people," she said vaguely. It was 1970, the start of a new decade, and she believed she had the right to make her own friends, starting with that awkward, skinny blonde girl named Mabel, with eyes as blue as the ocean.

"Did Charles have a good time?"

Ever since her parents had deemed Charles a worthy suitor for her, they'd been more involved in her social life. She missed the days when they were both so busy they didn't have time to constantly check on her activities.

"I guess so. He didn't really say." After faking a yawn to end the interrogation, Bonnie bid them good night.

As Bonnie brushed her teeth, she recalled Mabel's flustered behavior around her that evening. She had noticed her staring at her as they walked over to the refreshment table at the dance. She watched Mabel as she poured punch all over her hand. Smiling as she spit out the toothpaste, she knew Mabel was just the type of girl her mother didn't want her to have as a friend. That was too bad because Mabel was exactly the kind of girl Bonnie wanted to get to know better.

Her parents didn't know it but, before they moved to Wheatonville, she had been sneaking out to go to the clubs in Chicago with her friends. She looked older than sixteen, and her fake ID wasn't always examined closely in those smoky clubs.

While out with her friends one night, they talked about going to a new club that played more than just the popular disco music. They drove to The Hideout. It was hard to tell it was a club by the outside; it blended in so well with its brick wall surroundings. There was only a small sign in the window pointing to the entrance down a set of concrete steps. A hideout indeed. After the man at the door gave her ID a cursory glance, the first thing Bonnie noticed was the thumping bass and flashing lights. Then she spotted the couples dancing. She'd never before seen women intimately dancing and was excited by the way their bodies moved together.

As she crawled into bed, she wondered what it would be like to take Mabel to The Hideout. She lifted her sketchpad from the nightstand and thumbed through some of her drawings. Bonnie had an urge to capture Mabel's image before she fell asleep. As she quickly drew several lines of her face, the image started to take shape. Try as she might, she couldn't quite capture Mabel's eyes. Bonnie heard the harsh criticism of her mother ring in her head as she stared at the image she'd drawn.

'This little hobby of yours is a waste of time. No one is interested in your trivial drawings. Such mundane tasks are beneath you, Bonnie Jean. Your job is to buy great works of art, not to create them.'

Blinking back her tears of frustration, she recalled the way Mabel's eyes lit up as she talked about the stars. The moonlight had streamed down onto the bleachers with the two of them lost in easy conversation. The desire to touch and kiss Mabel coursed through her veins. Bonnie remembered the feeling of Mabel's leg pressed against hers, the heat of her skin, and the softness of her lips. She was devastated to have been interrupted just as she was about to kiss those soft lips.

Mabel had withdrawn after that. At the diner, Bonnie tried to engage her in conversation, but she only responded in one or two-word answers. She eventually gave up as the boys dominated the rest of the evening with talk of sports, cars, and movies.

Instead, she had turned her attention to Corrine. She discovered she had a lot in common with the friendly girl. Corrine offered to show Bonnie around Wheatonville, which earned a scoff out of Mabel. Bonnie asked if Mabel would like to join them, but she turned down the invitation.

The evening had ended too soon. Mabel had become anxious about her curfew, finally dragging Jay out of the diner mid-conversation. When Bonnie questioned the abrupt departure, all Corrine said was Mabel had a strict father. They said their goodbyes, and then Charles drove her home.

Bonnie put away her sketchpad and turned off the lights, but sleep was elusive. She kept thinking about the blue-eyed girl and her question about being different. Mabel was having an internal conflict over something important, and even though Bonnie suspected what it might be, she wasn't sure she was the best person to help with her struggle.

Chapter 5 - 1970

Mabel never felt more alive than at this moment. She whistled on her way to the drugstore where she worked as a part-time cashier, feeling lucky to have a job. It was her ticket out of this town. The money she saved would pay for college, preferably a university far away from Wheatonville. She dreamed of a life filled with great adventure, none of which she could see happening if she stuck around here.

It was a perfect autumn day. The sun played hide-and-seek in the billowy white clouds, dancing across the sky like dandelion seeds. The birds were singing songs of the harvests to come. Mabel loved autumn. The crispness in the morning air brought a rosy color to her cheeks. It was hard to tell if the redness was from the cool temperatures or from memories of that night a few weeks ago—images of a dancing Bonnie, the sensation of her touch forever burned to her lips. She could recall every minute detail, especially anytime she was near Bonnie.

Mabel took a shortcut through the alley running behind Mrs. Winterstein's house and stopped to watch a couple of rabbits eating their breakfast—Mrs. Winterstein's dahlias. "You better eat fast. I hear Mrs. Winterstein has a taste for rabbit." She chuckled as the rabbits looked up, twitching their noses at her in response.

Mabel tilted her head toward the sun before it hid again behind the clouds. She felt like dancing today. She had woken up this morning with dreams about dancing with Bonnie still running in her head; the vivid image of Bonnie kept her company on her walk to work. Mabel wondered how Bonnie would feel in her arms dancing across a big ballroom. In her dream, their bodies fit perfectly together, and Mabel led her effortlessly across the dance floor. Bonnie moved elegantly across the floor like a feather blowing in the wind, clad in a flowing white evening dress that floated around her like cotton candy. Mabel wore a black tuxedo, complete with tails and a top hat. Other people stopped dancing just to watch their graceful movements as they pirouetted across the floor.

Mabel felt so light and free today. Her happiness was bursting at the seams and it just had to find a release. Dancing into the back door of the drugstore, she clocked in for her shift. She pulled on her smock and adjusted her name tag as she went to the office to count in her drawer.

Time ticked by like drops of water clinging to a faucet as long as gravity would allow. She'd already straightened all the shelves in the entire store and was now trying to will the clock to move faster so she could take her lunch break. Mabel had spent most of the morning thinking about a pair of green eyes and a little pert nose with freckles. She was thrilled when the pharmacist said she could go on break early. She'd brought her homework along to finish during her lunch break. She was behind in her reading and needed to catch up so she didn't have to waste an entire Sunday finishing it before class came again on Monday.

Fifteen minutes later, Mabel was trying to memorize important battle dates from the Civil War for her history test on Monday when she heard her name over the PA system. She was being paged. Mabel slammed her history book shut in frustration and crammed the rest of her sandwich in her mouth before answering the page. Rushing to the front of the store, she saw Corrine flipping impatiently through the magazines in the rack by the front doors.

"There you are. What happened to you last night? You were supposed to meet us at the football game."

Corrine finally took a breath so Mabel could tell her that her dad wouldn't let her go to the game since she missed her curfew after the dance.

"Yeah," Corrine said. "I thought it might have been something like that. We missed you."

"What's up? I was trying to get caught up on my homework before I have to go back to work."

Corrine told her she came by to see if Mabel wanted to go to the movies after work. "Bonnie and I were thinking about a triple date."

Mabel's heart fluttered at the sound of Bonnie's name. The idea of spending more time with her filled her with joy. She pushed down her excitement, not wanting to raise Corrine's curiosity or make her feel jealous of their new friend.

"I'd have to check with my mom first. I might still be in trouble with my dad."

"I already did that for you. Here. She told me to give you these." Corrine handed Mabel a paper sack containing a set of clothes for her to change into after work. "She said to tell you to be sure to be home by eleven tonight. Jay is going to pick you up when your shift ends."

"Great," Mabel said. "Just what I need. Now he's going to think it's a date."

"What's wrong with that? It *is* a date. You act like going on a date is the worst thing in the world."

"Corrine, I've tried to tell you I'm not like every other girl in this town. I don't want to get married and pop out a brood of grandkids for my parents. Despite what my dad thinks, my dream of going to college isn't ridiculous. I'm going to be an astronomer."

"I'm sure you will, Mabel, but I don't see why you can't loosen up and have some fun along the way. What's the harm in going on a couple of dates? Jay is one of your best friends."

"Exactly. He's a *friend*. I know he wants more, but I'm not interested."

With an exasperated sigh, Corrine put the magazine she had been flipping through back on the rack and turned to go. "Later, gator," she said as she headed off to finish running errands for her mother.

As much as Mabel loved her best friend, she often didn't understand her, least of all Corrine's ideas on dating. She knew Corrine wanted to get married one day, but Mabel had no desire to be tied to the outdated notion of a woman needing a man—not when there were so many new opportunities opening up for women in this new decade.

* * *

Mabel glanced at the front door when she heard the entrance bell signaling another customer. With a greeting ready to roll off her lips, she saw Jay stroll through the door. Letting another cashier greet him, she ignored him and went back to ringing up her customer. As Mabel placed Mrs. Johnstone's items into a bag, Jay snuck up behind her and planted a kiss on her cheek.

"Hi, beautiful."

"Jay, I'm a little busy right now. Why don't you wait outside for me? I still have fifteen minutes left."

"Nah, I have some shopping to do first."

"Fine, then go shop and let me take care of my customers." Mrs. Johnstone gave her a smile and Mabel blushed. *'Great. Now everyone will think we are dating. I could punch Jay.'* The afternoon had seen a steady increase in customers, and Mabel had been kept busy ringing up purchases for the last couple of hours. She liked being busy. It kept her mind from wandering down dangerous paths.

Jay left so she could check out the people who had been patiently waiting in line. The last ten minutes flew by as she rang up each customer's purchases with practiced ease. Mabel was a fast, friendly, efficient cashier. Her boss had once told her she was one of his best workers, even better than some of his full-time staff. When the last person in her line had been rung up, she pulled her cash drawer and went to find Jay.

She found him in the aftershave and cologne aisle. She prayed he wasn't buying something for their outing tonight. Mabel couldn't bring herself to think of it as a date. Jay had an unfortunate tendency to think the more cologne he wore, the better it made him smell.

"I have to count my drawer before we go. It should take about ten minutes. I'm not going to change into what my mom sent with Corrine. She has no clue about what I like."

"Mabe, don't worry. You look fine in what you're wearing. Better than fine," he said, looking her up and down with a lopsided grin.

Spinning away from him in frustration, Mabel stomped to the office to cash out for the night. *Why does he always have to act like that? I never give him any encouragement to think we are more than friends.*

As she thought about their plans for the evening, Mabel looked in the bag Corrine had brought her earlier. Hearing Bonnie was coming with them made her unsure if she should change clothes after all. Mabel usually didn't care how she looked when she went out. Comfort was always more important to her than being fashionable. She wasn't sure she liked the thought of worrying about her appearance.

Inside the paper sack was her favorite shirt she wore for special occasions. She couldn't make her nervous fingers work to button it correctly; it took three times before she was able to fasten it properly. Looking at her reflection in the small mirror over the sink, she decided to take her hair out of the usual ponytail and comb it out.

Fifteen minutes later, Mabel and Jay walked out of the drugstore together. They decided to eat before meeting everyone at the movies, so they walked across the street to the other restaurant in town. It wasn't as good as Daisy's Diner, but it was a little cheaper. Jay had worked all summer with his dad and uncle doing construction and managed to save most of his money to help get him through football season. Mabel knew Jay would like to take her out without their friends always tagging along, but she really didn't want to encourage him.

Sitting at a booth in the back, Jay filled Mabel in on the rest of last night's football game. Jay was the starting cornerback. He was quick and had quite a knack for knowing where the ball was going to be and led the team in interceptions. Their season had only begun a few weeks ago.

"Charles is going to make us state champs, Mabe. The guy has a rocket for an arm and he's on target with most of his passes."

"That's nice," Mabel said. She was tired of hearing about Charles's greatness. She couldn't curb her jealousy toward him. He was good-looking, smart, friendly, and most importantly, dating the woman who brought her black-and-white existence into full Technicolor.

"What's wrong with you?"

"Nothing."

"Something's up. You've been acting weird for weeks now."

"No, I haven't."

"Yes, you have. You hardly talk to me anymore or want to hang out with me. Have I done something to make you mad?"

"No, nothing's wrong. Can you just drop it?"

"Geesh. You don't have to bite my head off. I was just trying to talk to you."

"I'm sorry, Jay. I just wish everyone would stop asking me what's wrong when nothing's wrong." Mabel regretted her outburst when she saw the hurt look in his eyes. How could she reveal the truth to him? She knew the pain it would cause and didn't want to hurt him. As much as their friendship meant to her, she would never love him the way he loved her and certainly not enough to marry him.

"How about we split a piece of apple pie à la mode for dessert?" It was Jay's favorite dessert and she knew it would make him happy.

As Mabel and Jay pulled into the parking lot of the movie theater, Mabel's eyes found Bonnie standing by the ticket counter. The strong pull she felt toward Bonnie both excited and terrified her. Mabel spent most of her time at work today trying to figure out what drew her to Bonnie. She felt a switch had been turned on inside from the moment they met. Mabel had read about girls who had romantic feelings for other girls. When she met Bonnie, she knew she must be one of those girls. She kept replaying the moment on the bleachers when they almost kissed. If her friends hadn't interrupted, would Bonnie have gone through with it? And why was the thought of kissing Bonnie a hundred times more appealing than the thought of kissing Jay? By the time they had parked Jay's truck and walked to the front of the theater, Corrine and her boyfriend, Oscar, had joined Charles and Bonnie. The foursome appeared deep in conversation.

"What's going on?" Jay asked.

"We don't know if we really want to see this movie," Oscar said.

"What movie do you want to see?" Mabel asked.

"*A Bullet for the General*," Oscar said.

"What do the two of you want to see?" Mabel asked Bonnie and Corrine.

"*Funny Girl*," Bonnie said.

"Well, why don't you guys go watch the movie you want and we can go see the movie we want, then meet up after. Does that work?" Mabel asked.

"Sounds good to me," Jay said.

Nodding their agreement, the guys purchased the tickets for the group. Mabel hoped she would be able to concentrate on the movie with Bonnie sitting so close and stirring up all of her emotions.

Chapter 6 - 1970

"What are you, a faggot or something?"

The words stung Mabel more than one of her father's backhands. Was she that awful word? She couldn't bear to bring herself to think it, let alone say it out loud. She felt humiliated as the group of girls she thought were her friends laughed and pointed fingers at her, chanting the ugly torment. The gym echoed the words faggot, lesbo, and dyke, and everyone turned to stare at her. *How can they know when I'm not even sure myself?'*

"We see the way you look all cow-eyed at Bonnie," Carla said. Mabel had known Carla her entire life. They'd been in every class together since kindergarten.

"Yeah, it's unnatural and disgusting," said Karen, another long-time friend.

"You even picked her for a square dance partner instead of Jay," Carla said, sticking her finger down her throat, pretending to throw up.

"My daddy says all queers fry in hell. Mabel's going to hell."

More laughter followed. Mabel tried to cover her ears to block out the taunts, but her hands wouldn't move so the taunts kept filling her mind.

"Girls! What's going on?" Mabel sighed in relief as Mrs. Howell, the gym teacher, walked up to the class.

"Mabel's a dyke," Carla said.

"Is that true, Mabel?" asked Mrs. Howell.

"I . . . I don't know. I'm not sure exactly what a dyke is."

The sounds of their mocking laughter increased, and Mabel wanted to run out of the gym. She had to get away, but where would she go? The girls had blocked her exit to the locker room and were surrounding her. Even Mrs. Howell joined in their taunts. Mabel couldn't stop the tears from falling down her face.

"Mabel. Mabel. Wake up. You're going to be late for work."

* * *

Mabel opened her eyes and saw her mother smiling down at her. "You've overslept, honey. You're supposed to be at work in thirty minutes."

Scrambling out of bed, Mabel rushed to get ready for work. She tried to shake the remnants of the dream, but the images burned in her mind. It had been a week since the triple date at the movies, and she was struggling with her growing feelings for Bonnie. Rushing down the stairs, she grabbed the toast her mom had made and ran out the back door. She'd be on time if she ran the whole way there.

"Where's the fire, Mabel?" Mrs. Winterstein asked.

"Late for work." Mabel barely waved as she raced past.

She tried to catch her breath as she ran into the back door of the pharmacy to clock in. Grabbing her side to stop the pain from her sprint to work, Mabel clocked in with two minutes to spare.

"There you are. I was beginning to wonder if you were sick today," the pharmacist said.

"I overslept."

"Get your drawer counted in now. I'm opening the doors."

Mabel quickly counted the money in her cash drawer and hurried to her register. By the time she finished her opening duties, the first customer was ready to be checked out. Mabel froze when she saw it was Carla.

"Hi, Mabel," Carla said.

Mabel mumbled some greetings to her and tried to quickly ring up her purchases. She was still hurt by the awful names Carla called her in her dream.

"Are you okay?"

"Fine. Here's your change." Mabel thrust the coins back to her classmate.

Her nervous fingers tore two paper sacks before she was able to bag Carla's items. She saw the puzzled look on Carla's face but was able to ignore further conversation with her when the next customer set her items on the counter. Mabel released the breath she'd been holding when the bell over the door signaled Carla's exit.

The day's steady stream of customers allowed Mabel to forget about her nightmare. The pharmacy was just one of the many stops the people in Wheatonville made on a Saturday, so she focused her efforts and concentration on getting the customers speedily checked out and on their way to the next errand.

"Why don't you go on break now?" the pharmacist said.

Mabel turned the key in her register to "off" and pocketed it in her smock, then headed to the break room. She really needed something to drink. Out of habit, she stopped to straighten one of the end caps on her way to the back of the store.

"Hello, Mabel."

Mabel jumped back in surprise, almost knocking over the shampoo bottles she'd been arranging. In front of her stood Mrs. Howell, her physical education teacher. It had only been a dream, but she half-expected the woman to cruelly taunt her as she had last night. Mabel's cheeks burned when she met Mrs. Howell's eyes.

"Hello."

"Looks like a busy day here. I hope you get to enjoy the beautiful fall weather we're having."

"Me too. Well, it was nice to see you, Mrs. Howell." Mabel hurried past her to the break room.

She only had five minutes left on her break. Putting a nickel into the vending machine, she hit the button and watched as her can of Coke tumbled down to the dispenser. She pulled the aluminum tab off slowly, so soda wouldn't spray everywhere, then took a long swallow of the sugary drink.

Mabel leaned against the machine. Why would Carla and Mrs. Howell come in today, of all days? If she believed in signs, she would think the universe was telling her something. Did they know about her growing feelings for Bonnie? Could they see how she gave her attention to Bonnie whenever she was around? Those awful names from her dream resounded in her head. Was she really a dyke or lesbo? Mabel needed to talk to someone about all of this. But who? She couldn't talk to her friends because it would be all over school in minutes. She pictured Jay's face when he heard the news—not a pretty sight. He would be angry and wounded, maybe even disgusted with her. A heavy weight settled in her heart as Mabel knew she would lose Jay's friendship over this.

She definitely couldn't talk to her family about this. In the past, her mom avoided her questions about love, and she wasn't interested in giving her dad more reasons to beat her. For the past few weeks, it had seemed any time she was at home she was in trouble. Her dad had a way of finding fault with her chores and then whipping her with his favorite leather belt. His temper was getting worse and she was more often than not on the receiving end of it. She was glad she didn't have physical education classes this semester. There was no way she could hide all the signs of the punishment he had unleashed on her body this past month. It was hard enough keeping all the bruises and welts hidden from her friends, even with the cooler temperatures.

Mabel wouldn't be getting any help from the youth minister at the Baptist church either. She didn't want to hear about sin and praying to take the evil demon from her soul. She might be able to talk to Bonnie about her feelings, but what if it only drove her closer to Charles? Mabel couldn't lose what little time she spent with her.

As she took another drink Mabel felt the whole world weighing on her small shoulders. She'd been telling herself for weeks to concentrate on getting into the astronomy program at UC Berkeley, but even her beloved stars couldn't compete with the emotions Bonnie stirred in her.

Sighing as she tossed the now-empty can into the trash, Mabel left the break room slowly as she walked back to the front of the store. In between the rush of customers, she tried to think of someone she could talk to. It saddened her to conclude there was no one in Wheatonville who could know her dark secret. Not even Bonnie. Mabel was truly alone with the knowledge she was different in a very dangerous way.

Lately, Mabel had been working a lot of hours at the drugstore after school and on weekends. She had to if she had any hope of escaping this tiny town. The money she earned not only helped her save for college and her future, but it would let her leave home.

That night, Mabel, Bonnie, Corrine, and the guys had plans to go to the movies again. Mabel had jumped at the invite when Corrine called about it last night. Her dad had been in a relatively good mood and said she could go. Now, once again, she daydreamed about the curvy brunette. Even as her attraction for Bonnie grew, she was uncertain if she could share her feelings. Maybe tonight she could find the courage to tell Bonnie how she felt.

* * *

After the movie, they drove out to Stephenson Lake where they built a bonfire, sat, and talked. The lake was bigger than the town that surrounded it. On any given weekend, carloads of teenagers could be found hanging out around bonfires dotting the shoreline. Corrine had brought marshmallows to roast, and the guys were greedily eating them. It was a clear, cool autumn night, and the starlight radiated off the lake like Japanese lanterns. Mabel's attention was once again drawn to the skies and she kept burning her marshmallows, but she didn't mind eating the charred goo.

"What are you looking at?" Bonnie asked.

"The constellation Aquila, the Eagle. You can tell by three bright stars that form a triangle." Mabel tried to ignore how close Bonnie was sitting to her. It felt as if all the air had left her lungs as she inhaled Bonnie's spicy perfume. Swallowing hard, Mabel said, "The bright star on the southern point is actually twice as big as our sun."

"How do you know so much about the stars?" Charles asked.

"It's always been something that's interested me," she said, pulling another charred marshmallow off her stick.

Jay put his arm around her and pulled her in for a kiss. Tonight especially, the thought of kissing him made her nauseous, and she turned away, announcing she was going for a walk, not caring about the hurt look on his face from her rejection. Walking briskly along the shore, she heard Bonnie call out to her to wait up.

"What are you really thinking about tonight?" Bonnie broke the silence between them.

"How I want different things than most people in this town," said Mabel, glancing up at the starlit night.

"Like what?" Bonnie slipped her arm around Mabel's. The simple gesture sent shocks of electricity to Mabel's skin and she felt thunder in her chest.

"I want to go to college far away from here."

"Why?"

"Because I want to be bigger than Wheatonville. I can't . . . be myself here," she whispered in the dark. As she stared out at the inky lake, Mabel could hear her father's sardonic voice in her head telling her how stupid, worthless, and unlovable she was. She felt it would be such a miracle if she ever found anyone who could love someone as useless as her.

Bonnie slipped her hand into Mabel's and turned to look into her eyes. "It's true I may not have known you long, but I can tell you are destined for big things in your life. Anyone who can't see that is a fool."

"If you say so," Mabel said, "but you're right, you barely know me." She turned to resume walking but didn't let go of Bonnie's hand. Mabel liked how Bonnie's long fingers fit perfectly in hers. Bonnie's touch felt like holding the live wire of an electrical fence. Glancing back, not seeing the light from the campfire anymore, she turned to face Bonnie, wanting to tell her some of the thoughts that constantly ran through her head. Once again, fear stopped her as she looked at the girl watching her. Taking a deep breath, Mabel said they should start to head back.

"I'm not ready yet," Bonnie said. Still with Mabel's hand in hers, Bonnie wrapped her other hand around Mabel's arm and put her head on her shoulder.

Mabel tried to ignore all the sensations overloading her body from Bonnie's closeness. "If we don't, it will be a long walk home."

Neither one attempted to turn around or head back. They stood listening to the waves crash against the rocky shoreline. Mabel took a deep breath to fill her lungs with air and quiet the beat of her racing heart. She was sure Bonnie could hear the speeding tempo beating in her chest. A slight breeze blew off the lake causing them to shiver. On the breeze, Mabel picked up the spicy scent of Bonnie's perfume. It smelled like the fruits of autumn mixed with the nearby pine trees and sent a different kind of shiver down her spine.

Mabel kissed the top of Bonnie's head, pulling her chin up so she could see the lips she had been dreaming about for weeks. Bending her head, she lightly placed hers on Bonnie's surprised mouth. The sensation of her mouth, soft as velvet, left her wanting more. Mabel deepened the kiss, craving the feel against her own. She coaxed Bonnie's mouth wider and as Mabel's tongue dipped into Bonnie's mouth, she could taste the sweetness left from the roasted marshmallows. She ran her tongue over her lips before pulling Bonnie closer to her.

Mabel breathed heavily and pulled away from the kiss. Bonnie's kiss excited her in a way Jay's never had. Realizing what she had done, Mabel started to apologize, but her apology was swallowed up by Bonnie's lips pressing firmly against hers again. Ignoring the words of caution running through her head, she allowed Bonnie to claim her mouth.

Hearing Bonnie moan as their tongues danced together, Mabel's knees began to shake. She couldn't get close enough to Bonnie. Strong fingers in her hair pulled her head closer as Bonnie nipped her bottom lip. A growl escaped her as the feeling of teeth on her lip drove her wild. Just when she thought she couldn't breathe another breath, velvety softness trailed along her neck. Her skin was on fire every place Bonnie kissed her.

Mabel's brain screamed at her to stop, but her body ignored the message until finally she pulled away from Bonnie and turned to face the lake. She stared at the water, feeling the cool mist on her face. Every nerve in her body was begging for the girl behind her. Mabel ran her fingers through her hair, trying to make sense of everything she was feeling. Bonnie's hand rested on her back, intensifying the sparks still coursing through her. She couldn't believe she'd actually kissed a girl—and liked it. A lot. All she could think about was doing it again.

"Why did you stop?" Bonnie asked, breathing heavily at the loss of contact.

"I'm sorry. I shouldn't have done that."

"I'm glad you did."

Mabel spun around, looking at her friend. Did Bonnie actually say she was glad she was kissed by a girl? *By me? No. No, that can't be right. She's just being polite.*

"You don't have to say that."

"Mabel, you said I barely know you. Well, you barely know me either. I've wanted to kiss you since I found you sitting all alone in the bleachers at the dance. Then when you asked me if I ever felt different, I knew you knew my secret."

"What secret?" Mabel could see Bonnie was struggling with what she'd revealed and seemed unsure to tell her the secret.

"I like girls," Bonnie said in the faintest whisper.

"But what about your boyfriend?" Mabel asked, her head reeling from the news.

Bonnie slipped her hand back into Mabel's. "It's complicated."

"Mabel? Bonnie? Where are you?" came voices from the group.

Bonnie quickly kissed Mabel's cheek and dropped her hand. "Here we are," she yelled back.

Mabel could feel her emotions playing out on her face. Kissing Bonnie had been better than she had ever dreamed. Jay looked at her strangely as she silently thanked the moon for hiding behind the clouds so he couldn't see her face. He was probably still upset about her walking away from his kiss. Her legs refused to move. She wanted to stay in the place where she discovered the reason she felt so different from other girls. Then, turning slowly, she started heading back to where Jay was standing. Jay shot Mabel a curious look, but turned without waiting for her and walked back to the warmth of the fire. Glancing once more at the stars and their reflection on the water, Mabel let the feeling of Bonnie's kiss warm her from the inside out. She wanted the dream to last as long as possible.

Chapter 7 - 1970

"Bobby, how do you know if you're not like other people?" Mabel asked.

"Mayflower, you ask the goofiest questions. Quiet now, you're scaring the fish."

Mabel had no hope of concentrating on fishing. She was too distracted by thoughts of Bonnie and their kiss at the lake on Saturday. Mabel wasn't good with all these new feelings. They made her uncomfortable and she didn't know what to do with them. At least now she knew why she felt different from the other girls at school. It had once been too much to hope someone else could feel like her, but Bonnie made her feel safe enough to be herself——and that opened a whole new set of anxieties.

She watched Bobby reel in a small-mouthed bass. Excited for fresh fish for dinner, she handed him the net to scoop it up onto the dock.

"That's a nice one, little brother." Bobby was two years younger than her and, until a couple of years ago, they looked enough alike to be twins. He had the same sapphire eyes and blond hair she did, but he'd grown six inches last summer and was now close to six feet tall. Thanks to football and wrestling, he had built up muscle tone on his slender frame.

"Thanks. Think we have enough for dinner now?"

Looking at their stringer, Mabel counted six fish they'd already caught. With Bobby's fresh catch, there would be plenty for their family to eat.

"We should go before Mom decides to make something else for dinner," he said.

* * *

Hurrying home, Mabel knew she'd dawdled too long in fishing with Bobby. She would have to speed through her chores now to finish by dinner time. Her dad would be furious if her chores weren't done by the time he came home from work. It was his unbreakable rule that all chores be done by the time dinner was on the table, except for cleaning the dinner dishes. Mabel was not sure his recent good mood would last, and she didn't want to be the one to provoke his anger, especially tonight when she had so much homework to finish. When her father's temper flared, it never ended well for Mabel.

Lately, it hadn't taken much to set him off, and she'd become his favorite target. When he stopped off for a drink at the bar, it took even less. Still, Mabel didn't want to feel his leather belt on her backside tonight. She'd struggle to sit down for a couple of days after one of his whippings. Twisted as it may seem, she preferred the belt over his fists. She could hide welts easier than bruises.

She'd barely made it into the house to start setting the table when he walked through the back door. The look on his face told Mabel it had not been a good day at work and she knew it would take very little to spark his anger tonight. She ate as quickly as she could so she could get started on her homework.

As she was asking to be excused, her sister said, "Don't forget it's your turn to clean the supper dishes tonight."

"No, it's not. I did them last night. You just think you're too good to wash dishes now that you've graduated high school."

"Girls, quit bickering," her mother scolded them both. "Can't you see your father has had a hard day at work? He doesn't need to come home to hear the two of you squabbling."

"But, Mom, it's Isabella's turn. She never does the dishes anymore."

"Mabel, just do the dishes," her father told her.

"I have homework to finish," Mabel said.

"Girl, did you just sass me?"

"No sir," she answered, casting her eyes downward so he wouldn't see the anger building in them. She bit the inside of her cheek and clenched her fist to keep from saying anything that would get her in further trouble.

"You can do your homework after you finish cleaning the kitchen."

"Dad! I have a science project to finish and two papers to write by Friday. Isabella already graduated, so being late to a date where she's just gonna kiss all over Jason Simmons won't be the end of the world for her, despite what she thinks."

"Mabel Ann! Enough!" her father bellowed. "One more word of back-talk from you and I will whip you until you can't sit down in class for a week. You know schooling isn't that important for girls. You should be spending more time at home helping your mother, instead of hanging out with the likes of that new Williams' girl. She's nothing but trouble. Why can't you be more like your sister and find a man to marry instead of always having your head in those damn books and looking at the stars all night?"

"Daddy, you know Jay Bradford wants to marry her and have a whole mess of grandbabies for you and Mom," said Isabella so sweetly it made Mabel's teeth hurt.

"Izzy, leave your sister alone. If you are going out, go get ready before I change my mind. Be back by eleven. I don't want you keeping your mother up all night worrying about you."

"Yes, Daddy. I love you." A retreating Isabella left the table, but the moment she was out of her parents' line of sight, she stuck her tongue out at her younger sister.

"I'll help you, sis," Bobby said.

"Don't you have to get to work, son?" his father said.

"I have time to help."

"Don't worry about the dishes. That's your sister's job. You get to work."

Getting up from the scratched wooden kitchen table, she took her dishes to the sink. In defiance of his father, Bobby helped her clear the rest of the table before going back to work at Mack's Garage. He squeezed her shoulder in support and whispered he could help her clean up. She shook her head no as she looked around at the mess waiting to be cleaned. She didn't want him to get in trouble for being late to work. Her homework would take her about two hours to finish, and she estimated this mess would take at least an hour to clean up. Angry tears welled in her eyes and she mumbled, "It's just not fair."

"I know, sis. I know. But Izzy isn't worth you getting another whipping." Squeezing her shoulder one more time, he left her alone in the kitchen.

Mabel became angrier at her dad's treatment of her as she continued to scrub the dishes. All Izzy had to do was talk so sweet to their dad to get out of doing her chores. It had been a month since Izzy washed the dishes. After drying and putting away the cast-iron skillet her mom had fried the fish in, she ran upstairs to start her homework.

She started working on her math problems since they would take her the longest to do, but soon she was again distracted by thoughts of Bonnie. She brushed her fingers against her lips as she remembered the kiss they'd shared. She couldn't wait to see Bonnie at school the next day and hoped they could find time to spend together alone. Her mind strayed back to her dad's comment at dinner about Bonnie being trouble. What did he mean by that?

"Mabel Ann, come down here," her father yelled up the stairs at her. Mabel's chest tightened with fear and the pit of her stomach fell. She knew that tone. Gathering her strength, she cautiously went downstairs to find her father waiting for her impatiently in the kitchen.

"I thought I told you to clean up this mess."

"I did clean it up."

She was unprepared for the backhand that landed on her cheek. Tears sprang to her eyes as her cheek burned from the stinging contact.

"I told you, one more word of back-talk from you and I will whip you until you can't sit down in class for a week. You didn't sweep or mop this filthy floor. Now, young lady, get the broom and mop, then finish cleaning up this mess. I'm going to stand right here to make sure you do it right this time."

"It's not my turn to do the floors. It wasn't even my turn to do the stupid dishes. It's Isabella's, but she never seems to have to do anything around here except get ready to go out on dates. It's not fair."

The words flew from her mouth before she could stop them. She sensed he had been pushed too far by her outburst and tried to prepare herself for what was coming. She didn't prepare quickly enough. He grabbed her wrist and twisted it so she had to bend over to keep it from breaking. Tears fell from her eyes at the unexpected pain.

"I'll show you what's fair," he spit out at her.

As he undid his belt, her mind shut down. Mabel squeezed her eyes shut to stop the flow of tears as the leather belt stung her skin. She could feel the welts forming on the backs of her legs and buttocks. She knew sitting would be extremely painful for the next couple of days. Because of the painful grip he still had on her wrist, she couldn't lessen the blows. Mabel was certain he was going to break her arm from the angle at which he was holding her. Her only hope now was for his anger to burn out before he drew blood. She promised herself she wouldn't give him the satisfaction of seeing how much he hurt her, no matter how bad the pain felt on her legs.

"Robert, that's enough," her mom said, grabbing his arm. "Isabella knew she had to clean the kitchen tonight. You are punishing the wrong daughter. You know I will clean the floors in the morning, and that the girls only have to wash the dishes."

"Hazel, I am trying to teach this one some responsibility. She needs to learn her place in this world. Nothing good is going to come from her having her head in those damn books all the time. She needs to find a man to take care of her, just like Izzy."

"Robert, let her go finish her homework. We can discuss this later."

Her dad released Mabel's wrist and told her to go upstairs and get ready for bed. As she was running from the room, Mabel saw Bobby standing in the kitchen door and knew he had witnessed their dad whipping her. She felt the shame of her brother seeing how weak she was and slammed the bathroom door shut before letting the tears flow freely. A handprint stained her cheek where her father had slapped her and her wrist was starting to show the bruises from where he held her while he beat her. Wringing out a washcloth with cool water, she tried to wash away the stinging from his belt. She gritted her teeth so she wouldn't cry out when the rough washcloth touched her tender skin. Luckily, her mom had intervened just in time.

Hearing a knock on the bathroom door, her brother asked quietly if she was okay.

"I'm fine," she lied through her tears.

"I'm sorry, Mayflower. You didn't deserve that. Isabella did."

"When does Isabella ever get punished for what she deserves?"

Silence greeted her in response. Seconds passed before he asked, "Is there anything I can do for you?"

Mabel opened the door to see the worry and concern on her brother's face. She knew he wanted to protect her from their dad. The fierceness of his loyalty to her flooded through her as he wrapped her in his arms, careful not to squeeze her too tight. It helped to lessen some of her shame.

"I'll be okay, Bobby. As long as you're my brother, nothing can really hurt me."

"Here. I brought some ice for your hand." After placing the plastic bag gently on her swollen wrist, Bobby slipped past her to wash the grease off his hands.

A moment of panic sparked in her chest as Mabel realized she'd only finished a couple of math problems and hadn't touched her other homework before her dad's interruption. She would have to get to school early tomorrow to finish so she wouldn't be penalized again for turning in a late assignment. Maybe Corrine would be able to help her with the math.

She laid down on her bed gingerly and tried to go to sleep, doing her best to ignore the sharp, stinging pain in her lower body. She couldn't wait to leave for college so she wouldn't have to worry about finding a comfortable sleeping position.

Chapter 8 - 1970

School was challenging today. Bonnie typically loved her art class, but nothing she drew today was correct. She struggled with getting the shading of the plant just right all class period.

"No, no, no," Mrs. McHenry yelled at her. "You are losing the leaves of the plant with your shading. Start over."

Bonnie ground her teeth together, biting back the sharp retort that sprung to mind. She wanted to tear up her sketch and walk out of class. It was hard to focus on drawing perfect leaves when thoughts of Mabel kept her mind preoccupied. Mabel inspired her creativity, but the art class was stifling that. Bonnie yearned for the freedom to create the images she saw in her mind.

Mabel had been unusually quiet during their English and Geometry classes. Bonnie noticed the extra sweatshirt she had with her today, using it as a seat cushion. When she asked Mabel if she was okay, Bonnie was met with stony silence and the stubborn set of Mabel's jaw. Bonnie couldn't help but feel uneasy about whatever was bothering her.

When the bell finally sounded, she headed to the lunchroom where, once again, she gave thanks that Charles had a different lunch period. This way, she didn't have to sit with all the jocks and pretend to be the perfect girlfriend. Bonnie liked having Mabel all to herself at lunch each day. Hopefully, Mabel would feel like telling her what was bothering her.

The thought of kissing Mabel ran through her mind as she found the girl sitting alone in the corner. She'd adored the softness of Mabel's lips on her. It drove her insane to be so close to her and not be able to kiss her. Bonnie wanted to do a lot more than just kiss her, but was Mabel ready for that?

Mabel waved as Bonnie wove her way through the students rushing to find a place to sit in the lunchroom. She noticed Mabel was still using her sweatshirt as a seat cushion. Something had to be wrong.

"Is everything okay?"

"I'm fine. Why?"

It wouldn't be smart to call attention to the sweatshirt. The last thing she wanted to do was embarrass or anger her. "You're really quiet today. Do you feel okay?"

"I'm a little sore." Mabel hedged on the truth.

"Anything I can do to make you feel better?" Bonnie waggled her eyebrows at Mabel hoping to charm a smile out of her. She was happy when a light blush crept its way up Mabel's neck. Bonnie's comment had the intended effect.

"Can you run an errand with me after school?" Mabel asked her.

"Don't you have to work today?"

"No, thank God," she whispered.

"Then I would love to. I just have to be home by six," Bonnie said.

"Great. Meet me at my locker after the last bell."

The girls ate their lunch in companionable silence. Bonnie could tell Mabel didn't really feel well, so she didn't push her into talking more. Besides, the silence gave her time to study Mabel's fingers pulling her sandwich apart. Luckily, the lunch bell signaled it was time for the next class before she could get into trouble with her thoughts.

After an afternoon that seemed to crawl by on its hands and knees, Bonnie threw her books in her locker, then raced to meet Mabel. Watching as Mabel gingerly put her books away, she tried to be patient, hoping Mabel would eventually tell her what was wrong.

"Did you drive or did Charles pick you up?" Mabel asked, turning her attention to her.

"I drove today. Where would you like to go?"

"It's a surprise."

"Oh, I love surprises!" Bonnie hopped from one foot to the other in excitement, hoping Mabel would share more details.

A tight-lipped Mabel steered her out the door and to the parking lot where she directed Bonnie to drive to Stephenson Lake. When they got there, they parked in the gravel lot and walked down a small dirt path until it split off into two directions. Turning left, Bonnie admired the bare trees leading them to the other side of the lake. Following the well-worn path towards the lake, Mabel stopped suddenly.

Several deer were getting a drink at the edge of the lake. They counted six of them. Mabel put her fingers to her lips and they stood watching the animals until a noise in another part of the woods startled them.

"Mabel, that was amazing! What a great surprise. I've never been so close to deer before."

"I knew you would like it." Mabel beamed.

Looking around, Bonnie noticed more bareness of the surrounding trees. Spring was her favorite season, but winter took a close second. She loved the cooler temperatures, the contrast of the trees without their leaves, and the snow that blanketed the ground. She couldn't wait until the leaves fell so she could capture the starkness of the wintertime during her art class, hoping her attempts wouldn't pale in comparison to the reality of nature.

"This is my favorite place," Mabel said.

"I can see why."

"Follow me."

They headed back to the path. At the fork in the trail, they turned right onto a new trail. This one wound deeper into the thickening trees. Bonnie looked down, trying not to trip on the exposed roots, and didn't notice Mabel had stopped in the middle of the trail. She ran right into her back, almost knocking her down. Mabel yelped at the contact but quickly regained her balance to stop them from falling.

"Sorry," Bonnie said.

"The place I'm about to show you is my special place. It's where I come when I need to be alone. I've only shared this place with one other person, and that's my brother. I spend a lot of my free time here and wanted to share it with you."

A small wooden structure in a state of abandoned disrepair stood before them. Mabel explained it was an old shack for runaway slaves and how there were still a few of them around the area.

"It doesn't look very sturdy, but the walls are pretty stable. The roof leaks in a couple of places. I put some plywood over the bigger holes, but the rain still manages to get in around the edges during a big storm."

"It looks quaint. Can we go inside? I'm a little chilly out here," Bonnie said shivering.

"Sure. Come in, but it may not be any warmer inside." Mabel grabbed Bonnie's hand to help her through the maze of vines to the front door. Bonnie held tight, careful not to fall through the rotting steps that led into the cabin. She tried to ignore the sparks of electricity flowing through her gloves from holding Mabel's hand.

"Watch your step. The porch may not be as sturdy as it looks. I don't want you falling through," Mabel warned her.

Once inside, they stood by the front door letting their eyes adjust to the darkened room. It was bigger than it looked from the outside. A small aluminum folding table stood by the only window in the shack. Four wooden crates turned on their sides were used as chairs. Against the back wall were a couple of old sleeping bags and a few blankets were scattered on the floor. Two lanterns hung on nails in the wall and on another wooden crate lay several burnt candles with matches.

"What do you think?" Mabel asked. She lit the lanterns and a soft glow fell over the room, chasing the shadows away, making it all feel cozier.

A warmth spread through Bonnie despite the cool temperatures as she imagined Mabel lying on the blankets, reading. She turned to answer Mabel.

"It's hard to picture people actually living here, but the space totally suits you."

"I know. I'm pretty sure they didn't live here on purpose or if they did, they didn't stay long." Mabel pointed to the ceiling, explaining how she painted several constellations on the ceiling and walls. She started walking to the door. "I guess we should go."

"Why? We just got here." Moving closer to Mabel, Bonnie suddenly noticed the bruise on Mabel's cheek. She had tried to cover it with makeup, but the purplish color showed through now. As she reached her hand out to caress the damaged area, Mabel jerked her head away.

"Don't."

Bonnie tried not to cringe at Mabel's harsh tone. It was her nature to offer comfort to those who suffered. She grabbed Mabel's wrist and jumped back when Mabel screamed.

"Mabel, what's wrong?"

"Nothing."

Bonnie pushed up the sleeve on Mabel's coat and shirt. Seeing an even nastier bruise encircling her swollen wrist, Bonnie couldn't stop the gasp from escaping her lips. Tears of pain poured out of Mabel's eyes. Bonnie enclosed her in a hug as Mabel's tears quickly turned into sobs. Leading them over to the sleeping bag, Bonnie eased them onto the floor. Stretching out on the makeshift bed, she pulled Mabel on top of her and let her cry. She didn't say a word through Mabel's tears. She just held her as tight as she could, placing tender kisses on the top of her head while stroking her silky blonde hair.

As Mabel's tears dissipated, she tried to unwrap herself from Bonnie's grasp. Bonnie just held her tighter. Soon Mabel quit struggling and allowed herself to be comforted by the girl who held her.

She whispered into Mabel's hair, "Tell me what happened."

"I can't," she said before crying again.

"Shh. It's okay. I've got you," Bonnie whispered to her, gently holding her in her embrace. "Are you okay?"

"Yes," Mabel said through clenched teeth.

The pain in Mabel's eyes showed she was lying. Bonnie could tell Mabel's wrist was in real pain. As swollen and bruised as it was, she worried it might be broken.

"Maybe you should go see the doctor?"

"I'm fine," Mabel snapped.

"Mabel, you're not fine. You are in a lot of pain. You don't have to tell me what happened, but I care about you. It hurts me to see you suffer."

Mabel tried to reassure her that everything was okay, but Bonnie wasn't buying any of her excuses. She could tell Mabel wasn't ready to tell her the truth yet. Staring up at the starry ceiling, she tried to ignore the pain on Mabel's face snuggling closer to her.

"Tell me more about the stars."

Mabel took a deep breath, turned over to lie next to Bonnie, and with a shaky voice began pointing out the various constellations drawn on the ceiling and the stories behind them.

When Mabel paused during her story, Bonnie leaned over and kissed her. It wasn't the gentle kiss she had planned. This kiss was filled with desire, on a mission to claim Mabel's lips for her own. When Bonnie sought entrance to Mabel's mouth, she gladly let her in. Bonnie stroked her tongue eagerly while she ran her fingers through her smooth hair. Bonnie continued to kiss with a dominance that belied her feminine physique. She never wanted this moment to end. A small cry escaped from Mabel's lips when Bonnie broke off contact. Looking down at her, Mabel could see the desire still flaming in her eyes. Leaning up, trying to kiss her again, Bonnie put a finger on her lips to stop her. Mabel slipped the finger into her mouth and gently sucked.

Bonnie tried pulling herself away, but the feelings Mabel created in her body made it almost impossible for her to move. She wanted this and more with this girl but now was truly not the time. Using all of her willpower, she pulled her finger out of Mabel's mouth. The pure desire still shining in her eyes almost broke Bonnie's resistance. "Mabel," she gasped through ragged breaths. "I hate to do this, but I have to go. I promised my mom I would help her fix dinner tonight. My dad has business people coming to our house and she needs my help."

Rolling off Mabel, she took several deep breaths to slow down her heartbeat. Looking over, she saw Mabel's eyes closed, struggling to bring her own body back under control. Bonnie ran her fingers across Mabel's jawline and down her neck. The small gasp she heard escape her lips was enough to bring a smile to Bonnie's face.

She stood up and pulled Mabel to her feet by her good arm. Wrapping her arms around her carefully, she stood willing her strength into her friend's body. Bonnie knew she was struggling with trusting her. It would take time for Mabel to feel safe enough with her and when she did, Bonnie would be here to support her. Before they left the cabin, Bonnie kissed her once more, promising there would be more to share in the future.

Chapter 9 - 1970

"Mabel, what's the answer to number three?"

"Bonnie, I can't keep giving you the answers. You have to figure it out on your own."

"You know math is a foreign language to me."

"All right, let me see what you've done so far."

As Mabel leaned over to see where she was stuck with her problem, Bonnie smelled the strawberry-scented shampoo in her hair. For a moment, she was distracted by the scent and stopped paying attention to Mabel's explanation of her equation. She stopped herself just in time from kissing her.

"Hey, Bonnie, why are you hanging out with this freak?" Stephanie, one of the popular cheerleaders asked. "Come sit with us."

"I'm good, Stephanie."

"Suit yourself, but she ain't like the rest of us cool cats."

Before Bonnie could respond, the librarian shushed them all. She saw Mabel's discomfort and wasn't surprised when her cheeks flushed in anger.

"I'm leaving." Mabel closed her math book and gathered her things.

She walked quickly past Carla's table so focused on the door she didn't see the foot sticking out to trip her. Her books scattered all around as she lost her balance and landed sprawled out on the floor by the table.

"Oops," Stephanie said. "The spaz took a tumble. Guess you had your head in the stars again."

Mabel gathered her books and papers quickly before being admonished again by the librarian. She ran to her locker, struggling to get it open. Mabel smacked it out of frustration.

"What did that locker ever do to you?"

"Not now, Bonnie." Mabel wouldn't look at her as she finally opened her locker and grabbed the rest of her books.

"Forget about them. Let's go to my house to study."

"Won't your mom be home?"

"Not today. It's her tennis day at the country club."

"Would she be okay with you having . . . friends over when she's not there?"

Bonnie knew her mother would not be okay with Mabel coming to her house, but she didn't care. She was struggling in geometry class and Mabel was one of the best students. She needed to understand geometry better to help her with her art. Her advisor recommended the class, and even though math was not her best subject, she didn't want to let him down. Besides, this was a way to spend time with Mabel without all their other friends being around.

"She's always on my case about not bringing my friends over. It will be fine."

"Sounds good, but I can only stay for an hour. I have to finish my chores before my dad gets home."

Bonnie drove them to her house and watched Mabel's reaction at seeing her house for the first time. She knew Mabel's family didn't have much money but, unlike her parents, Bonnie didn't care about money or possessions. She did care about making Mabel feel more at ease with the obvious differences in their financial status.

"Wow, you live in a mansion," Mabel said.

"It's just a building. Wood and brick make the structure; they don't make it a home."

Bonnie unlocked the door, threw her books on the kitchen table, and gave Mabel a brief tour of the house. Upstairs, she stopped before a closed door.

"This is my room," she said, opening the door.

"Wow."

Bonnie tried to see her room through Mabel's eyes. It looked like something out of an interior design magazine. Her mother had hired a decorator for the entire house, and Bonnie had little to do with the decisions made about her own room. The focal point of the room was a giant canopy bed covered with a pastel pink floral bedspread. Next to the bed stood a cherry-wood nightstand with a Tiffany lamp in the middle of it. On one wall was a matching six-drawer dresser. The hardwood floor gleamed and an accent rug that matched the bedspread kept the rolltop desk from scratching the pristine floor.

"I don't think it's such a good idea for me to be here," Mabel said as she moved to the door.

"Wait." Bonnie stepped in front of Mabel and kissed her. She had wanted to kiss her since doing their homework in the library. Mabel broke off the kiss by taking a step backward.

"What's wrong?"

"It's obvious that I don't belong here."

"Not to me, it isn't. Mabel, do you think I really care about all these things? Look at this room. It's like living in the middle of a magazine spread. It's you I care about."

"Easy to say you don't care about things when you have them. I might never own matching furniture."

"You have to believe me. I didn't ask for any of this. Don't judge me by what my parents have. I don't judge you by your parents."

"What's that supposed to mean?"

"Bonnie!" her mother yelled up the stairs.

"Crap. She's not supposed to be home yet."

"So, it's not fine I'm here, is it? I'm not going to be your dirty little secret."

Mabel stormed out of the room and ran down the stairs, almost knocking over Bonnie's mother on the staircase. Bonnie watched as she grabbed her books from the kitchen table and ran out the back door.

"Who was that girl dressed in those awful clothes?" her mother asked.

"My math tutor," Bonnie lied. She thought her mother might be more accepting of Mabel if she thought she was only helping her study.

"Why do you need a tutor? You know Charles is good at math."

"He's busy with football and trying to earn a scholarship. Besides, he's more interested in making out than helping me understand equations."

"Honey, that's a good thing. You will want your *fiancé* to find you irresistible."

Bonnie turned around and stormed back up to her bedroom. Her mother would never get it. The person she wanted to make out with just raced out of her house furious with her deception. Flopping backward onto the flowery bedspread, Bonnie traced her fingers over her lips remembering the feel of Mabel's pressed against hers.

Had she lost the best thing that had ever happened to her? Why did she lie? All she wanted was time alone with Mabel somewhere other than the cabin. Mabel had been so upset at the library and Bonnie thought she could help her get over Stephanie's teasing, but she should've known how uncomfortable Mabel would feel in her house. Heck, there were times *Bonnie* wasn't comfortable living here or with her parents' money. She wondered if Mabel would ever speak to her again.

* * *

"Bonnie, are you ready to go?"

"Almost."

"Hurry up. Your father's in the car waiting. We can't be late in meeting the Wilsons for dinner."

Bonnie rushed to finish her sketch. She couldn't quite get the features on paper to match the image in her head. It was her first serious attempt to draw Mabel. She'd tried a couple of times before right after they'd met, but they weren't any good. She hoped to surprise Mabel with it.

"Bonnie?" Her mother opened her bedroom door and staccato-marched in her high heels over to her desk. "Bonnie, put that away. Now's not the time to be working on this little hobby of yours. Let's go."

"Mother, how many times do I have to tell you? This isn't a hobby."

"I'm not fighting with you about this, Bonnie Jean. Your father is waiting."

Closing her sketchpad carefully, Bonnie tucked it into her desk drawer. Irritated with her mother for continually calling her drawings a hobby, she stalled by running a brush through her wavy brown curls one more time, then reapplied her lipstick. She hated dinner at the country club. It was her mother's lame attempt at parading her around like a prized cow at the county fair just waiting for the other Queen Debutants to award her the 'Mother of the Year' blue ribbon.

After her fight with Mabel today, she wasn't in the mood to see Charles tonight. She knew it upset Mabel every time she had a date with Charles, but she had no choice. She'd agreed to this arrangement to keep her parents happy. Lately, when she went out with him, all he did was talk about playing football at a major university. Bonnie was beginning to realize he was as boring as all the other country club members. It wasn't fair to keep comparing him to Mabel, but she had a sharp mind and she was inquisitive about so many things. She really was interested in Bonnie and cared what she thought.

'Too bad Mabel isn't a guy,' Bonnie thought, 'I'd marry her in a heartbeat.'

Chapter 10 - 1971

Ever since Bonnie had given her one of her sketches she'd drawn of Mabel, they'd grown closer. It was Bonnie's way of apologizing for lying. Mabel had only been able to stay mad at Bonnie for a couple of days after their fight. Her absence left too big of a hole in her heart and it hurt not being around her.

Today was the first day of summer vacation. In a few short weeks, Mabel would be a high school senior and then would one day head off to college. She planned on becoming an astronomer and working for NASA. Nothing was going to keep her from studying the planets and the stars. Her guidance counselor, Mr. Brown, tried steering her towards more traditional areas of study for women, like nursing and teaching, but she wouldn't be talked out of her dream. Finally relenting, Mr. Brown helped her research astronomy programs at different universities.

As excited as Mabel was about going to college, she was beyond thrilled at having Bonnie to herself this summer, even if she *had* gotten engaged to Charles in the spring. Charles had gotten a football scholarship at Michigan State University and was leaving right after graduation. The rest of their friends would be working or vacationing away from Wheatonville for most of the summer.

Mabel had the day off and asked Bonnie to go for a walk at Stephenson Lake with her. She couldn't stop thinking about the way Bonnie kissed her or held her hand when they went walking in the woods. Mabel felt Bonnie wanted to do more with her but always stopped when things got too heated between them. She knew it was because of her. Mabel was trying to sort out her feelings and come to terms with her burgeoning sexuality. She was terrified and excited all at once. She felt things with Bonnie she had never felt before. Mabel hoped she could convince Bonnie she was ready for the next step in their relationship.

"Mabel, hold still."

"I can't. My nose itches. Can't you draw any faster?"

"I could if my subject would hold still." Bonnie had brought her sketchpad to practice her drawing skills because she had signed up to take a class at the community college later this summer.

"Let me see what you've drawn so far."

"Absolutely not. An artist *never* reveals her masterpiece before it's complete."

"Masterpiece? Come on, Bonnie, we both know I'm no masterpiece."

"You definitely won't be if you don't hold still. I'm trying to capture the sunlight streaming through the trees and the reflection it's casting over your head. You look like an angel. Turn your head to the right a bit."

"Angel, huh? My dad would say I'm the devil in disguise." She would agree with him because her thoughts of Bonnie weren't anything resembling an angel's. There were too many sinful thoughts demanding her attention when Bonnie was near.

"How's this?" She wanted to make Bonnie happy and had agreed to allow her friend to sketch her under one of the old oak trees. Now she was antsy to see what Bonnie had drawn. Staying in one position was torture for her, but she would do anything Bonnie asked of her.

"It's no good. The sun isn't in the right spot now."

Sensing Bonnie's frustration, Mabel suggested they walk down to the lake. When they came to the fishing dock, Bonnie pulled out her sketchbook again and started drawing the landscape. The afternoon turned warmer than they expected, and soon sweat dripped down their bodies. The water looked so inviting. Mabel grinned.

"I'm going swimming," Mabel said, jumping up from the dock.

"I didn't bring a bathing suit."

"Neither did I."

Mabel shucked off her shorts and t-shirt. Forgetting about the scars on her legs, she stood on the edge of the dock, prepared to jump in wearing only her underwear. Mabel felt bold as she turned back to Bonnie, teasing her as she shimmied her hips and said, "See something you like?" Without waiting for Bonnie's reply, she jumped into the lake.

The coolness of the water hit her immediately and she broke the surface with chattering teeth. To warm up, she started swimming away from the dock. Treading water several yards from the dock, she heard a splash. Looking back, Bonnie's head popped out of the water. Mabel turned around and swam back to the dock until she came face to face with Bonnie standing in the shallow water.

"You were right, Mabel. The water feels great."

"Aren't you cold?" she asked, teeth still chattering.

"No, I like it when it's this temperature."

Mabel decided now was her chance and grabbed Bonnie around the waist. She forgot that she had taken her clothes off as well and was surprised to feel bare skin under her fingers. Trying to ignore the sensations shooting up her arms, she leaned in and gently placed her lips on Bonnie's. She loved the feeling of her lips and started teasing her with soft, feathery light kisses on her nose, cheeks, and forehead. Goosebumps broke out on her arms. Bonnie pulled her closer and they kissed again, gently at first, then more and more insistent as their tongues danced together.

Her senses ignited and left her hungering for more of the girl's touch. Bonnie pulled away, leaving her breathless and unable to stand on legs that were limp as noodles. If Bonnie's embrace hadn't held her upright, Mabel surely would have drowned in delirium.

Yearning for the fullness of Bonnie's lips on hers again, she leaned in to kiss her, aware of her hardened nipples pressing against Bonnie's chest, the last of her resistance slipping away as she pressed tighter against her.

As their kisses became more passionate, Mabel wrapped her shaky legs around Bonnie's waist. She moaned at the contact and nipped at Bonnie's bottom lip. Taking an ear lobe into her mouth, a sharp intake of breath escaped from Bonnie as Mabel's tongue traced the outer edges of her ear.

"Take me to the cabin," Bonnie whispered.

* * *

Hastily throwing their clothes on over their wet underwear, they raced to the cabin. Once inside, shyness overtook them. Then, slowly, Bonnie moved toward Mabel, and when she stood in front of her she ran her fingers along Mabel's strong jawline and down her neck, watching the shiver work its way down her spine. Leaning in for a kiss, Bonnie felt the desire radiating between them as a thousand sensations danced on her lips. Bonnie could spend the entire afternoon kissing Mabel. She ran her fingers through Mabel's unruly, wet hair, loving the way the blond silken strands wrapped easily around her fingers.

"I'm glad we finally have some time alone together," Bonnie said.

Bonnie leaned in for another kiss and their tongues danced together. Feeling her breath hitch for just a moment, she thought Mabel would break off the kiss, but instead, Mabel pulled her closer.

"I think we have too many clothes on," she said. Bonnie couldn't wait to see Mabel completely naked. She'd only gotten a brief glimpse of her at the dock and liked the way Mabel stood cockily, teasing her before jumping into the lake.

Bonnie pulled Mabel over to the sleeping bags spread out on the floor. Tugging Mabel's wet shirt over her head, she tossed it onto the floor. Then she pulled her own wet shirt off. Pulling Mabel back into her embrace, Bonnie's lips trailed along her jawline and down her neck. She let her hands roam over Mabel's exposed skin exploring the contours of her shoulders, running light caresses down her arms. Goosebumps rose under her fingertips. She reached around to undo Mabel's bra but felt a hand on her chest pushing her away.

"Mabel, what's wrong?" Bonnie was afraid Mabel was going to tell her to stop. Unease filled her as she looked down at Mabel.

"I've never done this before," Mabel said shyly. Bonnie could feel her tensing up under her and tried to get her to relax.

"I know, baby. Just trust me. We can stop anytime."

She then placed gentle kisses on her lips and neck until she felt Mabel relaxing. Bonnie began to caress her skin all the way to her hips. She enjoyed seeing the pleasure Mabel experienced at her touch. For a brief moment, Bonnie wished she could capture the look on her face with one of her sketches.

"Did you want me to stop?"

Shaking her head no, Mabel chewed on her bottom lip, clearly worried about something.

"What is it, honey? You can tell me anything," Bonnie said, trying to ignore her own needs.

"I . . . I don't know what to do."

"Shh, it's okay. You need to tell me if you don't like something I'm doing to you. It's going to be fine, Mabel. I promise."

Bonnie watched the internal debate play out in Mabel's eyes. She thought Mabel would end things right then and tried to prepare herself physically. Mabel was clearly nervous, and Bonnie didn't want to push her into anything she wasn't ready for yet. Brushing the hair out of Mabel's face, she kissed her along her jaw and down her neck to her collarbone, feeling her body relaxing under her lips. After a few moments, Mabel's lopsided grin showed she had put any of her fears to rest.

Bonnie stroked Mabel lightly until she got used to her touch. Since this was Mabel's first time, she wanted her to enjoy every touch, every sensation coursing through her body. Speeding up the tempo of her fingers, she watched the changes in Mabel's face and body as she climbed to her release. Arching her back, Mabel's muscles tightened as she exploded beneath her. Holding her as she rode her first waves of ecstasy, Bonnie quickly followed her with her own release against Mabel's thigh.

"Was that okay?" a shy Mabel asked after a few moments.

Bonnie could only smile as the intensity of her orgasm rendered her speechless. It was amazing. She pulled Mabel into an embrace, gently kissing her lips, cheeks, and neck. Drifting off to sleep curled around Mabel, Bonnie realized she'd just broken her promise to her parents.

Chapter 11 - 1972

Life was rapidly changing for Mabel and she couldn't stop it. The previous summer and her senior year had flown by, and now she only had a few short weeks left of high school. Sitting on the dock overlooking the lake, she held the envelope in her trembling hands. She thought back to last summer, when she sent off her college applications to the two out-of-state universities. The college in California had the best astronomy program, but it was highly competitive. She hoped her grades would be good enough for her to be admitted.

She held what could be the key to her future in her nervous hands. Turning the envelope from California over several times, Mabel tried to calm her nerves so she could open it. She gave herself time to prepare for whatever news was written on the letter inside. She thought about how exciting it would be to have a chance to study the stars in college.

"What's in the envelope, sis?"

Mabel screamed and just barely stopped herself from falling into the frigid water. She had been so focused on the envelope and her thoughts that she didn't hear her brother sneak up on her. Trying to still her racing heart, she held the envelope up for him to see.

"Hopefully, the answer to my prayers," she said with dreaminess in her voice.

"Hard to know if you don't open it, don't you think?"

Mabel squinted up at her brother grinning down at her. Moving over, she made room for him to sit down next to her on the dock. Bobby set his fishing pole down before joining her in dangling his feet over the edge of the dock.

Mabel told Bobby about her dreams of studying the stars and the colleges she applied to without their parents' knowledge. She'd repeatedly tried to talk with Corrine and Bonnie about her plans, but they always managed to change the subject when she brought it up.

"I'm working up my nerve to open it. It's from the University of California in Berkeley and this is their response. What if they turned me down and I'm stuck here? You know Mom and Dad won't allow me to go to college if I stay."

"California is a long ways from here, Mayflower," Bobby said quietly.

"Bobby, you know it's my dream to go to college." Her brother, of all people, should understand why she had to leave Wheatonville. He'd experienced firsthand the beatings from their dad just as much as she had.

"I do. I'm just wondering, why California?" Bobby stared across the lake.

Mabel took a deep breath and tried to explain why she picked a college that was thousands of miles from anything familiar to her.

"California might be a fun place to visit," he said. "Who knows? I might have to move out there myself after I graduate, just to keep an eye on my big sister to make sure she remembers us little people who don't live in the stars."

Mabel hugged her brother without warning. Kissing his cheek, she was so grateful he didn't try to argue her into staying. It was refreshing to have someone excited for her new adventure.

"Before we make plans for you to visit me, I probably should open this letter and find out if it's even going to be a reality," Mabel anxiously said.

Ripping open the envelope, she pulled out the letter typed on parchment paper. She ran her hands over the words, caressing the college seal at the top of the page. Jumping up from the dock as her eyes scanned down the page, she yelled, "I got in! I got in!"

She was jumping up and down when Bobby stood from the dock, grabbed her, and began swinging her around until they were both dizzy.

"Put me down," she said.

He set her down carefully on the dock lest she get tangled up in his fishing pole. They both tried to regain their balance from the dizzying spinning.

Grinning down at her, Bobby ruffled her hair, knowing how she hated that.

"I'm so happy for you, Mayflower. I know you are going to do great things in college. Just think, my sister, the star scientist."

"Thanks, Bobby. Promise me you'll keep this a secret. I don't want anyone else to know until I'm ready to tell them."

Mabel worried how her friends would take the news of her actually leaving town, now that this hypothetical was now going to be a reality. Before this moment, it had been only a dream, but now there was no question: she was going to California. She was scared to death of what her parents would do once they found out. Mabel had to keep quiet about leaving because she knew her father would do everything he could to stop her.

"I won't tell anyone. I promise," he said. "Will you be able to afford to leave? I bet college is expensive and mom and dad won't give you the money."

"That's the best part, Bobby. It says right here my grades were good enough for an academic scholarship that will pay the cost of attending college. All I have to do is find a place to live."

Mabel had worked as much as she could for the last two years, saving her money all along the way. Her goal was to have enough saved for at least one semester. With the scholarship, she should be able to find some type of cheap student housing.

"Don't you worry about that, sis. I will help you afford a place to live. You can have some of the money I'm making at Mack's shop."

"I can't take your money. You've worked too hard for it, and I'm sure you have plans for how you want to spend it."

"Mayflower, I'm choosing to spend it on you. I want to help you. My big sister deserves to go to California, and if I can help you do that, I will."

Mabel grabbed Bobby around the waist to hug him again. She told him he was the best brother a girl could ever hope to have. Before heading home, Mabel hid the letter in the cabin so Izzy or her parents wouldn't find it at home. She told Bobby she had an errand to run while he fished.

"I'll come right back here so we can walk home together," she told him, skipping off the dock and running to the cabin.

After hiding her letter in the wooden box under the floorboards at the cabin, Mabel took her time meeting up with Bobby. She was thinking about her chance to study the stars. She remembered it was her dad who first got her interested in the stars. He bought her a telescope for her seventh birthday. They'd spent hours in the backyard looking at the constellations and planets. For her eighth birthday, he had painted her bedroom ceiling with glow-in-the-dark stars, telling her it was so she'd always be able to fall asleep underneath them.

She wished she could tell him her good news but knew that version of her dad was in the past. Ever since he didn't get the promised promotion at the factory, her dad had changed. He began drinking and staying out after work with his buddies. On the nights he did make it home for dinner, it didn't take much to make him angry. Bobby was the only person in Wheatonville she could trust with her news.

On their way home, Mabel had a hard time holding in her excitement. She kept dancing and skipping around Bobby with a huge smile on her face.

They were almost home when Bobby asked her, "How do you think Bonnie is going to take the news?"

Mabel's excitement dissipated in an instant. Bobby was the only other person who knew about her relationship with Bonnie. He'd been so supportive when she told him. Mabel knew without a doubt she wanted Bonnie to go with her to California. They could build a life together there.

"I honestly don't know," Mabel said. As they walked through the back door of their house, Mabel considered the possibility of heading off to college alone, and suddenly the thought of leaving filled her with dread.

* * *

The following weeks flew by. Mabel was getting ready to graduate from high school and was excited to be giving a commencement speech as the salutatorian.

Looking around the stuffy gymnasium, Mabel saw many of her friends' families in the stands beaming with pride. She waved to Bobby and her mom, nervous, but nonetheless glad they had come.

She spotted Bonnie a few rows behind her and blushed when she blew a kiss in her direction. They had plans to spend the night together at the cabin. First, they had to make an appearance at the graduation party, and then they would drive out to the cabin. They had told their parents they were spending the night at Corrine's after the party. Mabel couldn't wait to wake up with Bonnie in her arms. It was going to be the best graduation gift she could receive.

As the last of her classmates filed in to the band's erratic rendition of "Pomp and Circumstance," Mabel took a deep breath and tried to enjoy her last moments of high school, but became so lost in thought she missed her name being called for her speech. It wasn't until she was nudged in the ribs that she moved to the stage.

As the last of the applause died down, Mabel returned to the safety of her seat. She couldn't remember half the words she said, but figured she must have done okay, as the audience had laughed at some of her funny memories. She also noticed several of her classmates wipe tears from their eyes during her speech.

Walking across the stage one more time, Mabel shook Principal Miller's sweaty hand as her diploma was handed to her. Raising both arms in the air in celebration, the satisfaction of graduating swelled in her chest. Turning back to the stage, she watched as Bonnie received her diploma, and her heart burst with pride and love for this woman.

Chapter 12 - 1972

Mabel loved the way Bonnie felt in her arms. *'If only there was a way to bottle this feeling.'* Mabel ran her fingers through Bonnie's long strands of hair. Bonnie had taught her so many wonderful things about her body. She was a patient teacher. Mabel had learned to explore a woman's body in sensual detail that wasn't always about sex.

She tried not to think about why Bonnie knew so much about sex. Mabel wouldn't allow her mind to entertain thoughts of Charles touching Bonnie in such an intimate manner. Anytime he was mentioned, a knife plunged into Mabel's heart.

She wanted today to last forever. They had spent the entire day together, first with Bonnie drawing, then making love most of the afternoon. Kissing the top of Bonnie's head, Mabel smiled at how easy it had been for Bonnie to convince her to be her model. It started out innocent enough as Bonnie explained to Mabel she needed to practice with a live model like they used in her art class at the community college last summer. From there, Bonnie convinced her that posing nude would help her become a better artist. Mabel wanted to do her part to help Bonnie improve her talent. She quickly recognized Bonnie would do anything she could to get Mabel out of her clothes.

Her smile widened as she thought about all the conversations about Bonnie's drawings. She was eager to know what her lover saw in her naked body. At first she had been self-conscious about all her scars, but Bonnie never saw them as imperfections. Looking down at the woman in her arms, she saw the bite marks that had been left across her breasts. Bonnie was a passionate lover and delighted in leaving her mark on Mabel's sensitive skin.

Mabel's lips sprinkled featherlight kisses on Bonnie's cheeks and neck as Bonnie snuggled closer to her. Intertwining their fingers, Mabel gently kissed them.

She'd been thinking of a way for months to ask Bonnie to come with her to California. She was positive they could build a life together, away from Wheatonville. Mabel was sure their love was strong enough to see them through any of life's challenges.

"It's hard to believe summer vacation is almost over," she said softly.

"Mm-hmm," Bonnie said, lazily running her fingers up and down Mabel's arm.

"Bonnie, I need to tell you something."

Propping herself on her elbow, Bonnie looked at Mabel lovingly. "What is it, sweetie?"

"I'm leaving for California in three weeks."

"What? For a vacation?"

"No." Mabel hesitated. "I'm leaving for college."

"What are you saying, Mabel? Why haven't you said anything before now? Were you even going to tell me, or were you just going to send me a postcard once you got there?" Bonnie pushed herself away from Mabel and sat up. She wrapped her arms around her knees, turning her back to Mabel.

Mabel tried reaching for her, but Bonnie moved farther away. Dropping her hand, Mabel picked at a loose thread in the blanket.

"I was accepted into the astronomy program at UC Berkeley. They offered me a scholarship that pays my tuition and books. I just have to pay for a place to live," Mabel explained with excitement.

"How long have you known?" Bonnie asked, petulant.

"Since March."

"You've known for five months you were going halfway across the country and never bothered to say one word about it to me? You thought today, of all days, would be the best time to spring this on me? You are unbelievable, Mabel Flanigan."

Mabel watched in disbelief as Bonnie got up and started dressing in a hurry. This was not how this conversation was supposed to go. Bonnie was almost out the door before Mabel realized what was happening.

"Wait! Don't go," she said, but Bonnie was out the door and racing to her car parked down by the lake. Mabel threw on her clothes and ran after her.

"Bonnie, please. We have to talk about this."

"Why? Seems like your mind is already made up."

Bonnie jerked open her car door. Sliding into the driver's seat, she shoved the key into the ignition and started the car. Mabel slid into the passenger seat.

"Get out," she said.

"No. Tell me why you're so mad at me."

"I don't want to talk about it," Bonnie said, pulling out of the parking lot.

"That's part of the problem. You never wanted to talk about our plans after graduation." Mabel ran her fingers through her hair in frustration. She had tried to bring this up several times, but whenever she did, Bonnie would change the subject. They had to talk about it now. There wasn't much time before Mabel left for California.

Bonnie turned up the radio to prevent further conversation. They listened to a couple of songs before a commercial came on. When it did, Mabel switched it off.

"Just listen to me. I want you to come with me. We could go to California together."

"Are you kidding me? What would I do in California? Stay home all day while you go to classes?"

"You could go to art school. Bonnie, you have an amazing talent."

"Mabel, we both know I'm not good enough for art school. You can stay here and go to community college with me and Corrine."

"This is my dream. You know I've always wanted to study the stars. Now I have the chance. I'm going to be somebody." Mabel grabbed Bonnie's hand and held it tightly.

"You can be somebody here."

"No, I can't. My life isn't in Wheatonville."

"But I am."

"You don't have to be. You can come with me. Don't you see? We can build the life we want once we get out of this town."

"And what kind of life is that, Mabel?"

Staring out the window at the passing landscape, Mabel couldn't understand why Bonnie was being so obstinate. She knew how Mabel's dad treated her. Why would that change if she stayed? He would always pressure her to conform to his standards of a woman's duty to get married and have children. If she didn't, Mabel was sure he'd try to beat it into her. Mabel was not only different in that she was attracted to girls; she also desperately needed a chance to explore other parts of the world.

"Mabel, you're asking me to leave behind everyone I know. I can't just run off with you like that. I'm still engaged to Charles, and we are getting married next spring. You know that."

Trying to be calm over the reminder of Charles, Mabel once again tried to explain her rationale. "Bonnie, we can create our own life. The world is changing for women. We don't have to follow traditional roles anymore."

"Can we really, Mabel? Let's say I agree and we run off to California. How would we support ourselves? You would be going to class all day and studying at night. What would I do? Then how do we explain it to our families? What if they found out the truth about our relationship? You do realize if we are caught or even suspected of an immoral relationship, we could be thrown in jail, or worse, an institution. Is that the kind of life you dreamed for us? Because it sure as hell isn't the life I see for myself."

Mabel tried to calm her erratic thoughts so she could help Bonnie understand what was at stake for them both. Turning in her seat to face her, she asked, "But do you love him?"

Bonnie bit her bottom lip and turned her head to the window, struggling with the answer. The person Mabel loved was slipping away from her and she was desperate to hold on.

"You know I care for Charles," Bonnie said.

A scream lodged in Mabel's throat. "So you would rather stay here and marry someone you don't even love?"

"It's time for you to face facts and stop thinking you get to do what you want in life. So you go off and study the stars. You will never become a working astronomer," Bonnie said. "The world hasn't changed as much as you think it has. Our lives are already determined for us by men who decide what we can do or become. Men will always decide what is best for your life. The sooner you accept that, the happier you will be."

Her words cut right to Mabel's heart. She never expected to hear from Bonnie that her dreams were worthless. Turning away to hide the tears forming in her eyes, Mabel realized the one person who mattered most to her in this world had just shown she had no faith in her. Bonnie was like everyone else in this godforsaken town. Mabel had foolishly believed their love was magical and would be enough. She'd truly believed Bonnie would choose her over Charles.

"Bonnie, do you love me?"

Bonnie grabbed onto Mabel's hand like it was a lifeline to her drowning soul, hanging on for dear life.

"Yes," she said. "With all my heart."

"Then I don't understand why you won't come with me."

Releasing her hand, Bonnie stared out the windshield, her knuckles turning white as she gripped the steering wheel. She hesitated before answering.

"Mabel, it's not that simple. I'm not strong like you. I have responsibilities here. All I can offer you now is my friendship."

"Bonnie, I can't lose you. It would destroy me."

"Honey, you aren't losing me. Only an aspect of our relationship is changing. We can still be friends."

Mabel couldn't believe what she was hearing. *Friends?* After everything they had shared the last two years, now all she wanted was to be friends? Glaring at Bonnie, Mabel ground her teeth to stop the flow of hateful thoughts running through her mind and took a deep breath. She had to give voice to the shattered emotions inside. Maybe it was the only way to get through to Bonnie.

"Bonnie, I wish Charles was dead!"

Bonnie gasped at the vehemence of her statement and the car swerved.

"I'm so jealous he can freely give you the life I deserve to give you—the life he takes for granted, that in this society is deemed his right. Bonnie, you make me feel alive. When you're in my arms, when you kiss me, you make me believe anything is possible. But you act like kissing you or making love to you is an easy thing for me to give up, throwing it away like an old shirt. I can't believe you think our friendship will be enough to sustain me. It's not even close!"

"Mabel, this isn't easy for me either. I wish I could give you what you want, but I can't. There's no reason for you to be jealous of Charles. You're the one I love."

"But that love isn't good enough for you, is it? I have every reason to be jealous, only you're too stupid to see it. I can't stay here and watch you throw your life away on some man just because you feel obligated to him. I won't do it and you have no right to ask me to. If I ever meant anything to you at all, Bonnie, you would think about what you are asking of me."

Mabel rolled down the window, no longer able to breathe the stifling air in the confined space. Wrapping her arms around her drawn-up knees, she gasped for breath, but her lungs weren't cooperating. She wanted to stop her tears, a sign of weakness in her mind, but she didn't have the strength to hold them back any longer. Overwhelming grief at Bonnie's betrayal consumed her.

Bonnie reached out to touch and comfort her.

"Don't!"

Bonnie shrank back from the violence in Mabel's tone. "Mabel," she said quietly.

"No. Not another word. You've said everything I need to hear. I get it. I'm not who you want. I probably never was. It's my own fault for believing you were different and what we had was real. I was just some game you were playing."

"That's not true, baby."

"Don't 'baby' me. I can't just be your friend, Bonnie. Don't you see that? Not when I love you like I do. Was any of it real to you? Or was I just a distraction while Charles was off at the university?" Mabel looked at Bonnie with pleading eyes, desperate to hear something that would glue the pieces of her shattered heart back together.

"I don't know for sure."

Bonnie's answer broke the final piece of Mabel's resolve and dissolved into a barely controlled rage. How could she be so cavalier about the intimacy they shared over the last two years? Well, if it was all a game to her, Mabel was changing the rules. Now she was going to be her father's daughter. His cruelty over the years had taught her a thing or two about vindictiveness.

"Fine, if that's the way it's going to be. I lied. I don't love you. You meant nothing to me. You are nothing like the woman I imagined. I used to admire you for your beauty and strength. Now all I see is an ugly, weak woman—a coward who hides behind her parents' beliefs and the world's expectations because she doesn't have any guts. You're a mindless puppet, parroting the thoughts of whoever is pulling your strings. You are just an empty shell of a small, scared, horrid, and obnoxious little girl. I'm glad I'm leaving for college. Maybe in California I'll meet a real woman, one who will love me for who I am and know that what she feels for me is real. Maybe I'll even meet one who is twice as beautiful with truly amazing artistic talent, instead of that amateur crap you draw. You are a talentless, conniving wench who makes me sick. I can't stand to be around you anymore. You can go straight to hell!"

Mabel was stunned and watched as tears fell down Bonnie's cheeks. She never thought she could say such nasty things to the woman she loved. The hateful words hung in the air between them like thick black tar.

"You don't really mean that, Mabel."

"The hell I don't. I wish I'd never met you, Bonnie. I hate you. Go run back to your mommy and daddy like the mindless princess you are."

* * *

A warning horn sounded too late. The sound of screeching brakes and crumpling metal filled the interior of the car. Screams of pain broke through the noise of the hissing hoses as the smell of gasoline permeated the air.

Feeling a wet substance on her cheek, Bonnie tried to wipe it away, but her arm wasn't moving. A razor-sharp pain radiated from her wrist to her elbow. Her head throbbed from where she'd struck the steering wheel.

"Mabel, are you okay?"

Silence greeted her, and she opened her eyes to see what had happened. Bonnie slightly turned her head to the passenger side of the car and ignored the pain in her head to see if Mabel was okay. Loud shouting from the outside barely registered through the shattered glass. She heard banging on her car door but didn't have the strength to turn her head in that direction. Where had Mabel gone?

She would later learn Mabel had been thrown from the vehicle on impact and now lie unconscious twenty feet down the steep embankment.

Bonnie was cold despite the warm humid summer day. She had to find Mabel. She hoped she was okay. Why couldn't she see her?

She heard Mabel calling her and finally found her waiting outside the passenger door dressed in a tuxedo, looking so dashing. Her lopsided grin, the one Bonnie found so endearing, was plastered on her face as she held out her hand. Bonnie took her hand and was lifted out of the car. She was wearing a flowing evening gown like Ginger Rogers. Together they danced among the clouds and stars to the most heavenly music.

"Miss. Miss. Can you hear me?"

Bonnie mumbled incoherently, wanting to keep dancing with Mabel, but a bright light shining in her eyes chased the images of her lover away. She tried to move away from the light, but strong fingers held her jaw.

"We're going to get you out of here."

She heard the start of a saw as she was wrapped in blankets by the strong fingers. The force of the impact had pinned her under the dashboard. Her right leg was trapped between the floorboard and the dash. It was badly mangled, and the firemen worked frantically to save it.

"Have you seen Mabel? She was with me a second ago."

"We're taking care of her. You need to concentrate on staying still while we cut you out of here."

Bonnie nodded, then closed her eyes. Mabel was going to be okay. She hurt everywhere, but the pain didn't matter as long as Mabel was fine.

Chapter 13 - 1972

Bobby sat in the hospital room holding his sister's hand. Mabel's nose was broken, along with several ribs and her left arm. Her eyes were swollen shut and she had several stitches to close a gash on her scalp. She was covered in scrapes and bruises. The doctors worried about the swelling in her brain. She had hit her head on a rock when she had been thrown from the car down the embankment. Mabel hadn't shown any signs of waking up.

Bobby needed a drink. He found the room stuffy with his mother and sister hovering over Mabel with anxious worry, so he went in search of a vending machine. He knelt down, staring at the vending machine, when a female voice asked, "Bobby?"

His head was in such a fog he thought maybe he might have been dreaming the sound. Then he felt a hand on his arm. Focusing his attention on the hand, he traced it up to its owner. Corrine's worried face filled his vision.

"Bobby, how's Mabel?"

The sound of his sister's name broke through the last of his resolve. Bobby collapsed against the vending machine and sobbed in front of Corrine. Kneeling next to him, she grabbed him by the shoulders and gently shook him, which brought his focus back to her.

"Take a deep breath," she said. Following her instructions, Bobby gulped in a big breath. He wiped his tears with the back of his hand and brought the hem of his shirt up to clean the snot off his nose. He took another deep breath and tried to stand, but Corrine held him firmly in place.

"Better?" she asked and Bobby nodded. "Tell me what's going on."

Bobby held his hands over his face for a moment to clear his thoughts. He raked his fingers through his hair before speaking. "Mabel's in a coma from the swelling in her brain and they don't know if she's ever going to wake up. It's bad, Corrine. She has broken bones, stitches, bruises, and casts everywhere."

"Oh, Bobby, I'm so sorry. Can I see her?"

"Right now only family members can see her. What about Bonnie?"

"She's in the operating room. The doctors are trying to save her leg. She was trapped in the car for over an hour and they're not sure she's going to make it."

"I can't believe this is happening." Bobby gave Corrine a hug and asked her to keep him updated on Bonnie. He was staying in the hospital with Mabel tonight, just in case she woke up. "I'll let you know if there's any change in her condition," he said.

"I'm going to the chapel now to pray for them. You're more than welcome to come with me."

"Nah, I ain't got much use for God right now." Bobby spun away from Corrine, jamming his hands in his pockets as he made his way back to Mabel's room.

"I'll be praying for you too, Bobby Flanigan."

Chapter 14 - 1972

"Corrine, where is she?" Bonnie asked.

It had been two weeks since the accident, and she was anxiously waiting for Mabel to come visit. The surgery went well, but her recovery from the accident was going to take months. The doctors kept a close watch on her right leg. They were concerned it might have to be amputated because of the damage from being trapped in such an awkward position.

"Bonnie, remember, I told you she was in intensive care."

"I want to see her." Bonnie was still on a lot of pain medication and having trouble remembering things, but it paled in comparison to her clutching heartache.

"You can't. Only family members are allowed."

Mabel still hadn't regained consciousness from the accident. Corrine had been meeting Bobby in the cafeteria over dinner for updates. The doctors were still worried about the swelling in her brain. They had to drill a hole in her head to relieve some of the pressure, but she showed no signs of waking up.

A knock on the door interrupted their conversation. Bobby stood with a bouquet of lilacs he pushed in Bonnie's direction. He was trying to avoid looking at all the bruises on her face. She didn't blame him because what wasn't covered in plaster or bandages was instead covered in purplish, green bruises.

"Thank you."

Corrine took the flowers from him, emptied a vase of dying flowers, and placed his bouquet on the small table next to Bonnie's bed. She quietly left the room, giving the two of them a chance to talk privately.

"How do you feel?" he asked.

"Like I've been run over by a truck."

Bobby laughed at the poor joke. Bonnie quickly filled him in on her prognosis.

"How's Mabel? Corrine said she was still in intensive care."

"Yeah, we're not sure how much longer she'll be there. The doctors are talking about long-term care if she doesn't wake up in the next couple of weeks."

"Bobby, this is entirely my fault."

"It was an accident."

"No, we were having an argument and I took my eyes off the road for a second. By the time I heard the horn, it was too late."

Bonnie could barely look at Bobby. He had the same sapphire-blue eyes as his sister, which made her feel responsible for putting Mabel in intensive care. The compassion in his eyes only made her feel worse.

"Bonnie, I know Mabel loves you and wouldn't want you to blame yourself for what happened."

"Don't be silly. We're just good friends."

"Bonnie, we both know my sister is in love with you. You can deny it all you want, but it's the truth. Were you arguing about her leaving for college? I tried to make her tell you weeks ago."

Bonnie stared at him, refusing to admit the truth. If only she'd said yes like she had wanted to, they'd be on their way to California, but she had ruined both their lives instead. Mabel may never wake up because of her. How could she live with what she'd done?

"I'm tired, Bobby. Thanks for the flowers and the visit. It was sweet of you."

"I don't blame you," Bobby stood. "And I know Mabel doesn't either."

"Yes, she does. You didn't hear the vicious things she said to me when I told her I couldn't run off to California with her on a whim like that. I've never heard her be that cruel."

"I'm sure if she could, she'd tell you how sorry she was."

"Don't count on it. She said she wished she'd never met me. Told me to go to hell."

"She probably said it in the heat of the moment without thinking. Anyway, I'll let you get some rest. I just wanted to stop by and wish you well."

"Bobby, if she ever wakes up tell her I'm sorry."

"I think that's something she needs to hear from you."

Bonnie was lifeless as a popped balloon as she watched him walk out of her room. He may not blame her for the accident, but she held enough blame for all of them.

"Who was that boy? Did he upset you? You look pale." Bonnie's mother came into the room with a cup of coffee from the cafeteria.

"Mother, I'm fine. Stop hovering over me."

"Bonnie Jean, you almost died. I'm allowed to hover."

She could sense her mother staring at her and tried not to feel so overwhelmed by her anxious behavior. It was going to take a long time for her to recover from her injuries, and she had a feeling her mother's naturally overprotective nature would be turned up several notches.

"What did that boy want, Bonnie?"

"He let me know how Mabel was doing."

"Well, I suppose that was a nice thing to do, but you need to concentrate on your own recovery and not worry about someone else right now, especially since I'm sure she's to blame for your accident."

Swallowing the sarcastic reply, Bonnie just closed her eyes. "I'm tired, Mother. I need to rest now." As she drifted off to sleep with images of Mabel in her head, her mother shifted in the chair by her bed, making herself comfortable. The sound of turning pages was the last thing Bonnie remembered as the scent of the lilacs pulled her back to a less painful time.

* * *

Bonnie had a fitful night of dreams imagining the pain Mabel was going through. The nurse had given her a sedative earlier, and she pretended to sleep through her mother's visit, hoping she would leave early.

Now she found herself caught in the nightmare she couldn't stop. Blinding lights came at her as she was driving on a narrow two-lane road. Jerking the steering wheel to the right, she felt her tires slipping off the shoulder, and her car began falling down a steep embankment. As the car fell end over end, finally coming to rest on a rocky ledge, Bonnie looked up and Mabel appeared at the edge of the road. Trying to wipe the blood from her eyes so she could see better, she saw her parents and Charles yelling at Mabel to stay away from her, driving her closer to the edge until she lost her footing. Mabel looked over her shoulder at Bonnie and sent a desperate plea for help. Bonnie frantically tried to open the car door but was trapped. She couldn't keep Mabel from falling off the steep embankment and ending up in a broken heap next to her car. Black pupils stared at her in rage for not saving her. Then the light went out of those eyes. Bonnie screamed Mabel's name.

"Bonnie . . . Bonnie . . . BONNIE!" The nurse was shaking her awake. Pulling the nurse to her quivering body, Bonnie cried as she remembered how battered and bruised Mabel looked lying next to her car as she was helpless to stop her fall. The guilt crushed her.

"There. There. Shhh. It was all a bad dream," the nurse said.

Bonnie shivered as the cold sweat dried on her skin. Brushing the tears away, she pulled back from the nurse's embrace. "So you mean it's all a bad dream that I was almost killed in a car accident and my best friend is in a coma right now?"

The look on the nurse's face told her everything she needed to know. She turned away from Bonnie, checking the readings on the machines. Satisfied everything was within normal parameters, she turned off the light and went to check on other patients.

Bonnie was too scared to go back to sleep in case the nightmare came back. She had relived the accident enough over the last two weeks. Her mom's constant questioning of why she'd been on that particular road at all wasn't helping her recovery. She couldn't believe it had only been two weeks since she last saw Mabel's beautiful face.

Once again the scent of lilacs drifted to her. Turning over so she could see the flowers Bobby had brought her, Bonnie's thoughts returned to the woman she loved. Mabel was the only one who saw *her*, not her father's money.

'Now who will see me?'

As their argument played out again in her head, she couldn't help counting everything her cowardice had cost her. There was no denying her attraction to Mabel. When they were together, everything was perfect. Remembering how strong and safe she felt wrapped in Mabel's arms, Bonnie finally allowed herself to fall back asleep. Her last thought before she drifted off was how much she loved Mabel. If she were given a second chance with her, she would be sure not to waste it.

Chapter 15 - 1972

"Are you ready to go, sweetheart?" Bonnie's mom asked as she entered the hospital room, accompanied by her dad and Charles. Bonnie's injuries were healing nicely and she was going home today. The doctors still had concerns about her right leg, the one that had been badly mangled in the accident, but it would be six more weeks before the casts could come off and they would know for sure if the bones had set properly. In the meantime, as the bones in her legs and pelvis continued to heal, she would need rehab to learn to walk again.

"Yes, I am sick to death of being here. I can't wait to sleep in my own bed tonight."

The nurse came in with Bonnie's discharge papers and a wheelchair to take her downstairs, and Charles came into the room just as her father signed the last release form.

"Is the most beautiful girl in the world ready to go home?" Charles asked.

"I don't know if she is, but I sure am," Bonnie said, cringing as Charles leaned in to kiss her cheek.

She couldn't wait to feel the sun on her face again. Being cooped up for two months had taken a toll on her usual cheery disposition. Ever since Bobby's visit, she had been longing to visit Mabel. When she asked her parents to visit her before they left, her dad told her they didn't have time today.

"Maybe you could come back another time," he said evasively. Bonnie sensed her parents were up to something, but assumed they had some kind of surprise party planned for her today. She would convince Charles to bring her back later to see Mabel.

As they left the hospital, Bonnie rolled down the window of the car to feel the breeze on her face. She felt like she was breathing for the first time in months. It had been agony being stuck in that room. Bonnie had to find a way to see Mabel. She had so many things to say to her, starting with the decision she made for her life.

"Bonnie, dear, roll up that window. You don't want to catch cold now that you're finally out of the hospital. You have to take it easy until you can get back on your feet," her mother said. Reluctantly, Bonnie rolled up her window, mumbling about her useless legs. She suddenly had a glimpse of what her life would be like as she recovered from the accident. Thinking about it made her shudder as she felt her freedom being stripped away. Her resolve to live life by her own rules grew stronger the farther they drove away from the hospital.

Bonnie stared down at her fingers entwined with Charles's. For the first time, she could not stand him touching her. His calloused fingers from the hours of football practice scratched against her sensitive skin. His possessive touch leeched onto her body, sucking away her own identity. She couldn't live with her parents' expectations to become his wife and the mother of his children. If they were to marry, there would be no more Bonnie, only a shell of the woman she used to be. She was determined that was never going to happen.

"Why are we getting on the highway?" she asked her father. "I thought we were going home." A look passed between her parents and she knew something was off. There was something they had not told her. It was so typical of her parents to keep her in the dark, thinking she was too fragile to handle anything upsetting.

Turning to face her from the front seat, her mother explained they were driving to Chicago. She and Bonnie would be living there over the next several months.

"Why?"

"You'll need extensive rehab if you ever want to walk again. The doctors recommended this facility as the best in the state."

"I found a two-bedroom apartment for you and your mother close to the rehab center. I will drive up on the weekends to see you," her father said.

"Bonnie, your parents are only doing the best they can for you," Charles said.

Yanking her hand away from Charles, she turned to the window to hide the tears threatening to fall. Bonnie had just become a prisoner of her parents and fiancé, with no chance of parole in sight. It was bad enough being trapped under all the plaster of her casts, but now she was going to be trapped with only her mother for company for the next several months. Bonnie's new plans for her life slipped away from her every mile they drove closer to Chicago. As tears of distress welled in her eyes, Charles tried to pull her to him, but she pushed him away.

Bonnie bit back her retort of wishing she'd died in the accident. Instead, she was being held hostage by three well-intentioned people who never took her wants or desires seriously. She could feel her spirit shattering just like her bones. Would she ever see Mabel again in this lifetime? She wiped at her tears. What was the point of living now? Without Mabel, life didn't really matter anymore.

* * *

As Bonnie's parents drove her to Chicago, the doctors talked to Mabel's parents about long-term care for their daughter. The swelling in her brain had finally gone down, but she still had not shown any signs of waking from her coma. She needed more care than the hospital could provide.

Mr. Flanigan told the doctor he would check out the options available and let him know their decision by the end of the week. He had been making calls to different facilities for the past several weeks and might have found the perfect one to treat Mabel. Ever since he found the sketch of his naked daughter in the arms of another woman, he knew he had to do something. There was no way a daughter of his was going to be a lesbian.

He would make sure of it, even if he had to take drastic measures.

Chapter 16 - 1972

"Bonnie, you've put it off long enough. It's time for you to start therapy." Her mother was losing her patience and didn't hide it very well.

"I don't want to," Bonnie said stubbornly. "I didn't ask to come here. What does it matter if I don't learn to walk again? Just leave me alone."

She sat looking at the dreary day outside the small window in her bedroom. It had been raining for three straight days. The weather outside matched her mood. She was still angry with her parents over their deception and had refused to leave her room except to eat and use the bathroom. Bonnie felt broken.

"You've been moping around here for weeks. The doctor said the sooner you start therapy, the better chance you have of learning to walk again. I made you an appointment for Thursday."

"That's in two days, Mother," Bonnie snapped. She didn't want to do therapy with her heavy, bulky casts. They weren't scheduled to come off for three more weeks. The smell and itching of her casts were driving her crazy. She longed to soak in a warm bubble bath instead of her mother having to bathe her carefully every day.

"I don't want to hear any more excuses why you can't go to therapy."

Bonnie felt no reason to walk when Mabel might never wake up from her coma. The bones in her legs had been badly damaged in the accident, leaving her once-beautiful legs trapped and desperately trying to heal in stinky plaster. An eight-inch angry red, jagged scar ran from her ribs to her hip bone, reminding her how much her life had changed. She was in constant pain, but her mother carefully doled out her pain medication, too worried about Bonnie's mental state to trust her with her own medications.

Bonnie would never be beautiful again, especially for Mabel. *'How could she love me now with all my scars? After all I've done, how can she ever forgive me?'* These gloomy thoughts kept her company as she watched the drizzly rain falling. She tuned out her mother's chatter, annoyed the woman just wouldn't let her be. Her mom had been constantly pushing her to go to therapy and she was tired of fighting about it.

"It's time for you to get back to your life. Charles is waiting to marry you, so you need to work on walking down the aisle."

"Get back to my life? Are you kidding me, Mother? You and Dad took me away from my life and are determined to make *your* life my life. I want no part of it." Bonnie spun away from the window and rolled past her stunned mother into the bathroom, slamming the door before allowing the tears of frustration to fall.

The thought of marrying Charles pressed down on her like a fifty-pound bag of cement permanently attached to her shoulders. She was being buried alive under the expectations of her mother and Charles. Bonnie just wanted a minute to herself where she didn't have to live up to someone else's expectations for her, a minute where she wasn't constantly reminded she was no longer the woman Mabel had plans for, a minute where her mother was fixated on something besides her. She was sick of her mother's constant hovering.

A few hours later, Bonnie wheeled herself into the kitchen to find something to eat.

"Let me help you," her mother offered, following her into the kitchen.

"NO! I don't need your help. Stop making me feel like an invalid. Back off and let me have some space, please."

Bonnie spun past her mother and returned to her bedroom. The hospital bed took up most of the space in the small room, a constant reminder of her helplessness. She let the tears fall down her cheeks in anger as she swept books off the battered desk. As they clattered to the floor, she berated herself for her foolishness. This was the price she'd pay for her cowardice.

Rolling over to the bed, she pulled the quilt over her legs and rolled back to the window, her thoughts turning to Mabel. The woman she loved was never far from her mind these days. What would her life be like now if she'd said yes? Would they both be in college, or would Bonnie have gone to work? Where would they be living? Staring out the window at the gray skies, Bonnie fell asleep in her wheelchair dreaming of living in sunny California just as Mabel had planned.

* * *

Bonnie's mom dragged her to her first physical therapy session later that week. She was grateful Phil, the therapist, wouldn't let her mom stay to watch her try to maneuver around in her bulky leg casts. Whatever she had expected from therapy, the pain was a shock. She cried in agony through most of the exercises as her long-dormant muscles were stretched and pulled in all directions. Phil explained her muscles had to get used to working again. Since she was still in her casts, they had to strengthen the muscles she would need to walk again. Bonnie didn't care; she just wanted the torture to end.

At the end of the session, Phil told her the pain was normal and that it would get better over time. He warned her she might feel stiff tomorrow from all the exercises they had done.

"Your muscles will get stronger. You haven't used them for a long time, so you're learning to retrain them," he said, gently encouraging her. Cautioning her not to overdo it, he went over some exercises she could do at home that would make their time together go more smoothly. Bonnie took her time to gather her things before leaving. This was the first moment she'd truly had to herself since moving here weeks ago. She loved the solitude she experienced as Phil went to speak to her mother.

Leaving therapy, her mother tried to engage her in conversation, but Bonnie was exhausted. Therapy had zapped all the energy she had, but she had found a two-fold silver lining in going along with it: she got a break from her mother, and because she had to focus so much on making her muscles move, her thoughts of Mabel got pushed to the back of her mind.

Bonnie fell asleep on the short ride back to the apartment. It was the only way not to get into an argument with her mother about how rude it was for the therapist to stop her from helping her own daughter.

Chapter 17 - 1972

The scent of lilacs. Mabel's nose struggled sending a message to her sluggish brain. She knew that smell. From where? If only she could open her eyes to find the source of the beautiful fragrance. Why was it so familiar? *'Bonnie.'* The name flashed in her mind. It was Bonnie. She was here. Mabel's limbs felt weighted in concrete. Why couldn't she move them?

Mabel tried getting her brain to function. Her eyelids were sewn shut; she couldn't will them open. What was going on? She had to see Bonnie again. Why weren't her eyes cooperating? A frustrated moan slipped out. Using all the strength she could muster, Mabel concentrated on forcing her eyelids open.

"Too bright. Too bright." Her brain screamed in pain. Her eyelids slammed shut, blocking out the blinding light.

"I think she tried to open her eyes, Bobby. It was just for a second, but I think she tried."

"It was probably a muscle spasm. She does that periodically."

* * *

Since their dad had discarded Mabel into Pleasant Meadows State Hospital weeks ago, the visits from family and friends had dwindled down to almost nothing. Only Bobby kept his vigil for his sister. He no longer spent the night with her because it was an hour drive to the facility and an hour drive back to Wheatonville. He came as often as he could, but between classes, football practice, and his hours at the garage, most of the time Mabel was left all alone in the deep, dark hole of her dad's brutality.

A few minutes later, Corrine swore Mabel tried to open her eyes again. "Bobby, come here. She just squinted at the light." Corrine stroked her hand with a feather-light touch, looking down to see Mabel's fingers trying to move. "I know you think I'm crazy, but she moved her fingers, Bobby."

He looked down at his sister's face and a beat later it happened. Squinting blue eyes stared at him through half-opened lids. He didn't want to get his hopes up. Mabel had opened her eyes before, but there had been no focus to them——now she was blinking rapidly. That was new.

"Quick, Bobby. Close the blinds. I think the light is hurting her eyes."

Bobby walked over to the window and tried to pull the shade down. It only came partway down, but it seemed to be enough. Mabel's eyes adjusted to the brightness, and she opened them for longer periods of time.

"I'll go get the doctor," he said. Bobby ran out of the room to find a nurse and had to explain to them three times what happened before they finally understood his excited recounting of events. Once the doctor was paged, Bobby paced nervously at the nurse's station.

"I'm Dr. Cantrell. How can I help you?"

"I think my sister is waking up." Bobby led Dr. Cantrell into Mabel's room.

"We'll need to run some tests to be sure, but it looks like she is starting to come out of the coma," Dr. Cantrell said after shining a light into Mabel's eyes.

Grinning from ear to ear, Bobby picked up Corrine and swung her around. He held out his hand to thank the doctor. Mabel was back.

* * *

The next time Mabel opened her eyes she saw her brother sitting alone watching her with a goofy grin on his face. He jumped up and placed a sloppy, wet kiss on her forehead. She wanted to wipe it off, but her arms still felt full of lead and she couldn't move them. The open display of affection was so unlike Bobby. Why was he acting so strange?

"I have a lot to tell you, Mayflower, but it will keep until later."

She tried to speak, but her throat was so dry and there was something in the way. Bobby placed a hand on her shoulder and told her to try not to talk.

"Mabel, you are in a hospital," he said. "You have a ventilator and feeding tubes in your throat so you can't talk. We are waiting for them to run some tests before they take them out."

She wasn't sure she'd heard him correctly. Why was she in the hospital? She should be getting ready to start her senior year in high school. Where was Bonnie? Mabel was so sure she'd been here or was it only a dream? A bouquet of lilacs sat on the table next to her bed. Were those the lilacs she smelled? Something just didn't feel right in her mind. Her brain was foggy and she started to panic about being pulled back into the darkness. Bobby grabbed her hand, trying to soothe her.

* * *

"I really need to speak to your parents, Mr. Flanigan," Dr. Cantrell said.

"Whatever it is, Doctor, you can tell me. As you may have noticed, my parents haven't been around to see their daughter much since they dumped her in this place. No offense."

"Still, they are paying for your sister's care and therefore, only they have the authority to make medical decisions for her."

"Doctor, if something is wrong with my sister, I need to know. I take full responsibility for whatever it is and will tell my parents I made you tell me."

Dr. Cantrell glanced down the hallway as he ran his fingers through his thinning brown hair. Flipping the pages in Mabel's medical chart he said, "This is highly unusual and I still don't feel comfortable talking to you about your sister, but I guess I'll have to trust you will do the right thing and tell your parents what we discuss."

"Sure thing, Doc. Now what did the tests show about Mabel? Is she going to be okay?"

"Mr. Flanigan, as you are aware, it does look like your sister has come out of her coma. Depending on how she does over the next twenty-four hours, we will take the tubes out. We won't know any long-term issues for another couple of weeks."

"That's great news. I would almost guarantee you she is going to be fine. Wait and see."

"There is one more thing, Mr. Flanigan. I'm not sure how to say it."

"Just spit it out, Doc."

"There is a note in your sister's chart that if she ever regains consciousness, she is to be moved to a different section of our facility."

"What are you saying?"

"Once the tubes come out and all the tests have been run, your sister will be moved to the psych ward of our hospital and you will have limited visiting privileges."

"What?" Bobby's legs buckled and he stumbled into the wall. He grabbed his head to keep the dizziness from releasing his stomach contents, fighting to understand the doctor's words.

This can't be happening. Mabel has been through enough already. Will her nightmare never end?

"I'm really sorry about this, Mr. Flanigan."

Bobby watched the doctor walk down the hallway to check on other patients. Needing a minute to pull himself together, Bobby went to the restroom and splashed cold water on his face. When he felt calm enough he returned to Mabel's room. He shared the good news about the respirator and feeding tubes being taken out soon. Waiting until Mabel had fallen back asleep, he wrote Mabel a note saying he would return tomorrow. He then ran out of the building as fast as he could because the walls of her room had started closing in on him and he couldn't catch his breath.

Bobby unlocked his car and sat staring unseeing straight ahead for several minutes. It wasn't fair. His dad had made sure he locked Mabel away for loving Bonnie and there wasn't a damn thing he could do about it. Bobby wiped the unshed tears from the corner of his eye and started the car. He left the institution and made the long drive home in the dark.

Chapter 18 - 1972

Mabel hadn't expected the removal of the tubes to be so painful. She tried squeezing Bobby's hands to ward off the pain, but didn't have much strength left in her fingers. When the tubes were finally out, he started feeding her ice chips as instructed to help soothe the rawness in her throat. The coolness of the melting ice did help some.

"It's okay, Mayflower," he said. She smiled at his pet name for her. He was the only one she allowed to call her that. "Be patient. Your voice will come back soon."

Mabel lay in bed, slowly sucking the ice chips as her eyes took in her surroundings. She saw a big water spot in the corner of the ceiling by the door to her room. The flat gray walls matched the dreariness of the clouds she saw outside her window.

"D-da-date," she managed to force past the soreness in her throat. A look of confusion crossed her brother's face. Mabel was barely able to breathe when she heard the date.

Bobby tried to ease her fear. "You've been in a coma for three months, sis. You were in the hospital for eight weeks and then Dad moved you to this place."

"Do my teachers know what happened? Will they let me make up my classes?" Mabel asked Bobby hoarsely. Now that she was awake, she needed to get back to school. She probably had a lot of homework to make up if she was going to graduate this spring with all her friends.

"The college deferred your enrollment for a year."

"College?" Mabel asked, confused. "Bobby, I have to finish high school first."

"Sis, I'm going to go get the doctor. I'll be right back." He left Mabel alone in her room.

Mabel tried processing what Bobby said. Had she really been in a coma for over a year?

Why was she here? And where exactly was *here*? What happened to her? Why couldn't she remember? It didn't look or have the smell of a real hospital. And where was her mom? Why was Bobby the only one here? She searched her memories for a fragment of information, but her mind was a dark night without moon or stars to be seen. Her head throbbed from all the questions and the exertion of trying to remember. She reached up with shaky fingers to rub her pounding temples.

* * *

At the nurse's station, Bobby had Dr. Cantrell paged. Walking hurriedly to the counter carrying several patients' charts, the doctor dropped the charts on the counter before acknowledging Bobby.

"Doctor, you need to come look at my sister right now."

"Mr. Flanigan, what is the problem? Did something go wrong when the tubes were taken out?"

"Please, Doc, call me Bobby. Mr. Flanigan is my worthless father. They didn't have any issues taking out the tubes. It's something else. Mabel and I were talking and I think something is wrong with her memory."

Dr. Cantrell asked the nurse to file the charts and followed Bobby back into Mabel's room. Along the way, Bobby explained Mabel had been asking him questions. He told the doctor she seemed shocked to hear that she had already graduated high school.

"It's like she doesn't remember what happened to her."

Dr. Cantrell stepped close to her bed. "Mabel, what is the last thing you remember before waking up yesterday?"

It took her a moment to understand the doctor's question. She asked him to repeat it. Looking at the concern on their faces, Mabel searched her mind for the last memory she had.

"Getting ready to start my senior year," she said. Glad to see her voice remembered how to work, Mabel overlooked the pain in her throat. She caught the small upward movement of the doctor's eyebrow at her answer.

"Can you remember anything after that, prior to you waking up yesterday?"

Mabel shook her throbbing head no. The movement sent more stabbing pain to her temples and she pressed down on the top of her head to lessen the pain.

She looked over at Bobby and noticed the frown lines increase on his forehead. There was something wrong with her they weren't sharing. Mabel could feel herself getting upset with them for their silence.

"Mabel, tell me what happens when you try to remember."

"It starts out with a flash of blinding light. Then there is just this darkness or black space. There's nothing there," she said.

After checking her vitals, the doctor asked Bobby to step outside with him for a moment.

Bobby felt her anxiety the moment he returned to Mabel's room and sat down. He knew she needed to follow the nurse's directions and eat to get better. The orderly brought in a bowl of chicken broth for her.

"Bobby, what am I going to do?" she asked, sounding so lost.

"First thing you are going to do is eat your soup," he said.

"I'm not hungry."

"Mayflower, please try. Remember the nurses said this is the first step in getting you back to solid foods."

Reluctantly, Mabel pulled the bowl closer to her. Bobby watched her frustration as her fingers kept dropping the spoon, splashing soup all over the front of her hospital gown. Taking the spoon from her, he slowly fed her the lukewarm broth.

"Mabel, the doctor says you might have something called retrograde amnesia. They are going to run more tests to be sure. What do you remember before school started?" Bobby asked when she had swallowed the last mouthful of broth.

"The annual End of Summer celebration," she said, "1971."

* * *

"Come on, Bonnie. We're gonna miss the fireworks." Mabel urged her to hurry. They sprinted the last hundred yards to the city park.

"I'm coming. I'm coming," Bonnie said breathlessly, trying to catch up with Mabel's long stride.

They ran the last hundred yards to the city park where the annual End of Summer celebration was taking place. It was the town leaders' way of saying goodbye to the summer tourists and giving the students a sendoff into a new school year. It looked like the entire town was here tonight.

In just a few days, Mabel and her friends would be starting their senior year. They looked for Corrine, who had returned from summer camp a couple days ago where she'd been working for the last three months. Out of the corner of her eye, Mabel saw Corrine waving them over to the spot she had reserved for the three of them. Corrine had called Mabel yesterday, wanting to meet at the festival. The three friends were eager to catch each other up on their summers.

"There she is! Let's go," Mabel dragged Bonnie through the crowd of people until they were able to weave their way to the spot Corrine had saved.

"What took you guys so long? We were supposed to meet thirty minutes ago," Corrine said.

Mabel purposely avoided looking at Bonnie, feeling the heat still coming from the young woman's body. It was her fault they were late. Bonnie had asked to sketch Mabel again and one thing led to another. They had soon found themselves naked, making love in the cabin, any ideas of art lost in the passion of exploring the physicality of their new relationship. Mabel had discovered an awakening sexuality simmering in her and explored it every chance she was alone with Bonnie. She didn't want to think about what they would do when the school year started. Their attraction was intense and hard to control. It was going to be difficult to pretend they were only friends, especially when they could barely keep their hands to themselves now. She caught Corrine's puzzled look and realized she was waiting for an answer.

"Bonnie was working on some sketches and we lost track of time." Mabel told the half-truth with ease.

"Oh, Bonnie. That sounds so artistic. I'd love to see some of your drawings. What were you drawing today that made you lose track of time?"

Bonnie's cheeks darkened to a bright cherry-red color. "It was a new piece," she finally admitted.

"I'm sorry. Did you say *nude* piece?" Mabel asked, tormenting Bonnie. She loved watching her get flustered with any mention of sexual nature.

"Gross, Mabel. God, sometimes you are such a child," Corrine said.

"It's okay, Corrine." Bonnie stuck her tongue out at Mabel. "I'm trying to capture the beauty of the natural landscape."

Mabel started coughing at Bonnie's reply because she knew she was the landscape Bonnie tried to capture. It was Bonnie's way of getting back at her for teasing her about their afternoon together. Corrine looked at Mabel as if to see she was okay, but before she could ask any more questions, Bonnie asked if Oscar and Jay were meeting them at the festivities. Charles had already started his second year of college, so he wouldn't be coming tonight. It still would bother Mabel when Bonnie talked about her relationship with him and the future they were planning. Corrine interrupted her jealous thoughts by saying the boys were helping with the fireworks and would catch up with them later at the carnival.

The drummers from the high school band signaled the beginning of the ceremonies with a rousing cadence. The band started with a traditional patriotic sing-along number that was, surprisingly, mostly in tune this year. Following that, the mayor gave his usual long-winded speech about appreciating the tourists helping the local economy and building excitement for the upcoming school year.

Mabel quit listening two minutes after he began talking. She was glad the boys weren't going to be joining them until later. It was getting harder and harder to play along enough to feign any interest in going out with Jay.

Right now she was trying to devise a not-so-obvious way to touch Bonnie.

Corrine had effectively put herself in between the two of them and kept moving so any attempt at a simple touch would be easily noticed.

The sound of applause interrupted Mabel's musings. She looked up as the mayor finally finished his speech.

"Where were you?" Corrine whispered in her ear.

"Nowhere," she replied. She couldn't tell Corrine her thoughts. Not that she didn't love her best friend, but Corrine came down on the side of hellfire and damnation where sin was concerned. And this one, this sexual thing between her and Bonnie, was a big sin, at least to everyone she knew in this town. Mabel was still having a hard time figuring out why God would allow her to love someone as beautiful and amazing as Bonnie, then call it bad. If she were truly created in the image and likeness of God, surely some part of him was just like this. Somehow, she didn't think the pastor at the Baptist church would ever see it that way. If Corrine knew, she would feel obligated to tell Mabel's parents for her own good. Mabel could only imagine the punishment her dad would give her for that. Sitting, she knew, would be the least of her worries. This relationship between her and Bonnie would have to remain their secret and theirs alone.

"How soon before the fireworks start?" Bonnie asked with a twinkle in her eye. Bonnie loved fireworks, but she wasn't just talking about the ones exploding in the sky tonight.

"I think around ten," Corrine answered. "Don't forget, after the fireworks show we're meeting the guys at the carnival on the other side of the park. I hear they have some new rides this year."

"That would be great. I love new rides," Bonnie said.

A flush immediately started up Mabel's neck. She was glad it had gotten dark enough that Corrine wouldn't notice. Bonnie smiled innocently at her over Corrine's head.

"Count me in, but I have to tell my parents first. Hopefully Dad's in a good mood tonight and will let me stay out longer," Mabel said. His mood had gotten worse over the summer. He had been passed over for a promotion at work, but she also thought her not being around to relieve his frustration was a part of it as well. Between her hours at the drugstore and the time she spent with Bonnie, Mabel had managed to mostly stay away from her dad for the last three months. The last time she'd been punished was before school let out for the summer, and she could tell he was like a powder keg, ready to explode. Mabel prayed she wouldn't be around when he erupted like the very fireworks she was watching overhead.

As the fireworks continued to explode, lighting up the humid summer sky, Mabel snuck a peek at Bonnie. Excitement danced in her eyes at the colorful display bursting across the sky. Why did the world have to be so complicated? She turned back to watch the multicolored show. She would have to think of a way for them to be together more permanently, because without Bonnie in her life, she couldn't imagine breathing, let alone being happy.

* * *

Mabel's mind jolted back to the present. She looked Bobby in the eye and asked the question that had been flitting around in the back of her mind since she'd woken up.

"Bobby, where's Bonnie?"

Chapter 19 - 1972

"Dr. Gilbert, a Dr. Cantrell is on line two," Nurse Duncan interrupted as the doctor was updating his patient notes. The nurse's staticky voice over the intercom grated on his nerves. Dr. Gilbert punched the flashing light on his phone as he picked up the receiver.

"Dr. Gilbert, here," he said gruffly. He tried to place Dr. Cantrell but couldn't bring to mind any recollection of the doctor. Dr. Gilbert listened as the other doctor explained he had a patient who just awoke from a coma and was experiencing retrograde amnesia.

"Her father thinks she would recover quicker under your care," Dr. Cantrell said.

"Who's her father?" Dr. Gilbert heard the shuffling of papers as Dr. Cantrell searched for the name.

"The father is listed as Robert Flanigan."

Dr. Gilbert smiled as he had been waiting for this phone call. He was about to get another subject for his research. "Ah, yes I have spoken with Mr. Flanigan about his daughter's particular case. Can you arrange to have her transferred to the psychiatric wing? We need to begin treatment immediately."

***

Mabel could feel someone watching her. Barely opening her eyes, she saw a skinny black girl in pigtails grinning at her.

"Oh good, you're awake. I thought maybe you were in another coma. It's not every day we have the excitement of someone coming out of a coma here. You're like a celebrity or something. It's all anyone talks about—the girl who woke up from a coma. I just had to sneak in and see for myself. My name's Nancy. I'm going to be your new best friend."

Mabel was glad when the young teenager took a breath. All her chatter was bringing on a headache.

Mabel tried putting distance between the two of them by pulling the covers over her head. She cringed when she felt the bed sink from Nancy's weight. She suddenly felt the covers being pulled off.

"Hey."

"So, you do talk. I heard a rumor you couldn't, cause you haven't said nothin' since you were brought here."

"Go away."

"No can do."

"Leave her alone, Nancy."

"But—"

"Scoot. I told you not to bother the new kid yet."

Mabel heard a metal chair scraping across the floor and the scent of Old Spice drifted to her. "Sorry about that. The kid gets so excited when new people show up."

"Who are you?" Mabel said, pulling the covers off her head.

"I am your official guide to this particular loony bin."

"I don't need a guide. Just leave me alone."

Mabel rolled over to the other side of the bed, covering her head with her pillow. Why couldn't she be left alone?

"Time to rise and shine."

"Go away," Mabel groaned, annoyed that she'd been woken up. She turned over, rubbing the sleep from her eyes.

Sitting on the chair was a curious-looking girl about the same age as Mabel. Her hair was shaved so close to her scalp it was hard to tell its natural color, and she was what Mabel's mom would call "on the husky side." She looked to be taller than Mabel's 5'6" frame, but it was hard to tell from her own prone position on the bed. The girl's outfit was what gave Mabel the most pause.

She wore a green and blue plaid wool skirt with a red and white gingham button-up shirt. She paired the outfit with black and bright gold argyle knee-length socks. Mabel may have misjudged her height because the girl wore four-inch wedge white sandals covered in glitter. She had never seen so many different colors and patterns in one outfit.

"Get dressed so we can go to breakfast."

Mabel tried to remember the last time she ate. Throwing back the covers, she sat up on the lumpy mattress. She looked around the gray room. The color reminded her of the B-52 bombers in Vietnam she saw on the nightly news. The ceiling and floor tiles were stained and pitted, adding to the drabness of the room. Even her bedding took on a gray hue. A small sliver of sunshine made its way through the barred window in the room but disappeared quickly, afraid to cast any light in the colorless room.

"Where am I?" she asked.

"Pleasant Meadows State Mental Hospital."

"How did I get here?"

"Beats me. Probably same as the rest of us."

Why was she in a mental hospital? Mabel searched her memory and was immediately hit with the pain of a pounding headache behind her eyes. She felt nauseous and sensitive to the light. The hammering behind her eyes and in her temples hurt so bad her eyes watered. The room spun. Closing her eyes, Mabel laid back down on the bed, pulling the covers over her head.

"Take it easy. That happens a lot with the drugs they give you when you first get here."

She tried remembering how she got here and was hit with more pain. Why did it hurt so much when she tried to remember? She tried lying down perfectly still. That eased the pain a little. From her position under the covers she asked, "Why am I here? I'm not crazy."

"None of us are. Rumor has it you have the same sickness as me."

"Why are you here?"

"Kinda personal question don't you think?"

Mabel pulled the covers down so one eye peered at the unique girl. The light didn't bother her as much now that she wasn't trying to remember. She pulled the covers off her head but didn't attempt to sit up yet. The strange girl was staring at her with a smirk on her face.

"Nancy seemed to know I just woke up from a coma."

"Yeah, we don't see that too much here. See a lot of catatonics, but not too many recovering from a coma," she said.

"Get a move on if we are going to make it to breakfast on time," said the girl in the colorful outfit.

"I'm not hungry." Mabel wasn't sure she could eat with her stomach feeling so upset from her headache. It occurred to her that she'd been talking to this girl but didn't know her name.

"I'm Mabel," she said.

"My name's Sammie. You can call me Sam or Sammie. I will stab you if you call me Samantha."

Mabel laughed until she saw Sammie wasn't laughing. There was no humor in her expression at all. Maybe this girl really was crazy. She wasn't sure she should be hanging out with her alone in her room.

"The shrink keeps calling me Samantha. Thinks it will cure me. Just makes me want to strangle him in his sleep."

"What's wrong with being called Sammie?"

"I knew I was going to like you, Mabel."

"How will calling you—," Mabel stopped, unsure if she should say the other name. Deciding against it, she finished, "by that other name cure you?"

"That's a longer story than we have time for right now. Hurry up and get dressed. We can't be late for mealtime."

Mabel stood slowly and moved toward the metal dresser in the corner. The room had stopped spinning, but her head still hurt. She opened one of the drawers and found only neatly folded skirts. She hadn't worn a skirt or dress since she was twelve——she always preferred the comfort of jeans and t-shirts. Opening the rest of the drawers, she found lacy undergarments, pantyhose, and frilly blouses. She would never wear any of these clothes. Looking around to see if there was a closet where her clothes might be, she heard Sammie laughing hysterically.

"Man, it never gets old watching the new kids' reaction when they find out all they have to wear is skirts and pantyhose."

"Where are my jeans?"

"Rule number one, Mabel—girls wear skirts at Pleasant Meadows until you are cured of your *disease.*"

"What disease?"

"Rule number two," Sammie continued, ignoring her. "Never say anything in therapy. Rule number three—never be late for meals. Rule number four—don't trust anyone here, not even me. And rule number five—it's the most important rule of all. *Never, ever* swallow the pills they give you. Follow my rules and you will have a chance of getting out of here with your brain intact."

A shiver of dread ran down her spine as she listened to Sammie. Again she wondered why she was even here. She had a feeling Sammie knew but was keeping it a secret on purpose. Mabel picked out the least girly outfit, quickly dressed, and followed Sammie to the cafeteria.

* * *

Mabel felt uncomfortable walking around in the skirt. It was itchy and made her feel exposed. She watched in awe as Sammie gracefully walked in her four-inch shoes with ease. The smell of Pine-Sol stung her nose and made her eyes water. The pungent smell didn't help her headache. It reminded her of Jay's aftershave. Mabel stopped in the middle of the hallway, startled by the memory.

"What's wrong?" Sammie asked.

"I just remembered something."

"Good, that means the drugs are starting to wear off. Now come on. I'm hungry and there's going to be a long line."

Mabel almost twisted her ankle as she hurried to catch up to Sammie. She wasn't used to wearing heels like these navy-blue ones she'd found in her room. Even though they had a small heel, it was higher than her beloved tennis shoes. While she focused on walking in her awkward shoes, Mabel ran into Sammie, who had suddenly stopped.

"Sorry."

"Here we are. The first stop on your tour."

Mabel looked around the big room. It was brighter than her room, but not by much. The ceiling and floor looked identical, but the walls had been painted a dull white. Long wooden tables lined up in perfect rows. Seated at the tables were around twenty girls her age, wearing similar outfits to her own. Nancy waved to her and Mabel returned the gesture. About a dozen boys dressed in slacks, button-up shirts, and ties sat among the girls.

"You're late, Samantha."

Mabel turned to the man talking to Sammie. He was a cross between Yosemite Sam and Sam Elliott with a bushy moustache and mutton chop sideburns. She watched Sammie grip her tan melamine tray so hard, sure it would break into several pieces as Sammie tried to control her temper. With a white-knuckled grip on her tray, Sammie began moving through the serving line but was blocked by the man who had called her Samantha.

"Move," she said between gritted teeth.

"Not until you tell me why you're late," he snarled, "Unless you want to lose some of your privileges."

Sammie jerked her thumb over her shoulder at Mabel. When his attention shifted to her, she felt like a specimen on display at the museum. He barely managed to hide the look of annoyance at Sammie as he addressed Mabel.

"Hello, I'm Dr. Gilbert," he said, holding out his hand for her to shake.

She tried to focus on what he said, but she was too distracted by the way his moustache moved cartoonishly while he spoke. It didn't help that he had a big glob of oatmeal stuck in it that attracted her attention like a magnet. She didn't want to shake his hand because it seemed disloyal to Sammie. Even though Sammie had said not to trust her, Mabel saw her reaction to the doctor.

"Welcome to Pleasant Meadows," he said, dropping his hand.

She watched as he tried to figure out what to do with his rejected body part, finally dipping it into the front pocket of his well-pressed herringbone slacks. He jingled the coins in his pocket, likely out of nervousness as she had yet to say anything to him.

"Well, I guess we will have a chance to get to know each other later in our session. I hope you enjoy your stay with us."

How odd. It was like he was welcoming her to a hotel instead of a mental institution. Why would anyone enjoy a stay here? Isn't this the kind of place people get locked away because they can't function in society? She recalled the way her uncle had been treated. Her family called him "slow" and "not right in the head." Was that what was wrong with her? Did something go wrong in her brain while she was in a coma?

A nudge on her shoulder shook her from her thoughts. She was holding up the line for the others behind her. Sammie was almost to the end of the line. Mabel made her way down the line, noticing the food was as lackluster as the rest of the surroundings. She'd never seen gray eggs before and opted for cold cereal instead. She would have considered the oatmeal, but seeing it stuck in Dr. Gilbert's moustache made her lose her appetite for it. Picking up her tray, she followed Sammie to an empty chair next to a boy who looked about fourteen years old.

"I'm Randy," he introduced himself.

"Mabel."

Randy had several pimples breaking out on his rotund face. He had spilled milk on his tie. His shirt was wrinkled and he had an overall disheveled appearance. She didn't know curly hair could stray in so many directions. He seemed happy she sat next to him.

The tasteless cornflakes made her miss her mother's cooking. She managed to choke down a few bites before a wave of nausea hit her again. Mabel rubbed her temples to ease the pounding, wondering if she would starve before she ever left this gloomy place.

"You'll get used to it," Sammie said.

Mabel doubted she would ever get used to such awful food. She couldn't imagine eating such tasteless cuisine day after day. Her small frame couldn't afford to lose any more weight. She'd been teased her whole life about being too skinny, but she liked the way she looked.

"You don't talk much, do you?" Randy asked.

"Leave her be, squirt. She's got a headache from all the drugs they pumped into her. Let her get used to being in the loony bin first," Sammie said.

Randy leaned his head on his hand, staring down at his plate. Mabel watched him move what she guessed were eggs around his plate. She felt bad she didn't talk to him, but Sammie was right. She was adjusting. No, adjusting wasn't the right word. She didn't understand why she was here and needed answers now. Determination swelled in her chest. Mabel would find the answers, even if she had to talk to the creepy Dr. Gilbert for them.

Chapter 20 - 1972

After breakfast, Sammie continued playing tour guide. Mabel was surprised at all the places they were allowed to go. She'd thought being in a mental institution meant you were locked in a room by yourself all day.

"This is the group therapy room. Dr. Gilbert will expect you to tell us your deep, dark secrets, but remember rule number two and don't tell him a thing. It drives him nuts when we all sit there staring at him."

"I don't have any deep dark secrets."

"Sure you do. That's why you're here. To be cured of your secret."

"You keep saying I need to be cured. Of what?"

"Come on," Sammie said, "let's check out the activity room."

Why did Sammie keep avoiding her questions? *What disease do I have? I don't feel sick . . . If only I could remember.*

Twenty minutes later, they were sneaking up a concrete staircase. Sammie had them take off their shoes so they wouldn't get caught. Looking at Sammie's socks, it looked like bumblebees had been attacking her legs.

"Why aren't you wearing pantyhose?" Mabel asked.

"Shh."

"Where are we going?"

"To see the real crazies."

Opening the door quietly, they snuck down the hall until they came to a padlocked metal door with the sign reading, "Authorized Personnel Only" painted in big red letters. Strange moaning carried through the glass window. Mabel tightly grasped Sammie's hand at all the tormented sounds on the other side.

"Where did you bring me?"

"I told you. To see the real crazies."

"Why can't you ever give me a straight answer?"

"Straight's not in my vocabulary, but this is the floor where they put all the soldiers with mental problems from the Vietnam War."

Mabel was shocked by this news. She had friends fighting over there, at least she thought she did. She worried her younger brother Bobby would be drafted and sent overseas.

"Come on, we gotta go."

"What?"

"If we get caught up here, we'll get into real trouble."

Mabel followed Sammie back down the staircase. When they reached their floor of the hospital, they sat on the rough bottom step to put their shoes back on. She was still thinking about the soldiers and her brother when they returned to their floor.

"That concludes your tour of PMS."

"PMS?"

"Pleasant Meadows Shithole." Sammie roared with laughter.

"What do we do now?" The tour had only taken an hour. With the rest of the day looming ahead, how did patients spend their time in this hospital?

"Now we go see how crazy you really are."

Chapter 21 - 1972

"Let's welcome our latest guest to Pleasant Meadows. Everyone, say hello to Mabel."

She listened as everyone mumbled greetings to her as instructed by Dr. Gilbert. Seated in a circle of folding chairs, she counted sixteen people in the group. Some she remembered seeing at breakfast this morning.

"Today we are going to talk about the roles of men and women in relationships," he said to begin the session.

Mabel watched as the group shifted uneasily in their chairs as he continued talking. No one was really paying attention to him. Several group members stared at their hands or feet and others stared off into space. Randy smiled at her from across the circle and she smiled back.

"Women are meant to create a home and raise families. They are not meant to go out and get a job."

Dr. Gilbert's statement captured her attention as she wasn't sure she'd heard him correctly. She thought she misunderstood him until she saw Sammie had balled her fingers into a tight fist.

"Our society has been sending mixed messages to women. Messages like 'you can do anything a man can do.' I'm telling you that is a *lie*. A lie you've been brainwashed into believing."

Mabel stared at Dr. Gilbert in disbelief. *'What kind of therapy is this?'*

"That's why you are here. To learn the truth about what it means to be proper men and women in our society."

Next to her, Sammie muttered something.

"Did you have something you wanted to share with the group, Samantha?"

She watched as Sammie struggled to control her anger. Sammie glared at Dr. Gilbert until he was forced to look away. Again, Mabel wondered why he couldn't just call her Sammie. She almost missed Dr. Gilbert's next sentence.

"Women are meant to be in relationships with men, not other women. The same goes for men. You are here at Pleasant Meadows to be cured of your sexually deviant ways."

Sammie's evasiveness suddenly all made sense, but something else didn't. *'Why would her family dump her in such a place?'* She hadn't told them about Bonnie, and she'd been very careful in hiding the mementos Bonnie had given her. How had they found out? Did Bobby let something slip? Or did they only suspect she loved a woman?

Loving Bonnie made her feel alive, more so than any man ever did. The reason she felt different from other girls didn't make her sick or deviant. It was a part of her, like her blue eyes or blond hair. Loving women wasn't a choice. Why on earth would she choose something that got her locked up in a mental institution? If it were a choice, she would've married Jay to make everyone else happy.

As Dr. Gilbert droned on about proper roles for men and women, Mabel's mind drifted to Jay. He'd crossed her mind earlier on the way to breakfast, and now she recalled one of their conversations.

* * *

Another Saturday night in small-town America. Mabel couldn't wait to get out of here because she was going to be bigger than Wheatonville after she graduated. Bonnie was visiting her grandmother this weekend and Corrine was doing something with her church youth group. Jay had stopped by the pharmacy as Mabel was getting off work.

"Want to go see a movie tonight?" he asked as they walked out the door together. They came to a stop on the sidewalk outside of Daisy's Diner.

"We've seen everything at the theater already."

"We could go bowling," he said, imitating rolling a strike.

"It's league night. We won't be able to get a lane until after nine."

"What do you want to do then?"

"There's nothing to do here, Jay." Mabel looked up and down Main Street. She watched as most of the stores closed up until Monday morning.

"Come on, Mabel. Just be glad your dad was okay with you going out after work tonight. Let's go have some fun." He jammed his hands into his back pockets and kicked at a rock on the sidewalk.

"There isn't anything fun in this podunk town. It's the same thing week after week."

"We could go to Oscar's party," he said excitedly.

"I can't. Not after the way he dumped Corrine. Besides, I don't want to listen to disco all night." Mabel scrunched up her nose at the thought of listening to the loud, synthesized music and watching her classmates making out all night.

"Our friends will be there."

"*Your* friends, Jay. You can go without me."

"Everyone will ask where you are."

"So?"

"Geez, Mabel. What do you want me to tell them? She couldn't come because she's going to college and doesn't have time to hang out with the *uneducated folk* of Wheatonville?"

"That's not fair."

"What's not fair is thinking you are the only one with plans for life after high school. Not all of us want to be stuck here like our parents!"

"Jay, I know you don't want to be part of your dad's construction business, but it's not the same thing."

"Why? Because I'd rather go into the Army instead of some fancy university like you?"

"No, because you have options." Mabel knew Jay would never understand what it was like to have parents who didn't believe in education.

"What options, Mabel? We both know I'm going to Vietnam and there's a chance I may not come back."

"Don't say that."

"It's true. You think I don't listen to the news? I know our chances of winning aren't good, but I'm still going."

"Why?"

"Because it may be my only chance to see the world outside of Wheatonville."

Mabel had never thought of Jay wanting to leave their hometown. They'd been friends since grade school but hadn't talked like this since they started high school. That's when Jay's feelings for her changed. She missed this side of him. Thinking about him leaving to go fight in a war they couldn't win on the other side of the world scared her. Mabel finally saw she had wanted her life to move forward but thought everyone else's would stay the same. Now she realized in a few months everything would change for all of them. Even in this town of stagnation.

"Let's go to the park," she said.

When Jay pulled his pickup into the parking lot of the only park in Wheatonville, it was getting dark, so most families were at home taking their Saturday night baths, cleaning up for church in the morning. She was glad to have a job so she didn't have to go anymore. She had no use for religion in her life, especially the fire and brimstone kind. To Mabel's thinking, the God the preacher talked about was a mean-spirited scorekeeper and she'd decided not to play his game.

As they walked along the darkened sidewalk, she let Jay slip his hand in hers. It felt different now, like a silent agreement had been reached. Mabel led them to the latest addition to the park, a 1960 Santa Fe restored caboose. These cars used to travel through Wheatonville daily until the railroad cut costs and took their town off the route. Mabel remembered standing on her dad's feet as the trains rushed by when she was a little girl. . She loved the way the air messed up her hair and the sound of the wheels on the tracks.

Her dad hadn't always been such a mean jerk. She had several other memories of the fun she had with him when she was a little girl. What had happened to the kind and funny man she once loved? Her mom said it was because life kicked him in the teeth one too many times. She wished he would be like that again, but she had a feeling that all the alcohol he consumed on a daily basis prevented that from happening.

Mabel let Jay climb to the top of the caboose first so he could pull her up. They pretended to ride the rails like they used to when they were kids. Jay called it *train surfing*.

"Watch out for the tunnel," he said.

Mabel ducked as the pretend tunnel approached. Popping back up, she saw Jay's confused expression as he looked at her.

"What?" she asked.

"How come we can't date and have fun like this?"

"Jay, don't ruin this."

"I'm not trying to, but I've never understood why you refuse to admit that we're dating."

There it was. The perfect opportunity to tell him why she would never be more than friends with him. She wanted to—the words sat on the tip of her tongue—but she knew he would never understand, would never accept her as she really was. He would try to convince her that her attraction for Bonnie wasn't real. She could hear him reminding her of how close they'd been growing up and how she'd promised him when she was ten that she would marry him.

Instead she said, "Come look at the stars with me." She was not only avoiding answering him this time, but she was also tired of always having to answer that same question. She could never give him the answer he wanted, so staying quiet seemed like the best solution.

He sat down beside her and together they pointed out the different constellations. Jay was almost as good as her at identifying each one. He should be, since they had been doing this together since they were eight. The half moon and its position in the sky told her it was time to head home.

"We have to go. I can't be late."

Climbing down the caboose first, Jay waited for her at the bottom without saying a word. The silent treatment continued on the ride home. She rolled down her window despite the cool temperatures outside to prolong watching the starry night.

Jay pulled into her driveway, barely waiting until she got out before he drove off. If he thought his silence bothered her, he was mistaken. She'd found comfort in not having to discuss his obsession with dating.

* * *

Startled back to the present by the scraping of chairs across the floor, Mabel stood and followed the group in putting her chair away. It was hard to believe everyone in her group was just like her. She now understood why no one spoke to Dr. Gilbert.

"How did you like our group session today, Mabel?" Dr. Gilbert asked.

Without answering she followed Sammie and several of the others to the activity room. She had to get out of this place—and soon.

'Bonnie must be worried sick.'

Chapter 22 - 1972

Bonnie couldn't wait for therapy today. The casts were finally off and today she would try taking her first steps since the accident. She made Phil promise not to tell her mother. Bonnie didn't want to hear all the conversations about walking down the aisle at her wedding to Charles. There wasn't going to be a wedding. She was determined to find Mabel right after she could walk again and beg her forgiveness for screwing everything up between them.

A drizzle of rain began to fall on the drive to the rehab clinic. Bonnie was sick of this gloomy weather, but it wouldn't dampen her spirits today. She smiled as she stared out the passenger side window, remembering a romantic summer afternoon spent with Mabel in the rain. Bonnie had convinced Mabel to pick wildflowers with her when the skies opened in a sudden downpour. Mabel started pirouetting her around in the rain. That girl loved being out in the rain. Bonnie began shivering, soaked to the skin, and Mabel grabbed her hand as they ran to the cabin. Once inside the door, they dripped water on the wooden floor. Luckily the roof hadn't been leaking that day. They stripped off their wet clothing and hung them to dry anywhere they could find. The girls ran to the sleeping bag and blankets, snuggling together to keep warm. Mabel had been so gentle that afternoon as they made love. It was like the rain brought out a different side of her, a more sensitive side. Bonnie remembered those tender kisses on her lips and skin. She'd felt so close to her that day. She knew that she belonged with Mabel and was going to do everything possible to make that a reality.

"You look happy today," her mother said, trying to politely start a conversation. "Is it because Charles is coming over later?"

Bonnie rolled her eyes. She remained frustrated with both her parents and fiancé. Ever since he finished his semester at college, Charles had been calling and coming over more often. Bonnie felt suffocated by the constant attention.

"Charles has nothing to do with it," she said. She wouldn't tell her mother the reason for her joyful mood. Once again, she turned her attention to the gray skies, still thinking about that afternoon with Mabel. All the things Bonnie had been afraid of losing no longer mattered to her. After almost dying, her priorities had shifted, and nothing was ever going to keep her from Mabel again.

* * *

"Are you ready, Bonnie?" Phil asked.

"Yes," she said excitedly.

Bonnie was nervous to take her first steps, but Mabel's voice echoed in her head encouraging her to try. She focused on that beautiful, inspiring voice as the therapist began their session with light stretches. Once they went through all the normal exercises to warm up her muscles, Phil led Bonnie over to a set of wooden parallel bars sitting three feet off the floor.

"These will help you regain your balance," he said.

Walking was all about balance, and Bonnie would need to practice balancing herself before she could take her first steps. He demonstrated the exercises they would do in preparation for that milestone.

"Don't get discouraged if you can't do everything today. Remember, we are *retraining* your muscles to do what they were intended for, and it may take a few sessions for them to catch up with your brain. I'm confident you will get there. Just be patient with yourself," he encouraged.

Finishing his explanation with a word of caution, he instructed Bonnie to tell him immediately if she had any sudden pain or felt anything unusual. They would stop right away, because those were indications something was wrong. When he asked if she was ready to try, Bonnie eagerly nodded.

She set her jaw in fierce determination: today marked the day she walked her way back into Mabel's arms. He locked her wheelchair in place, picked her up underneath her arms, and lifted her up close to the bars. As Phil instructed her to grab onto the wooden bars, he positioned Bonnie's body into the correct alignment. She was surprised how much upper body strength she had gained over the last several weeks as she held her body up on the bars as directed. This was the first time she had been able to hold herself in an upright position since the accident.

"Now, I want you to try to put your weight on your legs," he instructed, demonstrating what she needed to do.

Bonnie tried putting weight on her legs, but her knees buckled from the stress placed on them and she felt herself falling. He caught her as she pitched forward toward him. Heat flamed up in her cheeks because of her lack of coordination. She couldn't look at Phil. Bonnie chided herself for being so awkward.

"I should've warned you that might happen." He explained it was an automatic response when her body felt weight being distributed on muscles that hadn't been used in some time. He encouraged her to try again, this time holding the bars tighter until her legs adjusted to the sensation of holding her body's weight.

Bonnie tried doing it exactly as Phil demonstrated. Beads of sweat formed around her hairline as she concentrated on holding herself up. Her legs began to shake as the weight of her body traveled downwards. The sensation reminded her of how her legs felt after an afternoon of lovemaking with Mabel.

"Good job. See if you can hold yourself up for thirty more seconds."

She pictured Mabel standing right in front of her, grabbing the bars with her cockeyed grin and twinkling blue eyes, daring her to do as he directed. It was her favorite of Mabel's expressions because it was the look she usually had on her face right before she kissed her. It was just the inspiration Bonnie needed to block out the quivering muscles that were threatening to topple her over once more. Thirty seconds later, she was sitting back in the wheelchair to rest.

"How do you feel?" Phil asked.

"Exhausted," she said with a smile.

He laughed and told her it was a common reaction, but she had done very well for her first try. He added that as the bones continued to heal, the muscles would get stronger. They would try it again when she caught her breath. Bonnie scowled, but knew it was the only way she was going to learn to walk again.

"Today is more about you regaining your balance than walking. You will need to be able to stand for two minutes before we work on taking your first step."

"I'm ready," she said after her short rest, eager to try again. She was not leaving therapy today until she had taken a step.

Once again he helped her out of her chair and positioned her on the bars. Stepping in front of her in case she lost her balance again, he told her he was starting the clock and gave her a reminder to let him know about anything unusual. Bonnie heard the click of the stopwatch in his hand and concentrated on shifting her body weight to her legs.

The second time, she stood for ninety seconds before the trembling in her legs became too much to stay upright. The sweat poured freely down her face and neck now. She never would have believed the effort and concentration it took to convince her hips and legs just to stand in an upright position. Phil handed her a towel to wipe off her sweaty face while she rested again.

"It's okay if we don't take any steps today," he said.

"No, it's not." She'd been in this wheelchair long enough. Nothing was going to stand in her way of at least trying to take a step today.

With a quick reminder, he cautioned her once again about pushing herself too hard so as to avoid causing herself a setback. She stubbornly set her jaw as he left the remaining part of his caution to her unspoken. Once again he positioned her on the bars.

After two more tries, she made it to the magical two-minute mark. Bonnie slid Phil an "I told you so" look, then smiled brightly. She had stood for nearly eight minutes today!

"Since you did well with the balancing exercises, let's try taking a step today.

Bonnie, you should be proud of yourself for what you've accomplished. I know it may not feel like it, but it takes most people a couple of sessions to stand for the full two minutes."

"It must be the great instruction I got," she told him. Even though she was happy for what she accomplished with her balance, Bonnie wouldn't fully be happy until she took a step. In her mind, standing didn't seem like that big of a deal; it was actually taking a step that mattered. She needed that today. She needed to know she was taking a step back toward Mabel. This was crucial to Bonnie, even if she couldn't verbalize it to anyone else.

He went over the directions on what they were going to do to take a step. Once she was set, he started the stopwatch for thirty seconds of balancing. Bonnie's focus was totally on her legs now. He told her to take a step with her right foot and guided the movement of her arms along the bar. The tip of her tongue peeked through her lips in extreme concentration over her body movements as she leaned forward, briefly feeling a moment of panic that she was going to fall flat on the floor.

"Relax. Take a deep breath. You're not going to fall. I'm right here and I will catch you. I want you to move your right foot forward until it is even with your right hand on the bar."

Bonnie looked down at her feet, trying to will them to move forward, but nothing happened. Sweat dripped down her neck and face once again. She desperately wanted to wipe it away but knew letting go of the bar would cause her to fall even if it felt like her feet were stuck in thick mud.

Taking a deep breath as instructed, she directed all her attention on her right foot, urging it forward. Her brain finally received the message and relayed the request to her foot. Shuffling forward a few inches, Bonnie watched her foot slide minutely toward Phil.

"That was great, Bonnie. Now see if you can move your left foot even with your right foot."

Bonnie had taken a tiny step. If she could, she would jump up and down shouting her victory. Instead, she refocused her efforts on her left leg. Ignoring the burning sweat in her eyes, she willed the muscles in her left leg to join its partner just inches away. Her brain was tired and took its sweet time relaying the message to move her leg. She was about to give up when her left leg slowly inched forward. Soon she stood six inches farther down the bar than she was ten minutes ago.

Phil grabbed her in a huge hug, almost causing both of them to lose their balance. He exuded excitement for how much progress she'd made today. Apologizing for getting so carried away, he quickly brought her chair to her so she could sit and rest. He couldn't stop grinning as he handed her a fresh towel for her sweaty face.

"You did it," he said. "How do you feel?"

"Like I climbed Mt. Everest and planted a flag at the top," she said. She couldn't erase the smile on her face.

It had been exhausting, but today she had taken a step in the direction of her dreams. If only she could share this moment with Mabel. Though Mabel was hundreds of miles away, Bonnie hadn't felt this close to her in a long time.

Today's thoughts of Mabel put her in even less of a mood to see Charles tonight. He was a reminder of everything she was trying to escape. She had no hope of being able to cancel their date because her mother would always find a way for him to visit, despite her protests.

As Bonnie gathered her things, she reminded Phil once again not to say anything to her mother. She lied and told him it would be a Christmas present for her.

Phil ended that day's session by showing Bonnie some exercises to work on at home that would strengthen the muscles in her legs and ankles. With today's progress, he assured Bonnie she would be able to give her mom a special Christmas present.

'Oh, it will be a great present, all right—just not for my mother.'

Chapter 23 - 1972

Trapped. That's how Mabel felt. Like an animal caught in a snare, who knew they were about to become someone's dinner. The only difference she could identify was that she was unable to chew off her leg——if she could, Dr. Gilbert would no longer be able to rest his sweaty hand on her knee as he watched her responses to his movements.

Mabel at first thought Sammie had been overreacting about all the rules she told her on the first day, but Mabel quickly learned Sammie had been right all along. Mabel was foolish for taking the pills. It seemed like a good idea, since she wanted to be able to sleep, but now she was feeling the effects of the drugs.

Now she understood why the female patients were required to wear skirts. Watching as Dr. Gilbert's calloused fingers gently caressed their way up her thigh, she wished she were a black widow spider. She remembered reading in school how female spiders would kill and eat their mates. Right now she wanted to bite him and fill his body with paralyzing venom to get him to stop touching her. She was helpless as the effects of the potent drugs made her muscles lethargic and unresponsive to her mental commands. She hated the way his touch felt and wanted to shower off the slimy sensation.

At least she'd followed one of Sammie's rules and kept quiet. It did indeed frustrate him. He'd moved from his desk to sit close to her on the couch, but her silence got to him. He kept tapping his pen against his legal pad. The more she kept quiet, the faster he tapped. She could tell by the way he phrased his questions he was attempting to get her to let her guard down, but Mabel felt he was leading her to admit something that could be used against her. As her silence continued, he began touching her and making indecipherable notes.

A knock on the door interrupted his roaming hands. Dr. Gilbert slammed his legal pad on the coffee table in irritation and went to the door.

"I'm in a session," he said through the door.

"It's really important, Dr. Gilbert, otherwise I wouldn't have interrupted."

When he opened the door, Nurse Duncan, one of the floor nurses, stood wringing her hands. She kept looking over her shoulder as if someone were behind her.

"Well, what is it? I'm with a patient."

"We have a situation on the boys' floor and I was sent to get you. You're supposed to bring your medical bag."

"Mabel, we're done for today." Dr. Gilbert turned to get his bag. "Nurse Duncan will see you back to your room."

She watched in relief as Dr. Gilbert grabbed his bag and hurried from the room. She tried to move off the couch, but her heavy muscles refused to cooperate. After the third attempt, she felt an arm lift her up to a standing position. She swayed slightly, but thanked the nurse for the help. Walking back to her room with support, she desperately tried to think of a way to avoid being alone with Dr. Gilbert again.

* * *

'Not another gray and gloomy day,' she thought, but it did match her mood after her session with Dr. Gilbert. The dreary days blended into each other, and at this point, she wasn't sure how long she'd been locked up in Pleasant Meadows. Time was a challenge for her, especially with her memory loss. It was so hard to keep track of the days in this place.

"What a miserable day. So tired of all the gray. How do they expect crazy people to get better without sunshine?" Sammie said. "Think the cook feels it, too. Whoever heard of gray lasagna?"

Mabel smiled as she listened to Sammie's complaints. She was getting used to the way she spoke her mind. Sammie was the one bright spot left at

Pleasant Meadows——not that there had been many to begin with. Nancy had been released weeks ago, but she was not the same girl she first met when she arrived here. The drugs her family forced her to take made her little more than a zombie when she left. Randy's family transferred him to a different hospital a couple days ago. Mabel missed her new friends.

"Will you hurry up? There's only one piece of chocolate cake left and I want to get it before that prima donna Suzanne takes it."

Mabel wondered if she would ever eat a decent meal again. The food at Pleasant Meadows had singed all the taste buds off her tongue until blandness tasted like gourmet food to her. Even the desserts had no real flavor. Mabel longed for the days of high school cafeteria food. *'Now that's a sign I'm crazy.'*

She picked at the lasagna on her tray, in no mood to eat. She was scheduled for another session with Dr. Gilbert after lunch. *'Maybe I should eat so when he tries to put his hands on me, I will just throw up all over him.'* The mental image of the self-important doctor with vomit on his perfectly pressed pants made her laugh.

"What's so funny?" Sammie asked around a mouthful of lasagna.

"Just thinking my high school cafeteria had better food than this place."

Sammie laughed at her observation, then turned back to her conversation with Jason, another patient. Jason was a musical prodigy. When he was ten, he had played a concert at Carnegie Hall in New York City. The dark-haired boy was of Japanese descent and had brought shame on his family when he was caught kissing the stage assistant in his dressing room. Originally from Chicago, his family had him committed to Pleasant Meadows to "fix" his abhorrent ways. Jason wasn't allowed to play music until he proved he was "normal", but that didn't stop him from sneaking up to the ninth floor and practicing on the piano they put in for the soldiers.

Jason avoided looking anyone in the eye, nor did he ever smile. Mabel's heart cracked at his own sadness. The only time he didn't look like Eeyore was when the three of them snuck upstairs so he could play for the soldiers. Remembering what Jason looked like that day, she knew music was as vital to him as breathing. That was the thing about this stupid institution. If you showed an interest in something before you got here, it was assumed that was probably what made you gay, so you weren't allowed to participate in that activity anymore. Good thing Bonnie's parents hadn't sent her here, too. It broke Mabel's heart to think of Bonnie having to give up her art.

Chapter 24 - 1972

Thanksgiving saw the first snow of the year, making anxiety swirl in Mabel's stomach. It would be the first time she was allowed visitors, and she looked forward to seeing her family. She prayed the roads wouldn't be too bad for them because today she wasn't in the mood for the forced holiday cheeriness of the staff, so she hid out in her room after breakfast working on crossword puzzles.

From the window in her room, she watched the big flakes lazily make their way to the ground, feeling the urge to run out and play in the snow. When she and Bobby were younger, they would build snow forts and have snowball fights on days like this. The fights usually ended when their hands were too cold to form snowballs. She smiled at the memory.

Her family was scheduled to visit at two o'clock, but first she and Sammie would have Thanksgiving dinner in the cafeteria with the other patients. She missed being able to watch football games with her family. One of her family traditions was to bundle up and head to Main Street in Wheatonville for the annual Christmas Tree Lighting Ceremony. She could smell the apple cider and hot chocolate the Junior League sold at the event. Her heart lurched with homesickness and she prayed she wouldn't be stuck here next year so she could enjoy the holiday once again.

"What are you doing?" Sammie asked, coming into her room.

"Passing the time until my family gets here."

"If they show up at all."

"Why would you say that?"

"Don't get your hopes up is all I'm saying," Sammie said. "Come on. I want to show you something."

Mabel followed Sammie down the hall to her room. It was always a visual jolt entering her room. Where most of the other rooms were a dull gray, Sammie's room was filled with color, just like her outfits. There were dozens of magazine pictures of exotic locations taped to the wall and multicolored scarves hung from the ceiling like icicles. She even had a tie-dyed comforter on her bed.

"What do you think?" she asked.

On her bed was a pilgrim costume, only it was the kind the men wore in all the history books Mabel had seen in school.

"Are you crazy?"

"Yes, but that's not the point. Dr. Gillfish is going to blow a gasket when he sees me in it."

"Sammie, he'll take away your privileges."

"I don't care. It's totally worth it to bring some cheer to this depressing place. I got one for you, too." She pulled out a matching costume from under the bed.

"I can't wear this."

"Sure you can!"

"Sammie, I can't do anything to risk not seeing my family today."

"Suit yourself."

Sammie shoved the costume back under the bed. Mabel could tell Sammie was disappointed, but she was desperate to see her family . She had to convince them to get her out of here.

"I'll see you later, Sammie."

Mabel walked to the end of the hallway, stopping to watch the snow fall at the big window.

"We don't see much snow where I'm from in California. It sure is pretty coming down, isn't it?" Nurse Duncan said.

"Yes, I love watching any kind of storm," Mabel said.

"Me too, but only when I'm safely inside."

"It's more exciting to be outside in them." Mabel smiled at her and promised the nurse she would eat lunch in the dining room later.

The memory of kissing Bonnie during the falling snow in the woods by the cabin came to her mind like a welcomed guest. The way snowflakes caught in Bonnie's beautiful curls, then slowly melted. Mabel smiled at the image of Bonnie trying to catch the snowflakes on her tongue as she recalled how they ended up kissing in the falling snow.

Then suddenly her heart skipped for a different reason.

Mabel realized she had just recalled a memory from last year during the school break at Thanksgiving. She tried to see if there was anything else to the memory, but a blinding headache roared from the darkness, threatening to drag this brief image back to its murky depths. Closing her eyes in order to keep the headache at bay, she summoned the image of a rosy-cheeked Bonnie back to mind, replaying it over and over again to remember what it felt like to kiss the woman she loved.

Anger boiled just below the surface and bitterness crept into her mind. It was so unfair, all the things that had happened to her. Not only had she lost her memories, but the love of her life as well.

Allowing the falling snow to calm her raging emotions, she wondered now if her dream of studying astronomy would ever come true. *'Not if Dr. Gilbert has anything to say about it,'* she thought bitterly as she headed back to her room.

* * *

Mabel paced in the visitor's lounge. Her family was twenty minutes late. Sammie's warning was echoing through her head when Bobby walked through the door.

"Hey, Mayflower."

Mabel wrapped her arms around his waist and squeezed as hard as she could. Embarrassed by her emotional display, she let him go and led him to a table in the back of the room she had saved earlier. Looking past his shoulder, she searched for other family members.

"They're not coming," he said.

"Oh." She tried not to feel disappointed, but she was. It would be nice if just once her parents didn't let her down. "Doesn't matter. My favorite brother is here."

"I'm your only brother."

"Still makes you my favorite," she said with a wink.

They both laughed and Bobby asked her how she'd been doing. Mabel told him a little about what it was like to be in the mental institution.

"Why am I here, Bobby?"

"I don't know, sis."

"Did you say something to Dad about me and Bonnie?" she asked. It had been bugging her why their dad had dumped her in this particular place when she had been so careful to hide her relationship with Bonnie.

"Mayflower, I've kept your secret from everyone. They don't even know you aren't in a coma anymore."

"They don't know I'm here? I gotta get outta here, Bobby. Do you know what they're trying to do to me here? I heard a rumor that they take out part of people's brains to cure them. I'm not sick just because I love Bonnie."

"I thought it was best not to tell anyone where you were while I tried to figure out how to get you outta here, but I don't know what to do. Everyone I've talked to says there isn't anything that can be done. Short of you escaping, I don't have any solutions."

Mabel was grateful for Bobby's honesty, even if it wasn't what she wanted to hear.

"I know you'd help me if you could. How's Bonnie?"

Bobby didn't know much other than her family had taken her to Chicago to recover.

"From what? Is she sick?"

"You still don't remember? The two of you were in a car accident. She has to learn to walk again and you're stuck in here."

Mabel tried to remember but she only saw blackness. At least the headache that usually came when she forced herself to remember was a mild one. Mabel asked Bobby to fill her in on what had happened since she'd been at Pleasant Meadows. The two hours passed quickly, and the announcement signaling the end of visiting hours came over the loudspeakers. Mabel hugged Bobby goodbye. He promised he'd keep working on a way to get her out but wouldn't be able to see her again until Christmas.

'How could I last another month in this place?'

* * *

Bonnie couldn't wait for Thanksgiving to end. She'd been stuck inside all day because of the snow, and her mood only got worse as the day progressed. Her mother convinced her father to invite Charles and his family to Chicago for the holiday. Since there wasn't enough room in the tiny two-bedroom apartment for everyone, they would go out to a restaurant for Thanksgiving dinner——the worst way to celebrate a holiday. Bonnie was sick of her wheelchair, especially since she would have to use it in the restaurant where everyone would gawk at the poor crippled girl, but she was determined to her ability to walk a secret.

Her mom and Mrs. Wilson sat on the couch talking about the upcoming holiday season. Charles went with the men to watch the early football game at the bar down the street. Feeling depressed and useless, Bonnie went to her room and began doing the exercises Phil had shown her this week to further strengthen her legs. The sooner she could walk like a normal person, the sooner she would walk out of this apartment and never look back.

Bonnie cracked the bedroom door open, listening for her mother's footsteps indicating she was coming to check on her. Not hearing anything, she walked over to her desk and took out a sheet of paper and pencil. She began by doodling on the page. Her mind was filled with too many thoughts to focus on drawing anything specific. It felt good to hold a pencil, making artistic marks on the paper, especially since her drawings were the cause of one of the biggest fights she'd ever had with her mother.

While Bonnie was in the hospital, her mom had gone into her room in Wheatonville, supposedly looking for clothes for her to wear, and found her sketchbooks. Bonnie knew it was a lie because she had hidden them in a box of winter sweaters she stored under her bed. Bonnie remembered asking her mom to bring her a sketchpad and pencil while she was recuperating in the hospital, but her mother told her no. When she asked why, her mother repeated her refrain that a proper lady does not waste her time with such frivolous things like drawing, adding they especially don't spend time drawing obscenities about unnatural things. She said she wouldn't tell her father about the broken promise to stay away from other girls if she swore never to draw anything again. She even threatened to tell Charles so he would be forced to marry her sooner thinking it was a way to get over such foolishness. Bonnie's mother told her how she burned every last one of those disgusting drawings and if she ever did anything like that again she would be disinherited, kicked out of the house and never allowed back.

Bonnie had been livid. To her, it felt her mother had literally set Mabel on fire, trying to erase the young woman from her life, but Mabel would never be erased from Bonnie's memory or heart. Her mother would never see the beauty Bonnie saw when she looked at her. She tried to stand up to her mother that day, to tell her who she really was, but her mother wasn't having any of her "nonsense," as she called it. She told Bonnie she was going to marry Charles and that was final. Then came the mother's guilt card: "You promised your father you would stop those unnatural desires. If you don't marry Charles, it will break your father's heart."

As Bonnie recalled the memory, tears pricked the back of her eyes. Mabel had been the first person who saw her as an individual, not as someone's daughter or future wife. She wanted to be more than a label for someone else. Her mother had inadvertently succeeded that day in forging Bonnie to Mabel in a way that was ten times stronger than steel. There was no way she would ever marry Charles Wilson now.

Closing her eyes, Mabel's face immediately came to mind and she felt her body calm down. Turning the sheet of paper over, she let her hand move automatically across the page. She'd drawn the woman so many times her fingers could recall the lines of her jaw, the shape of her face, and the freckles on her nose. Mabel's image was permanently etched in her mind's eye.

A knock on the door startled her and she scrambled back into her wheelchair and hid the drawing in a book on the desk before her mother barged in. She didn't want to start another fight today about her artwork.

Bonnie was still seething over the memory of all the hours of hard work going up in flames by the hands of the woman standing in her bedroom now. Her parents didn't understand her talent and belittled it in order to get her to comply with their wishes for her life. Little did they know she had greater plans for her fanciful drawings.

"Why are you hiding in here, Bonnie?" her mother asked, stepping farther into the bedroom.

"Who said I was hiding?" Bonnie hissed. She didn't mean to snap at her mom, but the raw emotions of her burnt artwork still had her on edge. She wasn't a child who needed constant direction.

"I don't know what's gotten into you lately, young lady, but injuries or not, you will not speak to me that way. I've had it with your attitude. I am still your mother."

Fuming, Bonnie spun her wheelchair away from her mother. She didn't trust herself not to say something she would regret. Bonnie took some deep breaths to calm herself, but they didn't seem to work today. All she wanted to do was scream. She was sick to death of living up to everyone's expectations.

"Go wash up. We are almost ready to leave for dinner."

"I'm not hungry. Go on without me." She really wasn't. The thought of sitting at a table, having to pretend all was perfect with the world and that she was madly in love with Charles, made her head throb. She was tired of constantly being on display as the dutiful daughter and fiancée. Couldn't these people give her one moment of peace? *Is that too much to ask?*

"Bonnie Jean," her mother warned as Bonnie shut the door to her bedroom. "You will not embarrass me in front of company today, especially when they are going to be your in-laws soon. I have had enough of this foolish behavior. Now, I expect you to be ready in five minutes." Her mother flung the door open again, leaving an angry and frustrated Bonnie alone in her room trying to rein in her raging emotions.

Apparently, I can't embarrass you, but you have no problem doing that to me.

She gripped the wheels of her chair so tight her fingers turned white. If it weren't snowing, she would wheel herself right out of this apartment today and never come back. As she closed her eyes, she tried to recall Mabel's face, but it was no use. She was too upset at the moment to see anything but red. Bonnie skipped washing her hands, an act of stubborn defiance, and put on her jacket to leave for the restaurant.

132

Chapter 25 - 1972

It snowed for two days, covering the landscape in nine inches of a wintery blanket. Mabel was glad Bobby had been able to come for a visit a few weeks ago, as he was a great reminder of life existing outside of this place. The staff at the hospital was light this weekend due to the weather, so the patients had a little more freedom from their usual routine. Mabel decided to spend some quiet time alone in the small library off the activity room since Sammie had lost her privileges after the Thanksgiving incident with the pilgrim costume. Dr. Gilbert had not been amused and assigned her six more private therapy sessions. She also wasn't allowed to hang out with the other patients for a month.

"What are you doing in here all by yourself?" Dr. Gilbert asked and Mabel said nothing. She lifted the paperback over her face. "Sometimes I also prefer the company of a good book to that of people. What are you reading?"

Alone in the small room with him once again, a shiver traveled down Mabel's spine. It was unusual for him to be so friendly. He often tried getting her to talk about her preference for women. She kept reading her Jules Verne novel in hopes he would get the hint and leave her alone. She tried ignoring his piercing eyes that made the hairs on the back of her neck stand on end.

"Why won't you answer me? I know you can talk. I hear you talking to Samantha all the time," he said, standing in front of her with crossed arms and an icy glare.

Mabel wasn't surprised at the change in his tone. Dr. Gilbert hated being ignored, but she thought the less she said to him, the better her chances were of one day leaving this place.

"You can't be in here without supervision. I have to take you back to your room," he said, annoyed.

Dr. Gilbert wrapped Mabel's arm in the crook of his elbow and walked her down the long hallway to her room, whistling a Christmas carol. Once they were in her room, he shut the door. Mabel's eyes widened in fear, as she looked for a way to put distance between them.

In two strides, he was across the room pulling her into an embrace. She tried to break free but he held her tight as he lightly caressed her back. Humming a vaguely familiar tune, he began slow-dancing them across the small space. She could smell his English Leather aftershave mixed with coffee on his breath, reminding her of her dad. He leaned down, put his nose in her hair, and inhaled.

"Mm. You smell good. So clean. Just the way a woman should." With his right hand, he traced his finger down Mabel's jawline. She tried to turn her head away,but he grabbed her chin, forcing her to look in his eyes.

"You're pretty, Mabel. Much too pretty to be a lesbian."

She watched as his bushy moustache came closer to her face. He covered her lips with his thick ones and began kissing her. She tried to squirm away from him, but he pulled her closer.

'This can't be happening.' Dr. Gilbert danced her backwards into the wall and slipped his leg between hers. He slipped his tongue into her mouth for a bruising kiss. The door to the room creaked open behind them.

"Get the hell off her." Sammie grabbed Dr. Gilbert and punched him in the stomach.

"You'll regret that, Samantha."

"Screw you, Dr. Gillfish."

"Mabel, we will continue this in our next session together."

He left the room whistling the same tune, and Mabel slid down the wall, sobbing. Sammie sat next to her, reaching out to hold her hand.

"Are you okay? Did he hurt you? I will kill him if he did. I swear I will."

Mabel was touched by Sammie's protectiveness and was glad she had come in when she did. She didn't want to think what Dr. Gilbert would have done to her if Sammie hadn't interrupted him.

There was a knock on her door as two orderlies entered with Dr. Gilbert holding a white straitjacket and a syringe.

"Samantha, you need to come with us."

"The hell I do."

Mabel watched in alarm as Sammie jumped up and tackled the two orderlies. She wrestled them onto the floor, trying to get the needle away from them. Dr. Gilbert tried to separate them, but Sammie socked him in the eye. It took all three of them to put her in the restraining jacket.

"Remember the rules, Mabel!" she screamed as they sedated and dragged Sammie out of Mabel's room.

'What am I going to do now?'

Chapter 26 - 1972

"Imagine my surprise when I found out that my daughter, whom I love and care for deeply, came out of a coma, and I wasn't told. Makes me think she is ungrateful for all I have done for her. That's not true now, is it, Mabel?"

The voice speaking sent a shiver of terror up her spine while setting her teeth on edge. It was the voice of the devil she had no desire to ever hear again. Her father sat comfortably in the chair by her bed, calmly waiting for her as she returned from group therapy. She had been looking forward to spending quiet time reading her book from the small library, escaping into another world. Now every instinct she had screamed at her to run. He sensed her desire to escape and sprang out of the chair. Dr. Gilbert stood at the door, preventing her from leaving.

Mabel tried to swallow the lump of panic in her throat so she could scream for help, but no sound would come out except a harsh gasp. Her dad's towering strength loomed over her, and her limbs began to shake as she realized there was no escape from the two men.

"Is this any way to greet your father?" Dr. Gilbert whispered seductively in her ear. A wave of nausea washed over Mabel as he caressed her cheek. Not able to hold it back, she threw up on herself.

They just laughed at her, evil chortles sending alarms straight to her soul. The sound almost made her vomit again. Demons had come to claim her soul. A putrid smell drifted up to her nostrils as she felt herself being dragged into the tiny bathroom.

"Clean that stinking mess up," her father demanded. She hoped he would give her some privacy, but instead he and Dr. Gilbert barricaded her in the tiny room. She started hyperventilating as their immense presence imprisoned her. Watching her every move with leering eyes, Dr. Gilbert grew impatient with her stalling tactics. He grabbed her arm in his vise-like grip and told her to strip out of her smelly clothes before he did it for her. Mabel didn't want him to see any part of her body. Doing the best she could to wipe the drying vomit off her clothes while he lusted after her with desire-filled eyes, Mabel tried to figure out how to change her dirty clothes.

"Don't be modest with me, young lady. I've seen and sampled plenty of women. Just get out of those smelly clothes. NOW!"

Paralyzing fear tore through Mabel and her fingers wouldn't move fast enough in undoing the buttons on her shirt. Growing impatient, Dr. Gilbert ripped her shirt open, exposing her naked breasts. She tried to cover herself with the shredded cloth, but he pushed her hands away. Mabel felt like passing out from the lack of air in the tiny room, but the sting of her father's palm against her cheek brought her back to reality. Seeing him standing there, ready to strike again, loosened her stomach once more and she threw up again.

Grabbing a fistful of her sweat-covered blonde hair, he snapped her head back and said, "Let me tell you what's going to happen now: You are going to get married like a proper woman. If you defy me, you will stay right here for the rest of your life or I will bury you in a place ten times worse than this one."

"You'd make a perfect wife for me," Dr. Gilbert snarled.

Mabel felt the darkness coming up from the bottom of her mind. White blinding flashes appeared behind her eyes. The most intense throbbing pain seared through her temples. Trying to gulp in what little air there was in the bathroom, she wondered how her dad found out she had woken from her coma. She couldn't believe he was here, threatening her like this. She had to escape. She couldn't live the life he was demanding of her. Her eyes darted back and forth, searching desperately for a way out. She heard that evil laugh again and another tremor shook Mabel to her core.

"Silly child. There are no secrets from me. Dr. Gilbert tells me everything you do. Did you really think I was going to let you run off with that depraved dyke?" He smirked at her once more while she sat there in her own vomit with no shirt on, breasts fully on display. As Dr. Gilbert traced his fingers over her breasts again, a shiver of revulsion ran through her body and she had to bite back the urge to vomit yet again.

"You are never leaving Wheatonville." Glaring in her eyes, he told her if she didn't marry Dr. Gilbert, then her father would have no choice but to let the psychiatrist take a piece of her brain.

There really wasn't a choice in this for her. She couldn't get married and she wouldn't let them operate on her. Her only option was to die.

"I'll give you until the end of the week to make up your mind. Don't let your stubbornness or silly, childish ideas of love get in the way of making the right choice." Pulling her into the shower, he turned on the cold water to clean the vomit off her. The water made her shiver and the sharp needles from the spray bit into her skin. Leaning over her to turn the water off when she was cleaned to his satisfaction, he kissed her on the lips in the most unfatherly fashion.

"One more thing, Mabel. I am going to destroy the bitch who tried to turn you into a pervert and there is *nothing* you can do to stop me," he said, rubbing his calloused hands over her skin.

She could hear their evil laughter echoing in her room long after they'd left. The tears running down her cheeks turned into full, gut-wrenching sobs. Mabel felt something wet on her collar and the smell of bile filled her nose.

* * *

When Mabel woke up, she found her pillow dampened from her tears and something warm and sticky clinging to the sheets. She looked down where she had thrown up on her pajamas. Still dazed as she tried to wake up, Mabel thought she saw a flash of light from the hallway as someone left her room.

Relief replaced confusion as she realized it was only a dream. No, not a dream. That was a nightmare. Getting herself up, she went to the bathroom and stripped off her soiled clothes. She wanted to throw them away because she would think of her dad now every time she saw them. If only she could throw them away.

Mabel went to the nurses' station to let them know about her dirty bed linens. Nurse Duncan stood behind the counter filling out paperwork. She helped her get fresh sheets and remake the bed. After apologizing to Nurse Duncan for disturbing her, Mabel crawled back into bed and spread out on the clean sheets. She was scared to death to close her eyes in case her dad and Dr. Gilbert would return to haunt her.

Chapter 27 - 1973

Bonnie threw herself into therapy after the holidays were over. She was determined to walk back into Mabel's arms. At first it was frustrating to only be able to take one or two shuffling steps, but as she gradually regained the strength in her legs, taking steps became easier. Today was a great day. She'd walked the entire length of the wooden bar twice without any assistance from Phil.

She still wouldn't let him tell her mother about her progress. "My mother was sick over the holidays and my dad was too busy taking care of her to share my news," Bonnie told a curious Phil. "Her birthday is next month and I will be much better at walking by then."

Bonnie could feel her mother's frustration with the lack of information, but this was her own life, and she was taking control of it the best way she could. The *only* way she could. Thankfully Charles was busy again with classes at the university. It was his last semester before graduation and he was taking a full course load. He'd been upset with her lack of attention toward him while he visited her over Christmas. There were days when he was just as bad as her mother about hovering over her. Bonnie thought he might have suspected she had feelings for someone else, since she kept changing the subject every time he would mention the wedding, but he never asked or pushed her for an explanation. *'He probably just assumes I will be my old self once I'm done with therapy.'* Little did he realize the old Bonnie no longer existed.

Ever since Thanksgiving, Bonnie secretly worked on her drawings. She didn't draw Mabel now, but the hours she had spent drawing her over the last two years were ingrained in her ability—in her very soul. Now she spent time drawing things that would be more acceptable to her parents if they found her sketchbook: flowers, buildings, and landscapes. These things didn't stir her passion like drawing people, but at least it kept her practicing her skills. She was tired of her parents and Charles thinking her drawing was a cute little hobby. This "hobby" was going to be her ticket to the future. Bonnie had decided after her accident that being an artist was what she wanted to do with her life. Now she just had to figure out how to make that happen.

Her mother once again tried to engage her in conversation on the way home from therapy. Bonnie wished she could talk to her mother without feeling she was being probed for information. She knew her mother had been struggling with their relationship since the accident, but Bonnie needed more independence. That frightened her mother. She could see it in her eyes.

According to her mother, Bonnie's priority should be getting ready to marry Charles and raise a family. At one time she'd agreed to fulfill her parents' plan for her life because of the pain she had caused them, but since the accident, the immensity of those expectations suffocated her. She once told Mabel she didn't need adventure to be happy——that was a lie. The adventure she needed was building a life with the woman she loved despite the obstacles they faced. Walking back to Mabel on her own two feet was the motivation that got her through the days now.

ʏ ʏ ʏ

"Bonnie, I am running to the store to pick up something for dinner. Will you be okay by yourself for a few minutes?" her mother asked when they got home.

"Yes, Mother. I'm going to lie down for a little bit. I'm tired from therapy."

"I still don't see why I can't watch what you do. I could help you with the exercises Phil gives you."

Bonnie tried not to roll her eyes at her mother's definition of 'help.' She shrugged her shoulders and headed off to her bedroom to take a nap. A few minutes later, she heard a knock on the door and thought her mother might have forgotten her keys again. Pulling herself out of bed and back into her wheelchair, she rolled to the front door.

A delivery man stood on the other side with an envelope in his hand. "I'm looking for Bonnie Williams," he said.

"I'm Bonnie."

"Please sign here." He showed her where to sign on his clipboard.

Thanking him, she took the envelope and began shutting the door. When he cleared his throat, she realized he was waiting for a tip. She handed over two dollars and closed the door.

She looked down at the envelope addressed to her. It was from a law office right here in Chicago. Taking the letter to her room, she carefully opened it and read its contents. She didn't understand the legalese the first time and had to reread the document several more times for it to make sense. Apparently, the law firm had written a check for her from her accident. All she needed to do was come to their offices and pick it up. Hiding the letter in the pocket of one of her sweaters hanging in the closet, Bonnie contemplated how she was going to pick up the money without her parents' knowledge.

* * *

After her therapy session the next day, Bonnie asked Phil if she could make a phone call. Phil showed her into a small office with a phone. Nervously, Bonnie dialed the number she'd memorized and was soon connected with the attorney's office. After making arrangements to come in the following week to sign the paperwork, Bonnie hung up the phone. She sat in the small office, formulating a plan to find Mabel.

Chapter 28 - 1973

Mabel dreaded her next session with Dr. Gilbert. She considered pretending to be sick but knew he would stop by to check on her. She was deep in thought when she ran into Nurse Duncan——literally——knocking the patients' charts out of her hands.

"I'm sorry." She started to pick up the scattered paperwork.

"Is everything all right?" Nurse Duncan asked.

Mabel remembered Sammie's rule about not trusting anyone, but Nurse Duncan had always been kind to her. She'd helped her change her sheets after her nightmare a couple nights ago. Her thoughts were tangled like a knot in her tennis shoes she couldn't undo.

"Not really," she said.

"Come with me."

Nurse Duncan led her to a small file room behind the nurses' station. In the back of the musty room sat a square table with two folding chairs. Nurse Duncan indicated she should have a seat.

Mabel looked around the room at all the paperwork stored on the shelves. She couldn't imagine how many patients' lives were recorded on the pages sitting in the files. *What does my file say?*

"Want to tell me what's going on?"

Mabel hesitated, not confident she should tell her the truth. She wasn't sure if Nurse Duncan was on Dr. Gilbert's side and would tell him what she said. Maybe she could blame it on her memory loss, saying she didn't remember telling Nurse Duncan anything.

"Mabel, what's on your mind?"

"I'm worried about Sammie." It was easier to talk about her friend than her feelings.

"Why?"

"Because Dr. Gilbert was so mad when she interrupted him kissing me in my room."

"What are you talking about, Mabel?"

She explained to the nurse what happened with Dr. Gilbert and how Sammie had saved her.

"Then he had the orderlies sedate her and put her in a straitjacket. I haven't seen her for weeks, and I'm afraid they've done something terrible to her."

"Don't worry about Sammie. I'm sure she'll be fine."

"But I'm scared she might end up like Nancy or worse."

Nurse Duncan reached across the table to hold Mabel's hands. Mabel could see the compassion in her eyes and felt comforted by her touch. She was glad she'd talked to her and the knot of her thoughts began to unravel slightly.

"I'm afraid he will try to kiss me again, so I've been avoiding him. We have a private session this afternoon and I don't want to go."

"I know you're scared, but you are strong enough to handle this. Dr. Gilbert doesn't want you to believe you are, but he's wrong. Have faith everything will work out."

Did Mabel have that much faith? She wasn't sure, but she would do her best to be brave. Nurse Duncan showed her to the door, gave her a hug, and told her not to worry so much.

She wandered the halls until lunchtime. The rumbling of her stomach forced her to stand in line to get something to eat even if she didn't have much of an appetite. Mabel could not be late for mealtime.

* * *

Later in her session with Dr. Gilbert, she tried to have faith as Nurse Duncan suggested. It was hard seeing his excitement at being alone with her again. She heard the click of the lock and once again had the sensation of an animal trapped in a cage.

"I apologize we were interrupted after Thanksgiving, but rest assured, I have taken care of that nuisance." He came to sit by her on the couch and immediately put his hand under her skirt, resting his sweaty palm on her thigh.

'Be brave. Be brave. Be brave.'

"Mabel, I think you are confused about your sexuality and don't understand how wonderful relationships can be between men and women. Today we are going to explore how good a *physical* relationship can be between a man and a woman."

Mabel tried to put some distance between them, but Dr. Gilbert forcefully squeezed her leg until she was sure she'd have a bruise. The pain eased when she stopped moving away from him.

"Some men like a woman who plays hard to get. I am not one of those men."

He leaned in to kiss her and Mabel thought of herself as the main course for a Venus Flytrap. His fingers moved up the inside of her thigh as his moustache tickled her nose with his kiss.

As he tried to force his tongue into her mouth, a fire alarm sounded.

"Dammit," he said, racing to the door to unlock it.

The smell of hot smoke told her they needed to evacuate quickly.

"Follow me," he said.

Grabbing her hand, he pulled her into the hallway where she was able to loosen his grip on her in the crowds of evacuating patients. She followed them outside into the cold winter air. She didn't mind the cold, as it was the first fresh air she'd breathed in months. Scanning the crowd, she saw Nurse Duncan helping patients get out the door to safety.

"Miss me?"

Mabel squealed at the familiar voice. Sammie was standing behind her grinning and Mabel's heart soared at the sight of her friend in her usual colorful outfit. They hugged for a long moment before pulling away. Dark circles shadowed under Sammie's eyes and her skin had paled, but otherwise she looked great. *'She's okay.'* Relief, and the refreshing outdoor air, filled

Mabel's lungs.

"Are you responsible for this?"

"Nope."

The all-clear signal was given and they started back inside. They took their time re-entering the building, enjoying the freedom of being outside in companionable silence. Mabel was stepping inside when she felt herself being pulled back out. Dr. Gilbert had a hold on her wrist and was dragging her to the side of the building.

"I can see now the normal course of therapy isn't working for you. I have no other choice but to start drastic therapies with you. You are here to be cured of your homosexual desires and Samantha is only confusing you. Tomorrow, we begin aggressive conversion therapy."

He walked away, leaving a shaken Mabel leaning against the vine-covered brick wall. She had no idea what conversion therapy was, but it didn't sound like any therapy she wanted. Escaping wasn't an option. Several bands of razor-wire sat secured on top of the fences and thick, metal chains wrapped around all the gates. She had just run out of time.

Chapter 29 - 1973

"Bonnie, what are you *doing?*" her mother asked.

"What does it look like?" Bonnie bit back. "I'm packing."

"Packing? Where are you going?"

Bonnie relished the sight of her wide-eyed mother as the woman stood watching her move about her room without her wheelchair, filling up three large suitcases with all her belongings.

"I'm leaving Chicago, Mother."

Surprise turned to outrage on her mother's face, underscored by an icy tone. "How long have you been able to walk?"

"Long enough," Bonnie said coolly.

She stood in front of her closet, trying to decide whether she should take her winter clothes with her. Would she need them in California? This was the most impulsive thing Bonnie had ever done. She'd finished her physical therapy a few days ago and finding Mabel was the only thing filling her thoughts.

"What about Charles?" her mother asked.

"What about him? We broke up weeks ago."

"You did *what*? Why would you do that?"

"Because I don't love him. I love someone else." Bonnie looked her mother in the eye, daring her to say something more about her breaking off her engagement. The woman's face twisted as she tried to process what Bonnie had said, perhaps trying to figure out how Bonnie could be in love with someone else.

Bonnie pulled her sketchpad out of her desk drawer and regarded her mother's helpless stare at the offensive thing. When the pieces finally fell into place, Bonnie could tell her mother was struggling with her reaction, her expression dueling between confusion and anger, and something stronger, like hatred.

Anger won out. "I *forbid you* from going after that hussy. She will ruin your life. Have you not learned anything from the last time this happened?"

Bonnie glared at her mother and her self-righteous pose, arms crossed, eyes burning in sanctimony. It took all of Bonnie's control not to lash out at her. How dare she bring up the past? *'Why am I even surprised?'* This was exactly how she had reacted three years ago when she found Bonnie in bed making out with her best friend, Danielle.

"Mabel is *not* a hussy."

"Any girl who takes advantage of innocent young girls is a hussy in my book. Why must you always befriend those kinds of people? I don't even want to *think* about all the disgusting things she forced you to do with her. This will break your father's heart. Again! You do remember what you promised him last time, don't you?"

How could she forget? She'd spent the last three years feeling guilty over the way her relationship with Danielle ended. The worst part had been denying who she was to make her father happy. He blackmailed her into dating Charles, promising her if she married him and forgot about Danielle, he would give her ten thousand dollars. Bonnie had sold her soul to the lowest bidder. She knew it.

Things were going okay after that, until she met Mabel at that stupid dance her parents had forced her to attend. She'd tried to please her parents and Charles, even allowing him to have sex with her. Her body shuddered remembering the way he groped her before crawling on top of her to meet his needs. She never enjoyed being physical with him and had stopped letting him touch her during her senior year, telling him she felt guilty they didn't wait until their wedding night.

Those two summers spent with Mabel solidified an inflexible truth; she couldn't go back to her old relationship with Charles. She couldn't be with any man. Mabel had shown her how good sex could feel with someone she loved. Bonnie became insatiable, constantly coming up with excuses to run off with Mabel to the cabin to make love. Then, the accident happened—— in a split second, her entire life changed. All she could see for her future was being trapped in a loveless, miserable marriage that made everyone happy but her. She finally understood what Mabel had meant about throwing her life away for a stupid obligation.

She saw more for her life than being someone's wife or mother. She had a chance to do so many things with her own life, like become an artist. She'd never allowed herself to dream of anything for herself because of guilt. A gaping hole had grown in her heart for months now and it was time for Bonnie to begin healing more than just her body.

"I don't get you, Bonnie Jean. Your father and I have sacrificed so much for you. And this is how you repay us? By throwing everything away so you can chase that girl who caused your accident?"

"She didn't cause the accident, Mother."

"I'm sure you believe that, but she was only using you. Face it, Bonnie, you meant nothing to her. She has probably moved on to the next innocent girl by now."

"Stop it. You don't know a thing about her."

Her mother walked over to the window and watched the people walking by on the sidewalk below before she responded. "You're right. I don't. Do you know why? I would've stopped you from seeing her if I had known she had seduced you against your will."

"Mabel didn't seduce me, Mother. *I* seduced her."

Watching the horror of her words play across her mother's face gave Bonnie a moment of satisfaction. Her parents had treated her like fine china, so delicate and pretty. They never believed she could use her own mind to make decisions for herself. No, it wasn't Mabel who pursued her, just as it wasn't Danielle.

Bonnie knew her mother would struggle with this. She'd never gone against her wishes like this, but Bonnie was eighteen now and could decide for herself how to live her life. There was nothing her mother could do about it. Bonnie watched as the pain reached her mother's eyes.

"I don't even know who you are anymore, Bonnie Jean. You've done nothing but push me away since your accident."

"Do you wonder why, Mother? My life was shattered in a split second and your endless hovering, wanting to do every little thing for me is a constant reminder of how broken I am to you." Bonnie clutched her scalp in frustration. She didn't want to fight with her mother, but she could no longer be a prisoner to the woman's expectations.

"That is no reason to throw your life away like this. Don't be so dramatic."

"*I'm* the dramatic one? You act like my accident happened to *you*." Bonnie slammed the lid closed on one of her suitcases. "I'm sorry, but you weren't the one lying in the hospital for weeks, you weren't the one who needed to have someone wipe her butt every time she wanted to use the bathroom, you weren't the one who had to learn to walk again, but most of all, you weren't the one who became invisible sitting in that *damn* wheelchair."

"Watch your language, young lady!"

Rolling her eyes at her mother's reaction to the cuss word, Bonnie continued, "You never once talked to me without a look of pity in your eyes. I was just your poor, crippled daughter that was your burden until you could marry her off. All I ever saw and heard from you were my limitations."

"That's a horrible thing to say about me. I only wanted to help you recover."

"No, Mother. You didn't. You wanted me to stay broken so you could fix me. You thought if you made me dependent on you, I would see why I needed a man like Charles in my life. I would be coerced into living the life you and Dad decided for me years ago. All that mattered to you was the appearance of a perfect daughter for all your Junior League buddies at the country club."

"Bonnie Jean, I am sorry you believe I'm such a monster to you."

Bonnie had enough of her mother's pity-party. She had been listening to the woman's tale of woe since the day of her accident. She had no patience to listen to more.

"And you wonder why I pushed you away," Bonnie hissed. "Why would I *ever* want to share my feelings with you when you never take them seriously?"

Bonnie's mother ran from the room, slamming the door shut behind her, once again trying to make Bonnie feel guilty. But there was no time to waste on useless emotions—Bonnie needed to find Mabel. First, she had to go back to where it began all those months ago.

Wheatonville.

Chapter 30 - 1973

Bonnie paced along the front porch of the Millers' house, working up the courage to ring the doorbell. She hadn't heard from Corrine for several months, not since she moved to Chicago. She hoped her friend would be glad to see her. Shaking her arms to release the tension, she pressed the doorbell and waited.

"Bonnie!" Corrine ran out the door and threw her arms around her. She was caught off guard by Corrine's exuberance and barely had time to prepare her balance, recovering just in time to remain upright and return her hug. Corrine dragged Bonnie into the living room where her mom sat watching television. She exclaimed, "Mom, look who's here!"

"It's good to see you again, Bonnie. And you're walking! What a miracle!"

Bonnie told Mrs. Miller about her rehabilitation experience in Chicago. It had taken months just to be able to stand. They chatted a little about Chicago and everything Bonnie had been able to do while she was recuperating.

"How are your parents?"

She'd hoped not to have to discuss her parents, since they had seemed to disown her when she insisted on finding Mabel. The words sounded hollow in her head as she said they were fine.

"Did they come with you?"

"No, they are still in Chicago," she said.

"What are you doing in town?" Corrine said.

"I wanted to see all my friends now that I finished therapy." Bonnie would keep her real reason for the visit to herself until she could talk to Corrine alone. She took a seat on the couch.

"How long are you in town?" Mrs. Miller said.

"My plans are pretty flexible right now."

"I had sent you a bunch of cards and letters." Corrine turned off the television, then flopped down on the couch beside Bonnie.

"You did? I never got them."

"They all came back, labeled 'return to sender'. I thought you were mad at me."

"Oh Corrine, that wasn't it at all." Bonnie pieced together that her mother had sent back all the correspondence from her friend. It infuriated her to think of the lengths her mother went to so she would stay under her overbearing control. Bonnie was perfectly capable of making the right kind of friends. She tried to shrug off the anger she felt at her mother since she'd been told to leave and never come back.

"I'm sorry my mom did that."

"I'm glad you aren't mad at me. So, how's Charles? Handsome as ever?"

"We broke up a few weeks ago."

"I'm so sorry, Bonnie. I didn't mean to bring up something painful." Corrine placed her hand on Bonnie's arm.

"Don't be. I think we were both kind of relieved. Our parents really put a lot of pressure on us to get married as soon as I could walk again."

"Would you like something to drink?" Mrs. Miller asked.

"Iced tea would be great if it's not too much trouble."

"No trouble at all." She stood to fix the tea, which gave the girls some privacy.

"I can't believe you're here. I've been praying for you every night."

"It's good to see you, too."

"Do you feel like shopping?"

Bonnie laughed as she remembered all the hours they had spent in Wheatonville stores. Corrine loved to shop. Sometimes she could even convince a grumbling Mabel to go with them. Usually after an hour of Corrine's whirlwind energy, Mabel would either head to the library or Daisy's Diner to wait for them to finish.

"Here you go, dear."

"Thank you, Mrs. Miller."

After chatting with Mrs. Miller a few more minutes, the girls left for their shopping adventure. Corrine drove them through Wheatonville, pointing out the changes of the past few months. Bonnie found it strange that very little had changed in town when she had changed so much. When they drove past Stephenson Lake, images of Mabel and the accident ran through her mind. She wanted to talk to Corrine about Mabel but couldn't seem to bring up the topic. She was afraid Mabel had somehow told Corrine about their fight and that Corrine would also blame Bonnie for the accident. Bonnie didn't think she could handle losing her two closest friends.

"Want to stop at Daisy's for some chili fries for old times' sake?" Bonnie suggested.

Corrine pulled into the parking lot of the diner and raced Bonnie inside. Once they were seated in their favorite booth, Bonnie glanced over the menu of the same familiar dishes. After placing their order, she asked Corrine if she was seeing anyone.

"Yes, and he is the sweetest guy I have ever met."

"I'm so happy for you."

"It's actually because of you that we met."

"Me?"

Corrine explained to Bonnie how she'd gotten together with Mabel's brother Bobby.

"When you and Mabel were in the hospital, we kept running into each other in the hallway. One day he asked me to have dinner in the cafeteria, and we started talking. I can't say exactly when it happened, but one day, I stopped thinking of him as Mabel's little brother and saw him as his own person."

Bonnie thought about Corrine's story. She'd been so hurt when Oscar broke up with her and tried to play it off as no big deal, but she had been madly in love with him. She was thrilled to have found someone as special as Bobby. She wondered what it was about the Flanigan siblings that made it impossible not to love them.

The chili fries were as good as she remembered, but now she was stalling.

Taking a large sip of her Coke, she thought of how to phrase her question. Should she talk about their other friends and casually bring up Mabel? She could tell Corrine she'd been going through some of her things and found something belonging to Mabel she wanted to return. Would Corrine see through her attempts at playing "remember when"? Maybe she should ask her how Mabel feels about Corrine dating her younger brother. Realizing there would be no perfect way to ask, she just blurted out, "Corrine, do you know how I can find Mabel?"

"I'm sorry, but I don't. After you left for Chicago, her dad moved her to another facility."

"Does Bobby know where she is?"

"I'm really not sure."

It felt like losing Mabel all over again. She'd been so sure coming back here would bring them back together. Mabel had been close with Bobby and if he didn't know where she was, who would?

"I have to find her."

"Why?"

"Because I want to apologize for the accident and . . . to tell her I love her."

"I'm sure she knows you love her. Mabel is one of your closest friends."

"No, Corrine, I . . . " She took another fortifying sip of her Coke, then summoned the courage to finally admit the truth to her, "It's more like the way you love Bobby."

There, she'd said it. Out loud. As she watched Corrine struggle with her announcement, Bonnie debated whether she would ever say those words to anyone again.

"Bonnie, that's a sin. You can't love Mabel like that. You don't know what you're saying."

"Think what it would be like for you to live without Bobby. That's how I feel about Mabel. I don't care about eternal damnation because my life is hell without her."

"Does Bobby know?"

"Yes, we talked about it when he came to visit me in the hospital."

"What did he say about it?"

"Bobby loves his sister and wants her to be happy. He says there are worse things she could do."

"I don't know about this, Bonnie. I'm not sure we'll be able to remain friends."

"I'm sorry to hear that, Corrine, because you are a dear friend to me. But I blew it once with Mabel and if she'll give me a second chance, I'm going to spend every day of my life making it up to her."

* * *

Walking into the lobby of Mack's Garage after Corrine dropped her off, Bonnie looked around for Bobby. She found him sitting in an office studying a catalog, she tried to build up the courage to talk to him. Any hope she had of finding Mabel depended on his cooperation.

"Can I help you?" the receptionist asked.

"I'd like to speak with Bobby Flanigan."

A few moments later he came strolling up to the receptionist's desk.

"Bonnie! What are you doing here?"

He picked her up and spun her around the lobby. With a friendly laugh, she told him to put her down.

"Do you have someplace we can talk?" she asked.

"Certainly. Come on back to my office."

"Your office?"

"It's a long story. Would you like something to drink?"

He didn't wait for a response. He pulled a couple of bottles of soda out of the refrigerator in the employee break room, cracked them both open, and handed one to her. Bonnie felt him looking at her and squirmed under the scrutiny.

"I can't get over how great you look. You were a mess the last time I saw you."

She laughed at this assessment. She'd been covered in plaster and bandages when he visited in the hospital, so seeing her rehabilitated probably came as quite a shock.

"You look different now. More beautiful than I remember you."

"What a sweet thing to say. You look all grown up sitting behind that desk."

"Not sure how much of an adult it makes me, but thank you."

"Bobby, I came back to see Mabel," she said with the hope clear in her voice.

"She's gone."

No. *'It can't be true.'* Mabel was *dead?* Why didn't someone tell her sooner? And it was all Bonnie's fault. Her chest heaved, lungs gasping for a breath she couldn't draw in. *'What am I going to do now?'*

"Bonnie, are you all right?"

"No. Why didn't anyone tell me she died?"

"What are you talking about? She's not dead. She's fine as far as I know."

Relief flooded through Bonnie at hearing Mabel was still alive. Her own heart was beating again. Her lungs filled. "I thought by gone, you meant . . . you know." Bobby shook his head slowly. "So . . . tell me," Bonnie said.

Bobby spent the next several minutes disclosing the highlights of what happened in her absence. When he left out the specifics of what his sister went through in the mental institution, Bonnie didn't press for more.

"She headed to California after she left the institution. I got a postcard saying she made it safely. I'm not sure I still have it."

"How will I ever find her now?" Looking down into her lap, Bonnie couldn't help but feel the devastating loss of Mabel for the second time. How would she ever be able to locate her now? Would Mabel even want to see her again? She'd been so sure finding Mabel would be the answer. Now she only faced more problems.

"Mabel knew you would come looking for her."

"She did? I thought she'd hate me because of the accident."

"That's not true. All she remembers is the love she has for you."

"Huh?"

"You left before I could tell you the news, then several of Corrine's letters came back unopened so we couldn't let you know about her memory loss from the accident." He told Bonnie that the head injury Mabel suffered caused retrograde amnesia, that she did not remember anything from her senior year."

"Corrine told me about the letters. My mom sent them back without telling me."

"I'm so sorry, Bonnie. You probably thought we had forgotten you."

"Honestly, I was so focused on learning to walk again, I didn't even notice I didn't get any mail. And my mom constantly hovered over my every move, so I couldn't call to let you guys know I was okay."

"I bet Corrine was happy to hear you weren't mad at her."

"She was. Bobby, is there *any* way you can find out where your sister is?"

Instead of answering her, he took out a large wooden box from the bottom drawer of his metal desk. He pushed it toward her.

"What's this?"

"Open it."

Inside the box were two of her old sketch pads and several mementos that Mabel had saved for her. Bonnie teared up as she pulled each trinket out of the box, memories flooding her mind. "She saved everything."

"We both know my sister is not the sentimental type. You mean everything to her."

"I'm so happy to see my sketchbooks. My mom burned all my others. These are the only ones I have left."

"Give me a minute." Bobby excused himself and left the office. Bonnie thumbed through her drawings, replaying the details of each one in her mind. In each of the sketches she saw the love they shared. How foolish she'd been to carelessly throw it away.

Bobby came back into the room and handed her a slip of paper with a California address written on it. "I found the postcard with this address. I don't know if she is still there or has already moved somewhere else."

"Thanks, Bobby. I will start looking for her there."

Chapter 31 - 1973

Time had flown by quickly since first seeing the welcome signs for California. Spring was making its entrance early as Mabel continued to settle into her new life with the Chapmans. Sammie, Claire, and Mack had been nothing short of wonderful since leaving Wheatonville. Mabel had regained a lot of her strength during her trip out west, thanks to all the fresh air and rest she was able to get.

Claire had found Mabel a job as a cashier for the local Pacific Gas and Electric company. Her job was to process utility payments for the residents. She enjoyed getting to meet so many new people who knew nothing of her background. All she told her coworkers was she was from the Midwest and came to California because she was tired of the snow. It was hard to stand on her feet all day, but she wouldn't trade her aching muscles for anything. She loved her feeling of independence.

Sammie found a job as a mechanic working with Mack at the Western Auto store just a few blocks from Claire's house. She was as knowledgeable as Bobby about finding what was wrong with a car's engine just by how it sounded. Some days it was hard to believe the girl in the blue coveralls was the same girl who used to wear four-inch wedges.

On the weekends Mabel filled her time cleaning the house, walking to the neighborhood park, or going to the library. She volunteered sometimes with Claire at the community center, helping the girls with their homework. She liked knowing she could make a difference to someone else. When Sammie or Mack didn't have to work on Saturdays, they usually would go for a drive, discovering all the different points of interest in the area. Mabel loved when they would drive to the beach so she could see the ocean.

There were still many days when thoughts of Bonnie filled her with overwhelming sadness, painful reminders of the woman she loved and lost. She wondered if Bonnie ever thought of her. Did Bonnie know she had left Wheatonville? She considered going back to find her, but the chance of running into her dad squashed that idea. Oh how he would enjoy throwing her back into an institution, only this time it would be way worse than Pleasant Meadows.

Some recollections weren't as clear. Mabel couldn't be sure whether they were lost memories trying to resurface or wisps of dreams. Whenever she tried to grab hold of them, a migraine took root at the base of her skull. She had to let the ghostlike images float through her mind, believing one day they would all make sense to her.

* * *

One night, Mabel felt compelled to do something symbolic of the new person she was becoming. She sat on the back porch swing enjoying the warmer temperatures on this quiet and beautiful night and strove to work up the courage to talk to the Chapmans about an idea she'd been considering. She breathed in the scent of the blooming flowers in the yard and listened as the birds tweeted their joy for spring. When Mack asked about her day, it was the perfect opportunity to reveal her plan.

"I have something I would like to discuss with all of you," she said nervously, the weight of dinner lodged in her stomach like a brick. Mabel desperately wanted them to say yes because she was too afraid to wonder what she would do if they said no. Three pairs of eyes studied her and she swallowed trying to find moisture for her parched mouth.

"I hope you know how much I appreciate everything you've done for me these past few weeks. You didn't have to help me, but you did. You opened your hearts and home to me and made me feel welcomed and wanted. If it weren't for the three of you, I would still be rotting away in that loony bin where God-knows-what would've happened to me. I can't thank you enough for what you've done for me."

Claire reached over from her rocker to where Mabel was sitting on the porch swing with Sammie and squeezed her hand. "We've been happy to help. You have adjusted well to your new life."

"I'm glad you mentioned my new life, Claire because that has to do with what I want to discuss with the three of you."

Mabel explained that since she began living with them, she felt so many pieces of her old life fall away. Although she still didn't have her memory back, she was happy making new ones, happy ones, with them. Her memory loss was a blessing in disguise. Now she had a blank slate to create a new life, any life she wanted. To do that, she needed to rid herself of the things that reminded her of her old life.

"Like what?" Sammie asked.

"I want to ask if it would be okay with the three of you . . . if I changed my last name to Chapman. I feel I am becoming a brand-new person and I would like to have a name that reflects that."

Looking at Claire in hopeful anticipation, tears formed in the woman's green eyes. Turning her gaze, Sammie and Mack stared at her with matching goofy grins. Mabel's stomach turned flip-flops as she anxiously awaited their answer. She was too afraid to interpret their reactions as a good thing.

"I think that's a great idea," Mack said.

"You're already like a sister to me," Sammie said.

They turned to look at Claire, who had remained silent. She swiped at her eyes with the lace handkerchief tucked inside her dress. Standing abruptly, Claire went to the other side of the porch and bent over to inspect the flowers that were beginning to show their sprouts.

"Claire, is everything all right?" Mack asked.

"I'm sorry if I upset you. Just forget I asked," Mabel said, feeling her happiness leaving like the air in a deflated balloon.

"Upset me? Heavens no, you haven't upset me." Claire wiped the tears spilling out of her eyes, and attempted to explain her reaction.

"For the past couple of weeks, I have felt we were brought together for a reason, and I've been thinking if I had a daughter, I'd want her to be just like you. I'm so honored you want to be a part of this family."

"Will you help me fill out all the paperwork?"

"I'd be happy to."

"This calls for a celebration!" Mack beamed.

"What do you have in mind, cousin?"

"Ice cream, of course."

The women laughed. Mack, with his sweet tooth, would use just about any excuse he could find to have a bowl of his favorite dessert. It was a rare week when he didn't have a bowl of ice cream at least four times.

"That actually sounds great. I'm craving something sweet," Sammie said.

"Me too," said Mabel.

Mack and Sammie were already waiting in the car by the time Claire had grabbed her purse and Mabel locked the front door. Mabel was at peace for the first time in a long time and looked forward to celebrating as the newest member of the family.

Chapter 32 - 1973

Over the past few Sundays, Mabel had dinner with the entire Chapman clan, including Claire and Mack's brother Brian. She liked Brian's wife, Kate, and their two little boys. It became her and Sammie's unofficial duty to keep the boys entertained while the other adults sat around talking to each other. Mabel didn't mind hanging out with the energetic boys and watching Sammie come up with creative ways to keep her little cousins busy helping with chores. She could convince them easily by making a game out of the work. Hanging out with Sammie kept her away from the disapproving looks of Claire's father and brother. They were always civil to her, but there was no warmth in their eyes when they spoke to her. To them, she was only a nuisance.

One rainy Sunday, the boys had been corralled into one of the spare bedrooms to play with their toys by themselves while the three men sat in the living room watching a basketball game on Claire's new color television set. A cool breeze left over from the earlier rain showers blew through the open kitchen window where Claire, Sammie, Kate, and Mabel were preparing dinner. Kate made a tossed salad and Sammie cut up carrots and potatoes for the roast Claire was preparing, while Mabel washed the dishes.

"How's work, Sammie?" Kate asked.

"Busy. Seems the entire town is getting their cars ready for summer trips."

"I still can't believe you're a mechanic working at a garage!"

"Why? I can fix a car better than anyone there. Including Mack." She tossed the sliced carrots into a bowl.

"You know how hard the push is to get equal rights for women, Kate,"

Claire said.

"It will never happen."

"Don't be so negative," Sammie said.

"They were talking about it at work," Mabel added. "It's a big deal. There's even talk about making it an amendment." She put the last dish in the strainer and reached for the towel to dry her hands.

"That's ridiculous. Why do we need an amendment?" Kate asked in disbelief.

"Kate, you have the luxury of staying home and raising your family. How would you like to be in a career or job where you do the same work as a man but only make half as much money as he does?" Claire said.

"I don't think I'd like that."

"My high school counselor tried to get me to look at schools for nursing and teaching. He was frustrated that I refused," Mabel said, swiping a piece of tomato from the salad Kate was making. "I only ever wanted to study astronomy?"

"You were going to study astronomy? I didn't know that," Sammie said.

"Plans change." Mabel didn't want to think about her once-promising future. She wasn't sure she would be able to attend college now with her memory loss. She knew the sciences were still a male-dominated area, but with the recent passage of Title IX, more women were considering careers as scientists.

"I don't think it'll ever pass." Sammie threw the carrots and potatoes in the roasting pan, then put the lid on. "As much as I support it, men still rule the world."

"That's not why it will fail," Claire said. "It will fail because of the perception of what a feminist looks like."

"What do you mean?" Kate asked.

"People, men especially, fear strong females. In order to keep women as second-class citizens, they will turn the focus to fear or some irrelevant thing like looks. Watch the news and see if they ever show a beautiful woman when they talk about equal rights or feminism."

"That's crazy. Claire. We've evolved past looks determining everything about who we are," Sammie said.

"Are we? Look at the women on television or in magazines. Do they look like you and me? Or anyone we grew up with?"

"I see what you mean," Mabel said. She swept up the vegetable peels Sammie had dropped on the floor. "But I still support equal rights, even if it may lose."

Sammie got out a loaf of bread and arranged the slices on a plate. "You may have a point, Claire."

"How long before lunch is ready?" Mack asked coming into the kitchen for a drink.

"About twenty minutes. Tell the boys to go wash up," Claire said.

* * *

Mabel sat beside Kate instead of her usual place between the boys. She didn't say much at dinner; she was lost in thought about the earlier conversation in the kitchen. Maybe equal rights for women would include the right to love any person she chose.

The roast and vegetables were delicious. Mabel swallowed another buttery carrot covered in parsley and thought this may be the best meal she'd ever eaten. Claire was a good cook, maybe even better than her mom. She used a lot more spices than her mother, giving similar dishes different flavors.

Once most of the meal had disappeared, Mack inquired about dessert. Kate and Sammie cleared the dishes from the table while Mabel brought the homemade angel food cake with strawberries out from the kitchen. Scooping the cake and strawberries onto the dessert plates, she couldn't help laughing at Mack as he dug into his dessert like it was the first meal he was eating after a hunger strike. When he finished his slice, Mabel slid her uneaten piece to him as well. Winking at her he said, "Thanks, sis."

The deafening silence around the table after his comment was oppressive. With everyone looking at her, Mabel felt a deep scarlet blush creeping up the front of her neck.

Mack looked up to see everyone staring at him. "What?" he said around a mouthful of cake.

"Since when do you use a pet name for one of Claire's strays, Mack?" his father demanded, pointing his fork in his direction.

'Did I hear that correctly?' Before she could respond to Mr. Chapman's comment, Mack jumped to her defense.

"Mabel is not a stray and you will never call her that again," he vehemently said. Pushing his dessert plate away, he geared up to verbally tear into his father. Claire put a restraining hand on his forearm and squeezed.

"Father, I know you've never cared for my helping girls like Mabel. Especially since you believe my time would be better spent getting married and having my own children."

"Now, Claire, that's not what I meant."

"We both know it's exactly what you meant. You think my job as a social worker is less important than your job or Brian's or even Mack's. It doesn't matter to you how many people I help, how many people need me. All that matters to you is I'm a woman who doesn't belong in the workplace. My place is at home, in the kitchen, to be precise." Claire quoted her father's favorite saying about women.

"I never said that," her father grumbled.

"It's your favorite diatribe, Uncle Gary," Sammie said.

"I have news for you, dear Father. You'd better get used to Mabel being around. She is now a member of this family whether you like it or not." Claire glared at her father, almost daring him to say something else about Mabel.

"Congratulations, Mack, for finally acting like a man and settling down to start your own family. I thought you were just going to keep playing house in your sister's home."

Mabel could only stare incredulously at Mr. Chapman. Sammie started laughing at her uncle and almost choked on the piece of cake in her mouth. Mack threw his napkin over his half-eaten cake and stood up, almost knocking over his chair.

"I need some fresh air. Come on, boys. Let's go outside." He stormed out of the dining room with his nephews hurrying to keep up.

Sammie giggled at the drama.

"What's so funny, Samantha?"

"I have asked you a million times not to call me that."

"Why not? It's your name. I don't know why you keep insisting on being called that ridiculous nickname."

"Because I like it. That's why."

"How are you ever going to get married if you continually insist on being called a boy's name and wearing men's clothing?"

"Leave Sammie alone," Claire said.

"I have no desire to get married, Uncle Gary. I'm gay."

"No, you're not. You're just confused. I thought that hospital was supposed to help you become a woman."

"That hospital was more interested in cutting out my brain than helping me, Uncle Gary. I can't believe I let my parents convince me to go there in the first place. I don't need any help becoming a woman. And neither does Mabel."

"What are you saying?" Kate asked.

"She's saying I'm gay, too," Mabel said quietly.

"You can't be. You're too pretty," Mr. Chapman said.

"How do you know for sure?" Brian asked. "Don't you have memory loss?"

"I do, but I remember everything about the woman I love."

"Love?" Mr. Chapman snorted. "There's no way two women know anything about love. They can never survive without a man."

"I believe it's a choice," Kate said.

"Why would I choose to be this way, Kate?" Sammie asked

"It's because your mom died when you were so young and you didn't have any female role models," Mr. Chapman said.

"I had Aunt Phyllis."

"Leave my wife out of this."

"Why? You said I didn't have any female role models. And that's untrue."

"You're out of line, Dad," Claire said.

"Watch your tone, Claire."

Claire rolled her eyes and threw her napkin on the table. "Sexuality isn't a choice any more than the color of your eyes or your height is a choice. If it's a choice, tell me, Kate, when did you choose to be attracted to men?"

"I didn't choose, Claire. I've always been attracted to them."

"So, let me see if I understand this. It's not a choice for *you*, but it is for Sammie and Mabel? That makes no sense."

"You're twisting my words."

"No, she's not. She just wants to know why it's *natural* for you to be attracted to men and *a choice* for me to be attracted to women," Sammie said.

Mr. Chapman slammed a fist onto the table. "Because the Bible says so."

"It also has a lot of other rules we don't follow," Mabel said. She watched Mr. Chapman's head swivel in her direction like he'd forgotten she was even there. She was sick and tired of men telling her how to live her life. "The Bible has been used to justify all kinds of despicable acts like slavery and murder."

"That's enough out of you, young lady. Remember you are a guest in this house."

"STOP IT!" Claire banged her fists on the table, causing the water to slosh out of the drinking glasses and silverware to clatter to the floor. "Dad, you have no say in who is a guest in my house."

"You have gone too far this time."

"No. This is none of your business and we are not talking about this anymore. Mabel and Sammie can stay here as long as they want. This is their home."

Mr. Chapman slid a look toward Brian and Kate. "I would seriously think about the kind of influence these two are going to have on your children."

"That's not your decision to make," Brian said. "That's up to Kate and me."

Pushing his chair away from the table, Brian stood. "I think it's time for us to go. Claire, wonderful food as always." He left to go get the boys.

"Thank you for dinner, Claire. You've given me a lot to think about. Sammie and Mabel, I'm sorry if I said something inappropriate," Kate said as she got up from the table.

"Forget it," Sammie said.

"It's fine," Mabel said.

"Somehow, Claire, you've managed to turn everyone against me today. You always did have a wicked tongue," Mr. Chapman said with a scoff.

"It's time for you to go as well, Dad. I've had enough of your arrogance for one day. In fact, I think until you learn to respect the people who live in this house, you are no longer welcome here." She lifted his dessert plate and held his gaze.

"You're being a drama queen."

"I mean it. I no longer want your company at our family dinners."

"So you're siding with them? Figures you would take everyone else's side. You wouldn't know decent people if they were standing in front of you."

"Which at the moment they are not," she said.

"Why you . . . " Her father lunged for her, raising his arm to strike her. Brian had just re-entered the room and rushed to grab his dad's arm before he hit Claire.

"Pop what are you doing?" a shocked Brian asked.

"Let go of me, boy." His father tried to jerk his arm out of Brian's grasp. Brian instead tightened his grip on his dad's arm, spinning him away from the table and towards the front door.

"Claire asked you nicely to leave, Pop. I think it's a good idea you go before anything else happens today."

Mr. Chapman freed his arm from Brian's hold, storming out of the house slamming the front door shut in his wake. Kate and the boys came in just as the door slammed shut. She told the boys to say goodbye.

"Honey, take the boys to the car. I'll be out in just a minute," Brian said, giving his wife a kiss on the cheek.

Claire hugged Kate and the boys goodbye. Walking out the door, Sammie and Mabel waved goodbye to them, then went to the kitchen to clean up.

Brian stood with his hands in his pockets. "I'm sorry about Pop, sis."

"It's not your place to apologize for our father." Claire hugged him and walked with him out to the car.

From the kitchen window above the sink, the skies looked like they could open up any minute. Piling the dirty dishes in the hot, sudsy water, Mabel watched Brian and Kate leave as a slight breeze rustled through the trees.

"What's Claire doing?" Mabel asked Sammie. She watched as Claire opened her arms wide and skipped down the driveway, dodging the raindrops that had just started to fall.

"That's her dance of change. Usually does it when she wants change to happen."

Mabel hoped the change coming would be a good thing.

Chapter 33 - 1973

onnie watched the landscape fly by from her window seat on the train. She still couldn't believe she was on her way to California. She'd thought about driving out to find Mabel, but the very idea of driving still terrified her. Bonnie didn't know if she would ever be able to drive again. Every time she thought about it, a panic attack threatened to materialize. Anytime she thought about being in the driver's seat, all she could visualize was that truck headed right for her again. It had been eleven months since she'd last seen Mabel. She put her hands on her knees to keep them from bouncing in a fit of nervous energy. The stress of this morning settled in her neck and shoulders. Bonnie tried to stretch out her cramped muscles on the crowded train. She reminded herself this was the adventure Mabel always dreamed of taking with her—it helped to calm her nervous energy. Bonnie pulled out the book she planned on reading during her trip, but she couldn't focus on the words whatsoever. Her mind kept jumping from the past to the future. Bonnie wrapped her arms around herself, feeling the raised skin that formed the ugly scar along her ribcage. What would Mabel think of all the scars on her body from the accident? Would she still be beautiful to her? After the casts had come off, she'd been shocked to see all the mottled skin on her legs. The doctors said some of the scars might fade over time. Bonnie prayed they were right.

Reaching into her bag, Bonnie pulled out one of the sketchbooks Bobby had given her. Flipping to the last page, she smiled as the image of Mabel smiled back at her. Her rumbling stomach reminded her of the sack lunch Mrs. Miller made for her trip. As she nibbled on her sandwich, she was once again touched by the generosity of Corrine's parents. Crumbling up the aluminum foil, she brushed the remaining crumbs off her blouse, then leaned against the cool window. There, she let the rocking rhythm of the train pull her into a dreamless sleep.

* * *

Several hours later, Bonnie woke from her nap as the sun was making its western descent. She stared out the window at the bright pink and orange sky. She had never seen such a brilliant sunset. Soon she would be in California where rumor had it the sunsets were even more amazing. She couldn't wait to see Mabel. With the money she got from the insurance company, they could have the life of Mabel's dreams.

The conductor came by to announce dinner was being served in the dining car. It took her a few moments to work out her balance walking on the train. She had been sitting in one position for far too long and her right leg was throbbing again. Bonnie slowly found her way to the dining car where other passengers were enjoying quiet dinners.

She watched as shadows formed in the setting sun. After placing her order with the waiter, she turned back to the darkening landscape. When her salad arrived, she let her mind drift to the previous night's dinner with the Millers and Bobby. Corrine had been distant, but there was still so much laughter at the dining room table as Bobby and Deputy Miller regaled them with stories of customers and criminals. She couldn't remember the last time she'd laughed so much.

At one point during dinner, she secretly watched the animated conversation going on between Bobby and Corrine and only felt happiness for them. It had been a long time since she'd seen so much love between two people and tried not to let jealousy ruin her evening.

"Dessert, miss?" the waiter interrupted her musings.

Bonnie declined his offer and made her way back to her sleeping berth where the porter helped unfold her bed. Climbing in the lower bunk, she let the gentle swaying of the train rock her to sleep again, this time dreaming of her reunion with Mabel.

* * *

Two days later, Bonnie was beyond thrilled to step off the train for good. She looked around the station, trying to get a view of California while stretching the muscles of her cramped legs. Gathering her suitcases, she found her way to the front of the station where taxis were lined up waiting for the arriving passengers. One driver noticed her struggling with her heavy bags, walked up to her and asked if she needed assistance.

"Yes, please."

As she gave him the hotel address and two of her bags, she climbed into the back of the taxi. Bonnie could finally relax now that the hard part of her journey was over. Corrine had reluctantly helped her make arrangements for a place to stay. She had no idea how close it would be to Mabel, but was proud to decide the direction of her life without her parents' interference. Seeing the number of cars on the street whizzing by took her breath away. She'd never seen so many in one place. Bonnie rubbed her sweaty palms on her slacks and sat on her shaky hands. She forced herself to focus on the view she saw gliding past instead of all the cars. It helped to distract her from the number of vehicles on the road. California was way different than Wheatonville; it almost felt like a foreign country. It took her a few moments to comprehend what the cab driver was saying.

"I'm sorry. I didn't hear you," she said.

"Is this your first time in California?"

Bonnie nodded as she turned to look out the passenger window. Her leg still hurt from sitting in the same position for hours. "Are we almost at the hotel?"

The first thing she wanted to do was take a nice long bath to soothe her aching muscles—and her weary mind. Now that she was here, doubt about her decision crept in. Would she be brave enough to find Mabel tomorrow?

"Almost, miss."

Bonnie thought about her plan as she stretched her cramped muscles while waiting for her luggage to be unloaded. She was glad to finally be able to stand after sitting for three days.

"Is this address close to this hotel?" she asked the taxi driver.

"No, but here's my card. Call this number anytime you need a ride."

Bonnie thanked him and watched the bellhop drag her heavy suitcases into the lobby.

She was filling the tub in her room with warm water twenty minutes later. Opening one of her suitcases the first thing she saw when she opened one of her suitcases was her sketchbook. She'd been so grateful her mom hadn't destroyed all her drawings of Mabel.

She limped back into the bathroom, feeling the ache in her muscles from her long trip. Bonnie needed to work out the stiffness in her legs from sitting for so long. The bath worked wonders in loosening them. She stayed in the tub until the water turned cold, then dried off and dressed in a pair of sweats. Her mother would be appalled at her choice of clothing, but they were comfortable and that's what she needed now. For the first time in a week, Bonnie practiced all of her exercises Phil had instructed her to continue. It felt incredible to stretch her muscles. Bonnie smiled to herself as she remembered how difficult the exercises were in the beginning. She couldn't believe how second nature they had all become.

Midway through her stretches, her stomach started making noises. By the time she finished, she was starving. She ordered a club sandwich with French fries from the room service menu, then decided to splurge and order carrot cake for dessert. It would be her reward for accomplishing her first solo adventure.

* * *

A loud knock on the door woke her from her nap. She'd only meant to lie down for a minute. She opened the door to the room service worker and watched in fascination at the efficiency with which he placed her plate on the small table by the window. As she dug into her sandwich, it was halfway gone before she reminded herself to slow down, laughing about her lack of table manners. Looking out the window, Bonnie was once again amazed by the sheer number of cars speeding along the streets. She wondered if she would ever get used to so much traffic without always feeling her muscles tightening. Driving was the one thing no one had bothered mentioning in all her months of therapy. She wondered if her parents decided it would be a good way for her to be dependent on someone else to take care of her. Finding Mabel in all that traffic was going to be a challenge. The niggling doubt returned, creeping up her spine.

'Was coming here a huge mistake?'

Chapter 34 - 1973

Mabel hummed as she walked to the bus stop, feeling the best she had in weeks. She'd filed the paperwork to have her name changed, and today she'd been promoted to lead cashier at PG&E, which would net her fifteen cents more an hour. She was excited to take on the extra duties and the extra money would help especially since Sammie had moved out.

After the fight over her coming out, Sammie had withdrawn. When she wasn't at work, she'd spent most of her time alone in her room and refused to come down for dinner. Claire worried she was suffering from depression again, but always fixed Sammie a dinner plate and kept it warm in the oven for her. All Mabel knew was she missed her friend. Then one evening a few weeks ago, Sammie came down for dinner and announced she was moving to Oregon.

"I got a job in the timber industry."

"So you'll finally get some use out of all those flannel shirts you wear," Mack said.

"Very funny, cousin."

"What will you be doing?" Mabel asked.

"I'm going to be a mechanic for one of the logging companies. It'll be my job to keep the vehicles running. I may even get to work on some of the big machinery."

"That's great, Sammie. When does the job start?" Claire asked.

"Next week."

"So soon?" Mabel asked.

"Yeah, cutting season starts in a couple weeks, so they want to make sure all the vehicles are working properly."

"I'm going to miss you."

"We all will," Claire said.

"I say we need ice cream to celebrate," Mack said.

They piled into Mack's car and drove to the new Dairy Queen that had just opened in their neighborhood. Sammie gave herself an ice cream headache from the chocolate-dipped cone she ordered. Mabel tried to enjoy her hot fudge sundae, doing her best not to think about her friend leaving. Sammie was smiling again and that was all that mattered. Mabel sincerely hoped everything would work out for her.

* * *

Tonight, Mabel got off one stop before her usual one because she wanted to surprise Claire and Mack with the news of her promotion by making dinner. As she walked down the meat aisle at the grocery store, she tried to decide what would be good for a celebratory dinner. *'Pork chops.'* They hadn't had those in a long time and it was one of the few things she could cook without burning.

Mabel walked out of the store with the heavy bag pressed against her hip, she looked at the dazzling ball of fire in the sky. It had been raining for a week and it was nice to see the sun shining again. She took her time shuffling down the sidewalk with the extra weight, contemplating which vegetables would go best with the pork chops. Suddenly the hairs on the back of her neck stood up as if evil were lurking around the corner of the house she was passing. Mabel turned her head towards the street, watching the cars drive by in their usual frantic pace on the way to the next errand. That's why the dark sedan was so ominous. It crept along at a slow pace, as if the driver were lost or looking for someone.

When the driver turned his head in the opposite direction, Mabel felt her heart stop as she recognized the silhouette of the male driver. Her hands began to tremble and turned to ice as she dropped the bag of groceries. She scrambled to salvage the eggs and bruised vegetables, but her mind screamed, *'this can't be happening.' She crawled* slowly to pick up the dented cans of food that rolled away and dared herself to peek between the parked cars to see where the sedan was going.

Her nervous hands tried shoving the food back into the torn sack but she only managed to rip the bag further. Thoughts of the celebratory evening she'd planned were gone and all she could focus on was her escape.

'How could they have found me? I was so careful.' Mabel's thoughts paralyzed her. It was the pain from the muscle cramp in her leg that broke through her terror, screaming along her nerve endings. Daring to take another look, Mabel saw the car was now several blocks away turning left at the intersection down the block. As Mabel left the groceries on the sidewalk, she tried to push to her feet quickly. Thanks to the muscle spasm, her balance was off and she nearly toppled over before righting herself.

She darted into an alleyway that ran behind the houses in her neighborhood, hurrying as fast as she could to Claire's house. A stitch crawled up her right side from the exertion. Mabel needed to hide as quickly as possible before her dad and Dr. Gilbert cruised by again and found Claire's house. Almost out of breath and holding her hand on her aching side, Mabel worked feverishly to lift the rusty latch on the gate in the backyard. She ran across the wet grass, sliding through the rain-soaked sod, somehow managing to stay upright. As Mabel reached the back door, she flung it open, then slammed it shut and turned the lock into place.

As Mabel raced to the living room, she pulled the heavy drapes shut blocking out the waning sunlight. She put the chain on the front door and checked to make sure the door was securely locked.

"What's wrong?"

Mabel screamed and jumped in fright. She tried to tell Claire what she saw but her words were incoherent and instead she collapsed into Claire's arms.

"Slow down, Mabel. I can't understand you. Take a deep breath. Tell me why you look like you've seen a ghost," Claire said, using her professional tone.

Before Mabel could answer, there was a knock on the door. She grabbed onto Claire, dragging her away from the door and shoving her into the kitchen. Mabel stammered, shaking. "Don . . . Don't . . . Don't answer the door." She crumpled into one of the kitchen chairs.

Claire rushed to her side, trying to get her to calm down before her panic attack worsened. She held Mabel's hands and squeezed them, trying to get Mabel to focus.

"Look at me."

The knocking at the front door stopped momentarily but began again with a pounding that shook the door frame. When a man's voice yelled to open the door, Mabel felt the air leave the room and she collapsed on the kitchen floor. Her dad stood at the front door demanding entrance.

Claire had prevented her from falling on her face. "I won't let him hurt you again," she said pulling Mabel into a hug, rocking her. Mabel sobbed in fear. Claire told Mabel to hide in the pantry and she would take care of Mr. Flanigan.

"Don't leave me."

"I'm going to make a quick phone call. I will be right back."

"He's not alone."

"Your dad?"

"Dr. Gilbert is with him."

"Okay, get in the pantry. You'll be safe there." Claire went to use the telephone in the hallway where she quickly made two phone calls then hurried back to the kitchen to check on Mabel.

The pounding on the front door stopped as quickly as it began. They heard two car doors shut, then an engine rattled. Mabel wanted to check to see if her dad had really left, but she felt so dizzy. She put her head between her knees to stop from fainting and tried taking deep breaths. After a few moments, she felt good enough to stand up.

Mabel and Claire emerged from the pantry when Mack and Brian came racing through the back door with puzzled looks on their faces.

"Claire, what's the emergency?" Mack asked.

"Have a seat."

"Would someone please tell us what happened? Why did you need me to come here in my patrol car?" Brian said.

Mabel took a sip of water and tried to collect her scattered thoughts before recounting the terrifying events of the last hour. As she started telling the story, the fear she felt rising along her spine made her words come out jumbled. Claire placed a loving hand on her arm and Mack grabbed her left hand. It took several tries, but she was finally able to relay the story to them.

"I'm sorry, Claire," she said.

"You have nothing to be sorry for."

"I do. I was so afraid I dropped all the groceries I was going to use to make you and Mack a celebratory dinner tonight. This is not how I wanted my evening to go."

"What were we going to celebrate?" Mack asked.

"I got promoted at work today. It comes with a fifteen-cent raise."

"Mabel, that's great. Don't worry, we'll figure something out," Claire said.

"Are you sure it was your dad?" Brian asked.

"And Dr. Gilbert," she said as a shiver ran down her back.

"What do they want?" asked Brian.

"Me."

Chapter 35 - 1973

"I'm not hungry," Mabel said listlessly.

"Mabel, you need to eat. I'll fix something light. Soup and sandwiches sound good to everyone?" Claire said.

"That's fine," Mack said.

Mabel couldn't understand why they were being so kind to her. It was her fault they were in this situation. Feelings of despair swept over her as she thought of running away again. She felt Mack's comforting hand on her forearm and his kindness only made her feel worse.

"Why don't you go lie down for a bit? One of us will come get you when dinner's ready," he said.

Mabel went up to her room and shut the door. She heard their voices through the door in the other room and a weariness fell over her. Her father's pounding on the door echoed through her mind and her stomach clenched into a tight knot. She allowed herself a brief moment to hope things would work out as she drifted off into a fitful sleep filled with images of her enraged dad and Dr. Gilbert coming after her.

* * *

In the kitchen, Claire pulled a couple of cans of tomato soup out of the pantry and began heating them up on the stove. While waiting for the soup to cook, she pulled the lemonade from the refrigerator and poured each of her brothers a glass.

"Claire, what are we going to do?" Mack said.

"I will do whatever it takes to keep those men away from Mabel."

"I still don't understand why you two are going to all this trouble for her," Brian said. "Where's her own family?"

"She's better off without them," Mack said.

"Are you sure?"

"Brian, not everyone has a family they can turn to when they're in trouble," Claire said.

"Isn't it a good thing her father came looking for her? It must mean he cares about her."

"Brian, you've never met anyone like this bastard. He twists the truth to suit his purposes and he doesn't care who he hurts in the process."

"Why do you say that, Mack?"

"Because he had Mabel committed to the same institution as Sammie to undergo conversion therapy. She had escaped before he could operate on her," Claire answered for him.

"Conversion therapy?"

"It's the barbaric practice of trying to change an individual's sexual orientation."

"Can they do that?"

"Some unethical people in the mental health field believe it's possible. According to the American Psychiatric Association, homosexuality is considered a mental disorder and can be cured."

"Then I'm not sure I can help," Brian said.

"You have to, little brother. We can't let Mabel's dad take her," Mack said.

"Brian, there are some men—like our father—who are threatened by the changing roles of women and just want to control them so they are little more than slaves."

"I'll stick around, but if they have the legal paperwork, I may not be able to stop them from taking her."

***

Claire left her brothers to finish dinner and went to check on Mabel.

Satisfied she was resting, Claire went to her own room. She reached for the folder of papers she'd hidden in her chest of drawers, reading their contents one more time, hoping for an answer to the situation that was brewing for them. Sitting in her favorite wingback chair, she began arranging the papers in the folder.

She'd hired a private investigator to find out about Mabel's family after she asked to change her name. She needed the information to know the best way to protect Mabel. Turning the report over in her hands, she kept running his words of advice through her mind. He'd recommended filing a restraining order against Mr. Flanigan. Maybe it would give him notice he couldn't threaten his daughter any longer. If Dr. Gilbert was chasing after her as well, that threw in another complication. Claire flipped through the rest of the file and felt a thick envelope fall into her hands.

Staring at the envelope again, she wondered if now was the right time to give it to Mabel. It had arrived for her three weeks ago and Claire had a feeling whatever it contained would be exactly what Mabel needed to break her father's hold over her. Making up her mind, she went to wake her up.

Claire softly knocked on Mabel's door and entered when she heard her stirring inside. Walking over she sat down beside her on the bed.

"Were you able to rest?"

"A little. I kept having strange dreams. I was trying to get away from my dad, but I was carrying a twenty-five-pound iron ball. The faster I tried to run, the slower I went. Dr. Gilbert was laughing at me while he attached a giant magnet to my dad's car. I knew I would never be able to get away from them."

Claire watched Mabel shake her head, as if trying to erase the scary images from her mind. She reached over and took one of Mabel's trembling hands in hers. Pressing the envelope into her hands Claire said, "This came for you a few days ago."

"What is it? Is it something bad?"

Claire didn't know how to answer that. At first, she'd felt jealous to see the return address. She tried to justify keeping the letter from Mabel because she wasn't strong enough emotionally to handle whatever news the letter held. When Mabel had changed her last name, Claire relished the feeling of her new family. She felt she finally had the little sister she'd longed for over the past thirty years. When the private investigator's report arrived, she'd put it in the file and forgotten about the letter.

"I don't know if it's bad news. After some of our conversations, I didn't know if you wanted to hear from anyone in Wheatonville."

"Did Bonnie write me a letter?" she asked with expectation in her voice. Sitting up quickly, Mabel tucked the crocheted quilt tightly around her legs.

"No, it wasn't Bonnie," Claire said. She could see the disappointment on Mabel's face and hoped she wouldn't be too upset by seeing who had written her. Handing her the letter, Claire took a deep breath to calm her nervous stomach, knowing she'd taken a risk in keeping the letter a secret. Despite the rising temperatures outside, Claire was filled with cold dread. She hoped Mabel believed she'd had her best interests at heart.

Rotating the envelope over and over in her hands, Mabel tried to work up the courage to open the letter from her mother. Before she had the chance, Brian stuck his head into her room to let them know dinner was ready.

"Claire, I'm not very hungry." Mabel was still mesmerized by the letter in her hands.

"Come and try to at least eat some soup."

"Maybe in a few minutes. I want to read this first."

Claire wanted to say something, but decided Mabel needed time alone. Resigning herself to the consequences of her actions, she hugged Mabel and went downstairs to eat dinner with her brothers.

Chapter 36 - 1973

M abel sat on her trembling hands to control her nervous energy. *'Why had her mom written her now?'* She'd felt abandoned by her mom all those months she was in that horrible place her dad had dumped her. There were days she hated her mom for not protecting her and then there were days she'd missed her so much.

Now with her mom's correspondence sitting in her hands, teasing her with its contents, Mabel took a deep breath and slid her shaky fingers under the flap, pulling out several folded sheets of her mom's favorite stationary from the envelope. At the sight of the cream-colored paper with flowers stamped on the corner, tears sprang to Mabel's eyes. Mom only used this paper for special occasions, and holding the paper to her nose, she caught a brief scent of her mother's perfume. Carefully she unfolded the pages and began to read:

My Dearest Mabel,

I hope my letter reaches you in time. It took quite a bit of convincing for your brother to share your address with me. Bobby said you are doing well in California. I am happy to hear that. I have been so worried about you. Mabel, I'm writing to warn you that the man you think is your father is on his way to find you. I hope this letter finds you before more damage can be done.

Mabel, I would like to ask your forgiveness, but I don't think God himself will ever forgive me for what I've done. What I've allowed to happen.

Once, long ago, I left your father. It was after Isabella had been born. The reasons why don't matter, but I'm sure you can guess some of them. My family didn't approve of Robert and cut off all ties with me once we married. I couldn't turn to them for help and so I decided to move to Chicago. I wanted to lose myself in the crowded city, become invisible.

I found work as a typist for an insurance company and lived in a tiny apartment with Isabella and Daisy, my best friend now for almost 30 years. Things were hard for us, but we were surviving. One day at work, I literally ran into a man as I tried to catch the bus home and we hit it off right away. Mabel, I really loved David and I know he loved me and Isabella more than your father ever could. David wanted to get married, but we couldn't because I was still married. I had been told Robert died in the Korean War, but found out it was an Army clerical error. So I asked him for a divorce. He refused, of course, because Robert Flanigan hates to lose at anything. Back then, dear daughter, women had even less of a say over their lives than they do today.

Robert tracked down David and nearly beat him to death. He threatened to take Isabella away from me and said he would make sure I never saw her again. I was already pregnant with you but didn't tell Robert. Mabel, I couldn't lose my children. They were the one bright spot in my dull life. I was forced to make an impossible choice. I did the only thing I could. I gave up the man I loved and returned to your father a broken woman in order to save my children. He didn't know the truth until years later. David showed up at both my parents' funerals. After my dad's passing, David wrote me a letter begging me to leave my husband. Robert found it and read it. I think that was the final straw for him. His mother passed away and left everything to his mentally incapacitated brother, then he got injured and lost his job at the steel mill, and found out you weren't his child.

My dear, sweet daughter, I have not been the best mother to you. I will carry that guilt with me for the rest of my life. You are more like your real father than you will ever know. You are smart, kind, caring, and you are going to do many wonderful things in your life. Don't let Robert Flanigan break your beautiful spirit. I now know the truth of what was done to you. It sickens me to know I believed his lies and turned my own children against me. I am still a weak and broken woman he can bend and manipulate for his own purposes. I hate myself for my weakness.

Mabel, it will take everything in you, but stand up to him. Do the one thing I could not. You have it in you to do this. Bobby told me about your memory issue. You may not remember everything about who you were, but you were blessed with an unbreakable spirit. That scares Robert. Use it and you will break him and the hold he has on you.

I will always love you, my sweet and precious baby girl. I hope one day you will allow me to apologize to you in person. I pray when you find the person you love more than life itself, you don't turn your back on that love because I know your real father would want you to be happy. Take a chance on life and don't live in fear like I have for all these years. Take care, my daughter. I love you.

Mom

Mabel reread the letter two more times before returning it to the envelope. Her thoughts were a jumbled mess. Robert Flanigan was not her father. *'Is that why he hates me?'* The file folder at the end of the bed teased her with its open contents spilling out across the comforter. Curious, Mabel pulled it to her and began reading. Disbelief filled her mind. Unable to concentrate on the words, she shoved the papers back into the folder. *'What am I going to do now?'* Mabel looked out to the window and saw the petunias beginning to bloom in the planters on the porch.

She wished Bonnie were here to help her sort things out so she could see a solution. Mabel allowed a few tears to fall down her cheeks as she thought of the woman she still loved. She would give anything to see her one more time.

Her rumbling stomach interrupted her musings. As Mabel went down to dinner, she let go of the thoughts of Bonnie and let the loving words of her mom wash over her. A steely resolve found its way into her heart as her mom had provided the answer she needed.

Chapter 37 - 1973

Mabel and Claire cleared the dinner dishes from the kitchen table. She could tell Claire was dying to know the contents of her mom's letter but would not ask her to share until she was ready. She'd just finished rinsing off the dishes when they heard the pounding on the front door begin again, signaling her dad and Dr. Gilbert were back. She tried to be brave, but thoughts of the two men weakened her courage despite her mom's encouraging words. She almost dropped the bowls she was carrying to the refrigerator because her hands were shaking so much.

"What do we do now?"

"We stick to the plan," Claire said. "Are you guys ready?" Mack and Brian nodded. Claire took a deep breath, dried her hands on the kitchen towel, motioned for Mabel to hide again in the pantry, and went to answer the door.

"I know she's in there. You have no right to keep me from my daughter or this man's fiancée," Mr. Flanigan bellowed.

Claire slipped the chain on the door before opening it. Through the crack she saw a six- foot-tall man with curly brown hair and a moustache that mirrored his bushy eyebrows. He wore brown plaid pants with a mustard-colored shirt and green sweater vest. His cheeks were several different shades of red.

"Sir, I assure you no one else lives in my house," Claire said.

"Liar! I know it was you who kidnapped her. You stole her from the hospital and her family. She was under this doctor's care. As far as we know, she could be in danger from you and your perverted ways. It was *you* that turned my beautiful daughter into a dyke-whore. Listen to me, you filthy slut. My daughter is nothing like you. She is engaged to be married. Now let us see her."

"Claire, is everything okay?" Mack came up behind her and placed his hand on her back.

"Mack, these men refuse to believe me that his daughter isn't here. I tried telling him only you and I were having dinner, but then he started calling me nasty names for no reason. I was getting ready to call the police since he refuses to leave my property."

"Mister, my sister already told you no one is here. I suggest the two of you leave before she calls the cops," Mack said in a low, calm voice.

"I don't know who the hell you think you are, but we are not leaving without my daughter."

Mack, continued speaking calmly. "You will show some respect to my sister. You cannot come to my sister's home and threaten us. If you don't leave now, we will call the police."

He tried to shut the door in Flanigan's face, but the man managed to wedge his foot in it before it shut all the way.

"Claire, go call the police. NOW!"

Running to the kitchen to use the phone, Claire saw Brian already calling the station to have patrol units dispatched to the house. Mabel was shaking all over and had not hidden as directed. Claire watched as the color drained from Mabel's face. Before she or Brian could catch her, she fainted.

"Brian, go help your brother. I will take care of Mabel."

"Are you sure?"

"Yes, he's about to do something really stupid."

* * *

Brian raced out the back door and headed to the alley where he'd parked his patrol car as Claire instructed. Speeding to the front of the house with lights flashing and sirens blaring, he could see Mr. Flanigan was still trying to force his way into Claire's house. Dr. Gilbert was wringing his hands and swaying back and forth as he watched Flanigan's attempts to gain entry.

"Sir, do you live here?" he asked, walking up to the front porch.

He overheard Flanigan tell Dr. Gilbert to move as he took a couple of steps backward on the porch. Brian couldn't believe this man was going to ram his shoulder into the door and break into his sister's house. Since talking didn't seem to work with this guy, Brian pulled out his gun and pulled the hammer back, just as the man lowered his shoulder.

"Sir, I believe you are trespassing," Brian said. "The owner of this house called the police and has asked us to escort the two of you off her property."

Brian still had his gun drawn as he watched Flanigan ball his hands into fists. He prayed his backup would get here soon; he wasn't sure he would be able to handle this guy on his own. Flanigan flexed his fingers and stepped away from the front door.

"Officer, there's been a misunderstanding here," Flanigan said.

"I think the misunderstanding is yours. This is not your property and in this town, we frown upon strange men breaking down doors of our respectable citizens."

"Respectable? Do you know who lives here, Officer? Some bull dyke and her faggot brother, that's who. Officer, that woman repeatedly forced herself on my daughter, then kidnapped her and left the state of Illinois. It has taken me months to track her down. She's not a well girl and was under the care of Dr. Gilbert here. I need to bring her home so she can heal properly."

"No."

Flanigan and Dr. Gilbert turned to see Mabel standing outside.

"Brian, don't believe a word he says. That man is the one who put me in that awful institution and paid Dr. Gilbert to cut out part of my brain."

"Mabel, sweetheart, you don't remember because of your memory loss, but you were engaged to the doctor before your accident. You got engaged over spring break last year and were going to get married last fall."

"That's right, honey," Dr. Gilbert said with a nervous grin. "I was so worried about you when you were in a coma. When you woke up, I had your father transfer you to my hospital wing so I could help you mend. We were making good progress on your recovery, then you fell under the influence of that awful Samantha."

"You're both dirty liars. You're trying to manipulate me, but it's not going to work."

"Watch your mouth, young lady. I'll still take a belt to you for being disrespectful, engaged or not."

"Sir, you need to refrain from saying things like that or I will have to arrest you," Brian said.

"Arrest me? I don't think so. You should arrest the two perverts in this house for brainwashing an innocent child. They took advantage of my daughter and I'm going to make both of them pay for what they did to her."

Mack yanked open the front door and charged off the porch after the distracted older man. Mack tackled Flanigan to the ground, rearing back and punching him in the face. The cracking of bones in Flanigan's nose sounded like icicles falling off a metal roof.

Before Mack could hit him again, strong arms dragged him away. Blood dripped from Flanigan's nose and Mack smiled.

"Arrest him! Arrest him!" Flanigan said, pinching his bleeding nose. "That man just assaulted me."

"Mack, stop," Mabel said. She ran over to him to check out his rapidly swelling hand. "It's not up to you to protect me anymore. It's time I start protecting myself." Giving him a kiss on the cheek, she walked over to where her dad sat on the ground, trying to stop the bleeding.

"Don't just stand there like a statue or some kind of idiot. Help your dad."

"No."

"Girl, did you just back talk to me? You know what happens when you sass me. You're lucky I don't smack you across the mouth."

"You're lucky I didn't let Mack beat you to a pulp."

Mr. Flanigan got up and started after Mabel, but Brian was able to restrain him and place him in handcuffs. He moved the man away from Mabel.

"Officer, we have the paperwork to have Mabel committed back in Illinois. Like her father said, my fiancée is not well."

"May I see the paperwork?" Brian asked.

"You can't let them take her," Mack said, coming to stand between Mabel and her dad.

Claire came out of the house with a bag of ice. She gave it to Mack for his swelling hand. "Can I take a look at the commitment papers?" she asked. She quickly read through them and handed them back to Brian. "Gentlemen, I'm afraid you came all this way for nothing."

"What do you mean? That paperwork is in order and a judge already signed off on it," Dr. Gilbert said.

"I'm afraid it isn't."

Before Claire could explain, they heard sirens coming closer. Everyone turned to watch the police cruisers coming to a stop in the street with their lights flashing. Mabel saw several of their neighbors looking out their windows at the commotion in their quiet neighborhood. She watched as a familiar figure got out of a police car and made her way across the lawn. It was Nurse Duncan dressed in a police uniform, but not like the kind Brian wore.

"Hello, Brian. What's going on here?" Nurse Duncan asked.

"Hello, Sara. Why is a U.S. Marshal here?" Brian asked.

"Dr. Gilbert crossed state lines without notifying anyone, thereby revoking his bail. He is a wanted fugitive and I'm here to bring him back to jail in Illinois."

"You can't do this to me," Dr. Gilbert said.

"You did it to yourself when you deliberately disobeyed a direct order from the court. I'm just following procedures, Doctor."

Mabel watched in awe as Sara pulled out a pair of handcuffs and secured them around Dr. Gilbert's wrists. She listened as she read him his rights.

"I had to come and rescue my fiancée from this house of iniquity."

"Mabel is no more your fiancée than I am, Dr. Gilbert."

"My daughter is not well. These people have convinced her she's something she's not. I have papers to commit her until she is mentally sound again."

Brian handed the papers to Sara and she quickly scanned the documents then handed them back. Looking at the two men in handcuffs, she started laughing.

"What's so funny?" Flanigan said.

"These papers are forged."

"No, they're not. Dr. Gilbert filled them out himself."

"Mr. Flanigan, you really should've had an attorney fill out the legal paperwork. First of all, the birth date listed on the document states Mabel is now eighteen. She is legally an adult and unless she is a harm to herself or others, you cannot commit her."

"She is harming herself by her deviant sexual ways."

"Do you have proof of that, sir?"

"I don't need proof. It's why she was committed in the first place."

"I'm sorry, sir, but now that she is a legal adult you will need proof of how she is harming herself or others. The most important fact is your paperwork is for a Mabel Flanigan and there is no Mabel Flanigan here."

"The hell there isn't. She's standing right there. I know my own flesh and blood."

"I am *not* your flesh and blood," Mabel hissed.

"Do you see that? She's delusional. She can't even recognize her own father."

"You are not *my* father. I used to wonder why you hated me so much. Why you punished me more than Izzy or Bobby. Now I know."

"Girl, you are crazy and confused. This is why you need to be locked away in a mental hospital."

Mabel pulled her mom's letter from her back pocket and shoved it into her father's face. "I know you're not my father."

"Has that perverted dyke over there been spreading lies about me?"

Reacting to her dad's description of Claire, Mabel slapped him hard across the face twice. Flanigan boiled with a white-hot rage. Before he could say a thing, Mabel shouted, "Enough! I am no longer afraid of you or your threats. There is nothing you can do to hurt me anymore."

"I'm not leaving without you," he said.

Mabel turned and walked toward Mack, who stepped in front of her. Mr. Flanigan tried grabbing a surprised Mabel but was tackled to the ground again before he touched her. The officers ran over to the two men wrestling on the ground. Mack was doing everything he could to keep Flanigan away from Mabel. Finally, he was able to gain some leverage to throw the man off of him. Brian and the other officers quickly restrained the outraged and unreasonable man. Struggling against the refastened handcuffs, Flanigan let a stream of curses fly. When he ran out of steam, he knew that he'd made a grave mistake in coming here.

Chapter 38 - 1973

Today was the day. Bonnie was going to find Mabel. She tried ignoring the butterflies fluttering in her stomach. She gave up on the breakfast she'd had delivered and once again took out her old sketchpad. She gently caressed the pages as she flipped through each picture. She had spent several hours over the past couple of days studying her drawings, hoping they held some key answer for her. As she compared the drawings in her old sketchbook to her new ones, she could see the new ones held none of the emotional intensity she'd felt last summer.

Rooting around in the bottom of her purse, she found the business card the taxi driver had given her. She dialed the number and patiently waited until someone answered. She asked for Ralph, the driver who dropped her off at the hotel a few days ago, but was told he was on another call and wouldn't be available for at least two hours.

"That's fine. I'm in no rush. Please send him to the Thousand Oaks Hotel when he is available," she told the man on the other end of the phone.

As she hung up, Bonnie felt the urge for fresh air. Grabbing her purse and sketchbook, she walked across the street to the small park she'd seen from her hotel room. Luckily, not too many people were in the park this morning and she found an empty bench in the shade near the playground. It never occurred to her the weather would be so different in California. She'd been so focused on finding Mabel, the only consideration she'd given to the weather was when she decided not to pack her winter clothes. She'd heard several of the hotel employees talking about the unusually warm spring.

Bonnie took out her sketchbook and placed it on her lap as she searched for inspiration watching the smattering of people in the park. Twenty minutes, later the page remained blank. Thoughts of Mabel filled her mind and made it difficult to concentrate on the scenery surrounding her. Her mind's eye could so clearly see the face she loved and a whirlwind of emotions stirred inside over their upcoming reunion.

"It's going to be another scorcher," an older man said plopping down on the bench beside her. She was irritated he didn't wait for an invitation to invade her space. She swallowed her annoyance at his intrusion as she heard her mother's voice in her head telling her to be polite. As she smiled, she watched the man pull a small paper sack from his pants pocket and begin to tear pieces of bread into smaller pieces.

"I'm not used to all this sun," she said, trying to be friendly.

"It's the beauty of living in California," he said. "If you want bad weather, head east." Bonnie maintained her smile as he tossed pieces of bread to the nearby birds. Pigeons and sparrows gathered around his feet and he chatted with them as he fed them. She picked up her pencil and began to draw the man feeding the birds. She was intrigued by how brave the birds were as they took pieces of bread right from his hand. He soothingly told them not to crowd each other—he'd brought enough for everyone. Bonnie tuned out his conversation with the birds as she concentrated on her drawing. When he stood, the birds scattered like buckshot and she yelped in surprise.

"Sorry about that. I'm outta bread," he sheepishly said.

"It's okay. Guess I was too involved in my drawing to notice."

"I figured as much when you wouldn't answer my questions."

"I'm so sorry. I didn't mean to be rude."

"You weren't. What were you drawing?"

Bonnie flipped her sketchpad around so he could see the picture she'd drawn of him feeding the birds from his hand. He told her she was very good. He acted surprised at the amount of detail she was able to put into the picture in such a short amount of time. She tore the sheet of paper out of her book and gave it to him. He tried giving it back, saying she ought to keep it but Bonnie insisted he take it.

"Only on one condition. You have to sign it."

She laughed at him then dug around in her purse for a pen. "Should I just sign my name or include yours as well?"

"The name's Lawrence," he said, spelling it out for her.

"I'm Bonnie." She held out her hand to shake his, then signed the drawing: *To Lawrence, my new feathered friend.* Handing it back to him, she thanked him for the inspiration to draw this morning.

Tearing off a piece of paper from the old sack he'd brought, he borrowed her pen and scribbled a phone number on it, then handed the scrap of paper to her.

"What's this?"

"If you ever want to study drawing in more detail, this is the number of one of my best friends. She's an art teacher here in town and is always on the lookout for new talent. I think you would like her, and I know she would be excited to meet you. You really do have a lot of talent, Bonnie."

Bonnie was flabbergasted. Lawrence was the first person besides Mabel who ever said anything good about her drawing ability. She looked at the phone number for several seconds before Lawrence cleared his throat.

"I have to get going now."

"Thank you, but I don't know if I'll be staying in California after all. I don't want your friend to wait on my phone call. I don't know how my plans are going to work out. But thank you, Lawrence."

"I should thank you," he said. "I'm sure one day this little beauty would cost me a fortune."

She watched as he turned and walked out of the park, melting into the crowds of people on the sidewalk. Her eyes fell to the scrap of paper in her hands.

"Today is a special day," she said to the birds who had come back looking for more bread. "Someone actually thought I was talented."

Bonnie stuck the scrap of paper in her sketchbook as she replayed the brief conversation with Lawrence. *'Art school,'* she thought. *'Hmm, maybe I should give it a try.'*

Chapter 39 - 1973

Walking back to the hotel with a flutter in her belly, Bonnie smiled at everyone she passed. There was just one piece missing now. She prayed she would find her missing piece today. Back in her room, Bonnie was refreshing her makeup when the front desk called saying her taxi was waiting.

Hurrying downstairs, she found herself picking at her nail polish. What if Mabel refused to see her? What if her memories came back and Mabel remembered their awful fight? It was a very real possibility. Tired of all the chaotic thoughts, Bonnie handed Mabel's address to Ralph.

"Is it very far from here?"

"It's a little far, but not too bad. This time of day we should be able to get there in about forty minutes depending on the traffic."

"Will it cost a lot?" Bonnie was trying to be responsible with her finances. She'd heard taxis were a frivolous expense, but she didn't know any other way to get to Mabel.

"It won't be as cheap as from the train station, but since you called and asked specifically for me, I can give you a discount."

"Thank you, Ralph."

Bonnie climbed into the back seat. She was glad to only see a few cars on the road this morning. Anxious enough at the thought of seeing Mabel, Bonnie really didn't need extra anxiety over the traffic. Would she ever be brave enough to get behind the wheel of a car again?

"Have you enjoyed your stay here so far?"

"I have. The weather is perfect and I love seeing all the flowers blooming right now. Back home they would just be shooting up through the ground."

Ralph told her they had flowers here year-round. He shared the one thing he loved most about his job was seeing his home through the eyes of the people who visited.

"It always keeps my home new and fresh," he said with enthusiasm.

Bonnie liked how that sounded. They continued chatting about the community around them. Ralph recommended several places she should see before she left. He also mentioned a couple of his favorite restaurants to try.

"What's it like living here?"

"Everyone thinks California is filled with sunshine. Don't get me wrong, we do get our fair share of sun, but the best part of living here is being a direct descendant of one of the original gold miners in this area."

"Really?"

"Yes ma'am. My great-great-great-grandfather staked one of the first claims in this area before the gold rush started. He found several nuggets but gambled away any riches he had."

"How sad."

"I don't see it that way. He met my great-great-great-grandmother when he was penniless and they created a good life together. Family story is he always said he didn't have to worry if she married him for his money."

"That's a great story."

"I look at my job as prospecting gold nuggets of humanity. Sometimes I strike it rich with passengers like you and that makes the long hours worth it.

"That is a very sweet thing to say."

"We're here. Do you want me to wait?"

"That's not necessary."

"It's no trouble really. I will go grab a quick bite and come back in thirty minutes. It will take us longer to get back to the hotel because of the afternoon traffic."

"Okay, I'll see you soon."

Watching him drive away, Bonnie tried to still her racing heart. She turned to look at the brick house and noticed the big front porch. She didn't know what she had expected to see, but this house fit Mabel better than the one in Wheatonville. *If* this was the house where she lived.

Taking her time to allow her wobbly legs to steady, Bonnie noticed the number of flowers blooming in the yard. Everywhere she looked she saw yellow, red, pink, and blue poking up from several planters. A flash of purple caught her eye. In one of the planters were several lilac plants. Bonnie walked over to them, inhaling their sweet fragrant scent and knew this had to be where Mabel lived.

Bonnie grabbed the rail and climbed the four wooden steps to the front door. She could picture Mabel sitting on the wooden swing reading a book or watching the stars at night. Taking a deep breath, she smoothed out the front of her blouse and rang the doorbell. She was getting ready to ring the bell again when a beautiful auburn-haired woman answered the door. She had her hair in a ponytail, but it was the gold flecks in her hazel eyes that hypnotized Bonnie. She had not expected such a beautiful woman to answer the door and struggled to get her tongue unstuck from the roof of her mouth.

"Can I help you?"

"Is this 2137 North Sterling Avenue?"

"Yes."

"Is Mabel Flanigan here? I was just in the neighborhood and thought I'd say hello."

"No one by that name lives here."

"Oh." Now what was she going to do? This was the address Bobby had given her, but he had warned her she might not be living here now. Her hopes of a reunion crashed down around her like an imploding skyscraper. How wrong she'd been to think Mabel might still want her. Why would she want a recovering cripple with all her hideous scars? She was at a loss for what to do.

"Sorry to have bothered you." She turned and ran down the stairs as fast as she could, tears stinging the back of her eyes. She had to get away from here as the words of their fight echoed through her head. Bonnie knew now

Mabel had meant it when she said she would find someone else.

"Wait, I never got your name."

"Bonnie," she said, hurrying down the driveway.

At the end of the driveway Bonnie looked in both directions, unsure which way to go. Ralph wasn't supposed to be back for fifteen minutes, but she saw his taxi a few blocks away heading in her direction. She flagged him down.

"I got done early and thought I'd come back," he said as she climbed into the back seat.

"Take me back to the hotel."

"Are you okay?" he asked, looking at her in the rearview mirror.

"No and I don't want to talk about it."

An hour later, Bonnie crawled into bed and pulled the covers over her head. *What am I going to do now? How can I live without Mabel?'* She lay there for several hours, afraid of moving, lest the stabbing pain in her heart travel to the rest of her body. Coming to California had been the biggest mistake of her life.

* * *

"Kate, I'm back," Claire said coming into the kitchen with several bags of groceries.

"Did you get everything to make the cookies?"

"I did."

"Claire, I really appreciate you helping me bake them for Ethan's party at school tomorrow. We both know if I baked them, the kids would be eating charcoal bricks."

Nodding her head in agreement, Claire put the ingredients on the counter then went to dig out her mother's recipe card for snickerdoodles. As she mixed the butter and sugar together, she asked Kate about the taxi she'd seen pulling away from the house as she drove up.

"Some girl was looking for Mabel Flanigan. I said no one by that name lives here."

"Did she give you her name?"

"I think she said it was Connie."

"You mean Bonnie."

"That's it."

"Did she say anything else?"

"No, she just left. You said not to tell anyone looking for Mabel she was here. Did I do something wrong?"

"Not at all. Let's get these cookies made."

While the cookies baked, Claire thought about Bonnie's visit. She was sure it was Mabel's Bonnie and wondered if she should mention it to her. Would she still want to see her? After her dad's arrest, Mabel had become quieter. She wasn't much of a talker normally, but now unless she was asked a question, she rarely spoke at all, let alone started a conversation. Claire decided she needed to find out if Mabel still had feelings for Bonnie. If she did, Claire would find a way to bring them together and if she didn't, Mabel never had to know Bonnie was in California.

* * *

A few nights later, Claire took Mabel out to dinner at her favorite Chinese restaurant. Mabel ordered her usual beef and broccoli over rice, while Claire opted for Kung Pao Chicken.

"How's work?" Claire asked as they were eating their egg drop soup.

"Good. I'm learning a lot about our utility bills."

"I hope you're learning how we can make them cheaper."

"Have Mack find his own place." Mabel laughed.

"Is college still in your future?"

"Claire, I know you keep hoping I'll change my mind about going to college with all the brochures you try to sneak into my mail. I don't honestly know if I will. I like my job. The money is good and I like my coworkers, but I'm not sure I can see myself doing this for the next thirty years. At this point, I can't even see myself thirty years older."

"You have plenty of time to decide. I just don't want you to give up your options. You're a smart girl, Mabel. You can do anything you want. Provided you get an education first."

They continued talking about projects for the house and places they'd like to visit, only briefly stopping as their entrees were served. When they'd almost finished eating, Claire broached the real reason for the dinner.

"How's your love life?" She grinned behind her hands as Mabel almost choked on a piece of broccoli. Mabel never talked about dating and she was curious what she'd say to the unexpected question.

"Non-existent."

"Really? You're young and attractive. You really are quite the catch."

"I have no interest in dating."

"Why not?"

"Claire, why the sudden interest in my love life?"

"I was just curious, that's all."

After a pause, Mabel said, "Listen, there's something else I need to talk to you about."

"Sure. What is it?" Claire watched as Mabel twisted her paper napkin in her lap, then spun her glass on the table around the watery circle underneath it.

"My memories came back. The day after my dad was arrested."

"That's great!"

"Not really."

"Why would you say that? You've wanted them to come back for a long time."

"I know, but I remembered Bonnie and I had a huge fight while she was driving. We were breaking up because she wouldn't come with me to college and I think that was what distracted her. It's my fault we were in that accident. Bobby said she went to Chicago, but he didn't know where. I have no way to tell her how sorry I am for all the awful things I said."

"Mabel, I'm sure she knows and doesn't blame you."

"You don't know that for sure. For all I know she could've married Charles like she said she was going to and has forgotten all about me."

Claire had her answer. Mabel was clearly in love with Bonnie, but the guilt she felt over the accident was keeping her from doing anything besides punishing herself. Claire paid the check. She needed to find Bonnie for Mabel and she knew just where to start looking.

* * *

Claire and Mabel were watching *Marcus Welby, M.D.* after returning home from the restaurant. There was a knock on the door and Mabel got up to answer it. Standing on the porch were Brian and Sara Duncan.

"Come in."

"I apologize for such a late visit, Claire, but we wanted to stop by and give Mabel an update."

Claire turned off the television set and asked if anyone needed anything to eat or drink.

"I'm fine," Sara said.

"Me too," said Brian.

"How are you doing?" Sara asked Mabel.

"I'm doing okay, I think."

"I have some information for you and wanted to make sure you got it before I left town. Obviously by now you know I'm not really a nurse."

"I was so worried about you when you were caught at Pleasant Meadows."

"I was working undercover and couldn't say anything."

Sara explained Dr. Gilbert had arrest warrants out in North Carolina, Washington, Texas, and Ohio for practicing without a medical license. "Doctor" Gilbert had attended Columbia University but never graduated. He told various mental hospital administrators he had in order to have access to vulnerable patients.

"The hospital administrators we interviewed said they checked his credentials. We called the number he gave them and found out your father was the one who verified his background."

"What?"

"Mabel, your father and Dr. Gilbert grew up together. Your dad enlisted in the Army, while Dr. Gilbert went to college. Apparently, your Uncle Victor was a homosexual and your dad found out. He asked Dr. Gilbert to cure him. Something went wrong with the treatment and your uncle ended up with brain damage."

"He's not my father."

"Right. I know. I'm sorry."

Sara continued explaining that Robert Flanigan and Dr. Gilbert decided the treatment was a success and they had found a way to cure homosexuality. Dr. Gilbert's mother became ill in his last semester of college and he had to drop out and never went back. He got in touch with Robert Flanigan after he was discharged from the Army and together they decided they would cure as many deviants as they could.

"Dr. Gilbert would bill insurance companies for his procedure and split the reimbursement with Flanigan, who brought the patients to Gilbert," Brian said.

"Parents became suspicious when they got their insurance bills and were being charged for a treatment they never authorized. Several law enforcement agencies were called in to work on this case, but someone was needed on the inside to get the evidence. Dr. Gilbert doesn't trust men and you know firsthand his view on women, so I was chosen to go undercover."

"That was very brave of you," Mabel said.

"The good news is these two are facing criminal charges in several states and will not see the light of day for a long time."

"That is good news," Claire said.

"Well, it's late and you two have to go to work tomorrow. We just wanted to stop by and let you know these two men will not bother you again," Sara said.

Relief flooded through Mabel and she couldn't thank Sara and Brian enough. Ever since her memories returned, she'd been worried the men would come back to torture her again. Now they would be locked away for a long time, just like they had planned for her. She wanted to feel vindicated for all she'd suffered at their hands, but all she felt was sadness over everything she'd lost.

Chapter 40 - 1973

With nervous hands, Bonnie dialed the number on the crumpled piece of brown paper. As she waited, she paced in the small space by her bed in the hotel room. She kept telling herself she could do this.

"Hello."

"Hello, is this the Artist Training Institute?" she asked in a shaky voice.

"Yes. This is Maggie Craigson. I'm the director."

"Lawrence said I should call you. About art lessons. My name is Bonnie."

"Oh yes. I've been expecting your call."

"You have?"

"If Larry told you to call me, that means he saw something he liked in your drawing."

"Larry?" Bonnie asked.

"Sorry, Lawrence. He only gives my number to people he thinks show artistic promise."

Bonnie was surprised to hear such a high recommendation for a silly little sketch she'd done in the park. So few people believed in her talent. Closing her mind to the distracting thoughts, she focused on Maggie's voice.

"I would like to meet you in person. Can you come by my studio tomorrow around two o'clock?"

Bonnie chewed on her lip, on edge about going out into traffic again. She would need to take another taxi to get there and she couldn't be sure Ralph was available. Besides, taxis cost money and Bonnie didn't know how much she would need for art school if she were accepted.

"Would you be willing to come to my hotel instead? I'm not from here, I don't know the area very well, and I'm terrible with directions."

Silence greeted her on the other end of the phone. She could hear a cigarette being lit, then the intake of breath as Maggie drew smoke into her lungs.

"Tell you what. I will send Lawrence over to pick you up."

"I guess that would be okay." She hesitated, feeling uneasy about being picked up by a stranger, but decided to take the risk for the sake of her future.

"Great. Tell me which hotel you're at and he will be there at one-thirty to bring you to my studio. Bring any samples of work you've done."

After getting a few more directions from Maggie, she hung up the phone. Bonnie threw herself face down on the bed, letting the tears of grief fall. This should be one of the happiest moments of her life, but she felt only emptiness.

* * *

A sharp knock on the door pulled Bonnie's attention back into the room. She stopped drawing the pigeon that landed outside her window and went to answer the door. Lawrence stood smiling on the other side.

"Hello."

"Hello again. Come in." Bonnie stepped aside letting him enter the room. "I'm almost ready."

Taking one last look at the bird she'd been drawing, she closed her book, unsatisfied with the way the head had turned out. On a whim, as they were walking out the door, Bonnie grabbed the sketchbook that held all the pictures of Mabel. There were also a couple of sketches in the book of Wheatonville that might impress Maggie. She thought it might seem silly, but she wanted to have a piece of Mabel with her as she tried moving forward.

Chapter 41 - 1973

"No, this is rubbish, Bonnie. Your shading isn't correct. Try again."

Bonnie took a deep breath to keep the sarcastic reply from escaping. Three months of studying at the Artist Institute and she still had yet to get through one day without being yelled at for her lack of skill or talent. Most days she wanted to toss her art supplies in the trash and walk away from art forever.

She knew she wouldn't. Not after Lawrence had gone to so much trouble on her behalf. Besides if she quit, what would she do? It's not like she had many options available. She had no family, no marketable skills, and no desire to attend a traditional college.

Bonnie had been excited about her first day of classes, but since then it had been one disaster after another. She found it difficult to translate the concepts demonstrated in the different art mediums into a recognizable form, and she was tired of being constantly criticized. She couldn't believe she ever dreamed of becoming an artist when it seemed she couldn't even draw a straight line to the instructors' satisfaction. Looking at the tall buildings she should be drawing, Bonnie's mind wandered down a familiar path.

* * *

"Let me see," Mabel said.

"Not until I finish. If you'd quit squirming, I would finish quicker." As Bonnie set her sketchpad down, she walked over to the bed where she'd posed Mabel for the last hour.

"It's not fair. You always make me stay so still. Are you done yet? My arm fell asleep twenty minutes ago."

Bonnie placed feathery kisses on Mabel's cheeks and forehead. Smiling as she felt Mabel squirm even more, she kept up the torment of sensations on her skin. Without warning, she kissed Mabel's lips, letting the sensations fill her mind. The silky feel of her lips had a way of silencing all the distractions.

As the kiss deepened, Bonnie felt Mabel's tongue seeking entry. She opened her mouth and a moan escaped as their tongues danced their exotic dance of passion against each other.

"Mm. That feels heavenly. What a way to come home from a bad day of school."

Pushing Mabel against the bedroom door, she felt her gasping for air and reluctantly released her plump lips. Her lips grazed Mabel's cheek, traveling a path down her neck and across her shoulders. She stared into Mabel's desire-filled blue orbs. The emotions this woman brought out in her never ceased to amaze Bonnie.

"I love you, Mabel," she said as she went in for another kiss.

"Bonnie, are you even listening to me? Bonnie?"

* * *

Snapping out of her delicious daydream, Bonnie's attention returned to Maggie, who was staring at her in frustration. Bonnie nodded absently at the question. She had not been listening since she knew it was yet another lecture about her incorrect technique.

"Until you learn perspective, you will never be able to draw humans."

Here they were again, sitting in the middle of a park in a futile effort drawing skyscrapers she had no interest in capturing. A smile spread across her face as she picked up her pencil, remembering who she'd been drawing in her daydreams.

Chapter 42 - 1973

"We are having a girls' night out this Friday!" Claire exclaimed. Mabel tried not to let her frustration show as she continued to weed the flower beds. She knew Claire had her best interests at heart, but she was in no mood to socialize. "Thanks for the invitation, but I'm not in the mood to go out."

"You haven't been anywhere in weeks, Mabel. Kate has been asking you to do stuff with her and it's time for you to do something besides stay at home."

"Claire—"

"Not another word. You are going out with us Friday night and that's final."

"Fine."

Later that afternoon, Mabel locked herself in her bedroom. She had no desire to put on a happy face and go out, but Claire hadn't given her a choice. It would be so much easier to do as she asked than to fight her on this. Lying on her bed staring up at the ceiling, Mabel tried not to think about the effort it would take her to make small talk all night long because she didn't feel she had anything left to say. She wondered if she would ever move past her feelings for Bonnie and not feel so sad.

Mabel's eyes caught the big white envelope from the university sitting on the desk unopened. It had come a couple days ago, but Mabel couldn't bring herself to open it yet. The response from her application was sitting there, daring her.

Mabel tried ignoring the envelope but kept sneaking sidelong glances at it. She remembered feeling the same way last year as she waited to hear from

UC Berkeley. As long as the letter remained sealed, she didn't have to think about all the dreams that had been taken from her. Once she opened the envelope she would have a choice to make—give up a job she really liked or pursue the dream she'd had since she was nine years old. *'Could I do both?'* Times were changing. Billie Jean King just defeated Bobby Riggs, showing the world what women were capable of. *'Surely, I could study the stars and keep being a supervisor.'* Tired of the tormenting thoughts, Mabel decided to take a bubble bath.

* * *

Friday night came too soon. Mabel stared at the clothes in her closet for thirty minutes without really seeing any of them. She knew Claire wouldn't let her out of the house in shorts and a t-shirt tonight. Completely frustrated, she slammed the closet door shut.

Hearing a soft knock on her door, she was surprised to see Kate standing on the other side. With a big box in her hands, she bumped Mabel out of the way to enter the room. Smiling, she heaved the box onto Mabel's bed.

"I'm guessing you're not ready because you can't find a thing to wear."

"How'd you know?"

"Here, see if this meets your standards."

Mabel opened the box and saw new clothes lying in a bed of tissue paper. She picked up a blue striped button-down blouse, the perfect size. She pushed the tissue paper farther aside, revealing a pair of navy-blue slacks that matched the shirt, along with two other outfits.

"Kate, this is too much. I can't accept all this."

"Hush now. I know you hate shopping for clothes and thought you might like these."

"I don't know what to say."

"How about thank you for starters?"

Mabel hugged her friend as she realized how much she'd missed Kate's bubbly energy and changed her mind about tonight. It would be fun to go out with Claire and Kate. Shooing her out of the bedroom, Mabel quickly got dressed. Ten minutes later she rushed downstairs where Kate waited for her in the living room, but not Claire. Kate grinned as Mack let out a wolf whistle when he saw Mabel.

"Looking great, Mabel."

"Thanks to Kate." Kate's face flushed at the compliment.

"What's thanks to Kate?" Claire asked as she entered into the room.

"My outfit for this evening's festivities."

"You do look good in that color."

"What time will you be home?" Mack said.

Claire slid him a look. "Depends on how my surprise turns out."

Chapter 43 - 1973

Bonnie still couldn't believe it. Her first art show. She'd only been studying at the institute for a few months now. As she slowly walked through the gallery, she analyzed the works of her classmates, comparing their work to hers.

'God, they're so much more talented.'

Coming around the corner of the new-student exhibit, she nearly fainted when she saw her drawings of Mabel professionally framed and hanging there for the whole world to see at tonight's opening. Bonnie quickly turned away and ran in search of Maggie in the workroom in the back of the gallery. Maggie stood talking to the gallery owner while Bonnie waited impatiently for her turn to talk to her instructor.

"Is something wrong?" Maggie said.

"How could you, Maggie? Those were never meant for public display!" Bonnie felt violated as Maggie had totally gone against her wishes and decided to show her private sketches. Maggie dragged her into the small office to the left of the workroom and shut the door.

"I know you're upset with me, but I am asking you to trust me," Maggie said.

"Trust you? How can I trust you when you pull a stunt like this? I specifically told you I didn't want these sketches displayed at this show."

Bonnie felt her emotions tighten into an angry ball of fury. She was dealing with her mother all over again, caught in a situation where her desires didn't matter. She felt helpless and betrayed by the woman who was supposed to be looking out for her best interests.

"Why? Why did you do it?" She had to know what made her mentor totally disregard her feelings.

"Because those sketches are some of your best work and you need to see how people will react to them."

Bonnie stared at her not trusting herself to speak. She was furious she wasn't being taken seriously and thought about taking all her work out of the show. Slamming the office door shut, Bonnie raced out of the building wondering why everyone seemed to think they knew what was best for her.

* * *

"Uh, Mabel. You've got to see this."

Mabel heard Kate talking to her from around the corner. Claire had suggested they go to a student art show in one of the downtown galleries after dinner. It was a small gallery with bright lights displaying a variety of sculptures, paintings, and drawings created by the students. Mabel was impressed with a few of the items on display. As she turned the corner, she saw Kate staring intently at the framed picture on the wall.

"So what has your undivided attention, my friend?" She followed Kate's finger as she pointed at the wall.

It was a charcoal drawing of a girl smelling a bouquet of flowers. Focusing more closely at the drawing, she noticed it wasn't just any girl. It was her. Tilting her head to the side to study the picture more closely, she tried to speak but nothing came out. Why would a picture of her be hanging on a wall in an art gallery in this town?

"Is that really you?" Kate asked.

A thousand thoughts raced through her mind, and her heart fluttered as she stared at six of Bonnie's sketches of her, now framed and hanging on the wall. There was only one way they could've ended up here. Bonnie had come looking for her and she was now here in California. Scanning the crowd in attendance, desperate to find her, she was disappointed she couldn't see Bonnie anywhere.

"Mabel, who drew these? They are really good," Kate said.

"I'll be right back."

Mabel hurried back through the exhibits searching everywhere for Bonnie. Where could she be? The gallery wasn't that big and most of the art students were in attendance for the event. That meant Bonnie had to be here somewhere.

"I remember how she used to complain about having to sit in one position for hours."

Racing back to the display, Mabel finally found her talking to a small group of people gathered around the drawings. Rushing forward, Mabel elbowed people out of the way until she stood in front of her, face to face with the woman she loved. Bonnie took her breath away and she was still as beautiful as she remembered. Mabel gathered her in her arms and kissed her, pressing Bonnie's soft lips against her own. She reluctantly broke off the kiss, but still held on to her embrace.

"Kate, why don't we go grab something to drink?" Claire said quietly, steering Kate away.

"I can't believe you're here," Mabel said as she leaned in to kiss Bonnie again.

Chapter 44 - 1973

Bonnie struggled to breathe. Mabel was here, at her art show, kissing her in front of all these strangers. Was she dreaming? When she'd broken off the kiss, Bonnie immediately missed the contact.

"Is it really you?" she asked.

In response, she felt Mabel's hands wrap around her head, then pull her in for a fiery and passionate kiss. Bonnie returned the kiss with fervor, ignoring the gasps of surprise from the people around her. Dizzy from the emotions stirring inside her, she stepped away from Mabel, trying to stop the spinning sensations that threatened to topple her.

"Let's get out of here," Mabel said.

Bonnie nodded and went to get her things. In the back workroom, she hurried to grab her purse and jacket, afraid Mabel might disappear again. Rushing out the door she almost knocked Maggie to the ground.

"Thank you for not listening to me. I have to go." Bonnie sprinted back into the gallery and found Mabel talking to two women by the refreshment table. One looked familiar to her, but she couldn't remember where they'd met. She watched Mabel sense her presence and turn towards her, happiness radiating from her in waves. Mabel strode toward her with confidence, took her by the hand and led her out the door into the warm summer night.

"Where to?"

"I know just the place." Bonnie slipped her arm into Mabel's as they walked down the street.

* * *

Twenty minutes later, they were seated in a booth in the back of the all-night diner Bonnie frequented. Several of the art classes were held in the evening and on weekends due to the limited availability of the faculty. Whenever Bonnie had a night class, she would usually stop by for a quick bite before heading home.

She tried her best not to stare as she sat across from Mabel, but was having a hard time believing she'd found her. Bonnie gave up all pretense and allowed her eyes to study the face that had haunted her dreams for the past several months. Mabel looked the same but different, older perhaps. No, that wasn't quite what she was seeing. It was her eyes. They lacked the normal mischievous twinkle she'd grown to love. She'd spent many hours unsuccessfully trying to catch that twinkle in her drawings.

"You are as beautiful as I remember," Mabel said as she took Bonnie's hand across the table. "I had given up hope of ever seeing you again."

Bonnie rubbed her thumb over the back of Mabel's knuckles, enjoying the feel of her skin, remembering what those hands could do to her. When the waitress approached, she jerked her hand away and put it in her lap, keeping it there until the waitress finished taking their order. Bonnie sought out Mabel's hand again, feeling her heart thumping as Mabel pulled her hand to her lips and kissed it tenderly. Bonnie fought the urge to pull away from the intimate gesture as she felt everyone in the diner staring at them. Looking away from Mabel, she saw the diner was mostly empty, and the tension she'd been holding left her body like wisps of smoke.

"Guess I'm not used to being out in public with you like this."

"Like what?"

"It's hard for me to touch you when others are around. Mabel, we had to hide our feelings for so long."

"A lot changed for us this last year."

She thought about all the promises she'd made to herself in therapy about doing things differently if she ever got a second chance with Mabel. The second chance was now sitting across from her, watching her intently. And here she was, acting ashamed of loving Mabel.

"You were right about one thing. I was a coward. Still am."

"No, you're not. You are the bravest woman I know."

Bonnie laughed at Mabel's assessment of her. Brave was not an adjective she would ever use to describe herself. That's how she would describe Mabel.

"I want to apologize for all the awful things I said that day in the car. It was my fault we were in the accident," Mabel said.

"The accident wasn't anyone's fault. The truck driver crossed the centerline. Besides, I think I'm the one who should apologize to you. I was so afraid of losing a life I didn't really want and couldn't say yes to the one I did want."

The waitress set their plates down, refilled the water glasses, and asked if they needed anything else before she went to check on the four other diners. Bonnie had a hard time swallowing her scrambled eggs around the lump in her throat. She had so many things to tell Mabel but no idea where to begin.

"How's your French toast?" she said.

"Fine."

"Really? You've hardly taken two bites."

"I'm too excited to eat. I'm having a hard time accepting you're really sitting here with me."

"I actually came looking for you a couple months ago."

"You did?"

"I went back to Wheatonville and Bobby told me you were gone. I begged him to give me your address. It took me a week to work up the courage to look you up. When I did, the woman who answered the door said you didn't live there, so I thought you'd moved on without me."

"What was the address he gave you?"

"2137 North Sterling Avenue."

"That's my address."

"But the woman said Mabel Flanigan didn't live there."

"That's because Mabel Flanigan doesn't exist anymore. I changed my name to keep my dad from finding me, but it didn't work."

"Your dad found you here?"

"It's a long story. Do you know a place we can talk?"

* * *

Thirty minutes later, a taxi pulled into the driveway of a small cottage with a bay window and wraparound porch. Half a dozen saplings dotted across the large front lawn. Bonnie watched as Mabel exited the cab, then stood looking around while she paid the fare.

"Is this your house?" Mabel asked when the taxi left.

"Yep," Bonnie said as she unlocked the front door. Leading them inside, she set her purse on the small oak table by the entryway, then headed to the kitchen.

"Would you like a cup of tea?" she asked, leaning against the door jamb. She watched Mabel taking in the decorations of her house. Bonnie had never thought of this place as home. To her, Mabel was home. Her eyes widened as Mabel picked up the delicate snow globe.

"You kept this?"

"Of course. You won that for me at the carnival after our first summer together. That night is one of my favorite memories of you."

"I remember Jay and Oscar kept bugging us to ride the Ferris wheel with them, but I wanted to win this for you. I saw the way your eyes lit up when you spotted it as one of the prizes."

"I was surprised how quickly you won it. I never knew you had such good aim." Bonnie smiled as she watched Mabel carefully set it back on the shelf. The kettle whistled and she told Mabel to make herself comfortable. She poured the hot water into two mismatched mugs, watching as the tea bags turned the water brown and she tried to gather her scattered thoughts. Mabel was here and now Bonnie had to tell her the truth.

"Here we go," she said handing Mabel her cup. "I have sugar, lemon, honey, or milk if you like."

"No, this is fine. Thank you." Mabel blew on the hot liquid before taking a small sip, then rested the cup on her knee.

"It's not too hot, is it?"

"No, it's good."

Before Bonnie sat in the threadbare recliner, she set a coaster on the coffee table in front of Mabel as she took another sip. She smiled as she watched her trying to find a comfortable way to sit on the lumpy couch. It was a bargain she'd picked up in a neighborhood garage sale, and had only taken a couple of days to figure out why the couch had been so cheap.

The silence stretched between them, each lost in her own thoughts, not wanting to be the first to speak. Bonnie set her mug of tea on a coaster. *'It's now or never.'*

"I'm flunking out of art school."

"But . . . the drawings I saw. They were good."

"Mabel, most of those drawings are crap. The only good ones were the ones of you. All my instructors say I lack passion in my work. Everything I've drawn since I began taking classes is dull and boring lines on a page. One day I accidentally handed one of my old sketchbooks that Bobby gave me to my instructor. She wanted to know who the beautiful woman was in the sketches and why I couldn't draw like that now."

"I'm glad Bobby saved them for you. I told him to give them to you if you ever came looking for me."

"If it wasn't for you, I wouldn't have any of my old sketches. When I was in the hospital, my mom found them and burned them."

"Why?"

Over the next hour, while holding Mabel's hands in hers, Bonnie told Mabel about Danielle, why they had really moved to Wheatonville, and how her parents blackmailed her into marrying Charles. She told her how her parents took her to Chicago for rehabilitation from the accident, but it was really to break all ties she had with her friends. She told her about the attorney's letter and how she went to see him on her own.

"When they told me how much money I was due, it gave me new hope. I knew I would use the money to find you, even if I had to spend every last penny to do it. When my parents found out I was going to look for you, they disowned me."

"I'm so sorry about that."

"I'm not. I was so excited thinking I'd finally found you, then so heartbroken when you weren't there. It took me a week to get out of bed, I was so devastated. I knew I didn't have a home to go back to, so I decided to stay here and try to make a life without you."

She shared how she'd met Lawrence in the park and how he helped her get into art school where she'd been struggling to keep up in her classes. She told Mabel the drawings she saw of herself weren't even supposed to be a part of tonight's art show.

"I'm glad Maggie didn't listen to me."

"So am I."

Mabel left the couch and knelt in front of Bonnie, putting her head in her lap. Bonnie ran her fingers through the short, golden tresses, loving the silky feeling caressing her fingers.

"Suppose it's my turn now."

Mabel moved until she was sitting between Bonnie's legs with her back against the recliner. Bonnie lightly massaged her scalp and patiently waited for Mabel to begin.

"I'm not sure how much you know, but I was in a coma for a couple of months from the accident. When I woke up, I'd lost all my memories from the past year. My dad had me committed to a mental institution because he suspected I was a lesbian. Apparently, he found one of your sketches in my room. Thank goodness he didn't find all of them. The place was called Pleasant Meadows and was anything but pleasant."

She told Bonnie about Dr. Gilbert, the patients and staff at Pleasant Meadows, and the conversion therapy treatment she was supposed to have. She shared her fear of almost being discovered before she and Sammie could escape and how she was able to say goodbye to Bobby before leaving for California. She told her about the Chapmans and how they helped her to build a new life here.

"Then everything was almost taken away from me."

"How?"

"The man I thought was my father showed up with Dr. Gilbert at Claire's house. They brought commitment papers to take me back to Illinois. Dr. Gilbert tried to convince them he was my fiancé."

"What happened?"

Mabel told Bonnie about her mother's letter and how she was finally able to stand up to Robert Flanigan, the awful man she'd always been told was her biological father. She shared that Nurse Duncan was actually an undercover cop working to expose the fraud Dr. Gilbert and her father were committing.

"That bastard will never touch me again. I hope he rots in jail until his dying breath."

Bonnie wasn't surprised by the vehemence in Mabel's words. She'd seen firsthand the abuse Robert Flanigan had inflicted on her. It was good he was in prison where he couldn't hurt her anymore.

"My memories came back all of a sudden the day after his arrest. I felt terrible for all the nasty things I said to you that day, hoping I'd have the chance to apologize."

"I'm sorry, too."

Mabel stood up and pulled Bonnie into her arms. She felt soft, velvety lips placing tender kisses on her cheeks and neck. When Mabel's lips found their way to her mouth, Bonnie's knees wobbled, and they almost fell to the floor. The recliner broke their fall and they collapsed in a heap on top of one another.

"Stay with me tonight," Bonnie said.

Chapter 45 - 1973

The smell of bacon drifted up to Mabel's nose. Waking from a deep sleep, she couldn't remember the last time she'd slept all the way through the night without any nightmares. Stretching her cramped limbs, she listened as the birds sang songs of welcome to the new day.

The familiar scent of perfume, faint on the sheets covering her, stirred her memory of the night before. After talking with Bonnie, her world suddenly tilted the right way. She'd been broken into a million pieces, but something extraordinary had breathed life into her again. The scent of lilacs drifted up through the open window and she inhaled their sweet fragrance.

She brushed her fingers across her lips, remembering the kisses they'd shared before climbing the stairs to the bedroom. Mabel had wanted to make love, but Bonnie had stopped her.

"I have hundreds of scars all over my body now from my accident. I remember how you used to love to touch me and have worried for months whether you would still want to, if you would still find me beautiful when you saw my scars. I could never love anyone the way I love you, Mabel. I decided weeks ago if we couldn't be together, your happiness was all that mattered to me. I thought you had moved on and to me that meant you were happy."

Mabel had taken her time touching and kissing each scar. She'd given extra loving attention on the long, ragged scar running from her ribcage to her hip bone. She wanted Bonnie to feel the love she'd carried in her heart for her for the past year.

Mabel sat up and looked around the unfamiliar room. Rubbing her eyes to clear the sleep still left in them, she stared in disbelief at the opposite wall. A mural of lilacs covered the wall in many shades of purple. It had to have taken Bonnie several hours to paint this wall. She noticed a face among the lilacs, a face she was accustomed to seeing every day in the bathroom mirror at Claire's house.

Bonnie had used her bedroom wall as a giant canvas and painted Mabel surrounded by thousands of lilacs in various stages of bloom. It was strange seeing her own face staring back at her among all the flowers. She felt awe, just like she did any time she witnessed something Bonnie had created. She was totally mesmerized by the display and didn't hear Bonnie enter the room.

"Oh good, you're up. I was just coming to wake you."

Mabel mumbled something unintelligible in response. She couldn't draw her attention away from the mural.

"Are you hungry?"

Right on cue, Mabel's stomach growled, breaking the spell of the mural. They both laughed as Bonnie set the tray she'd been carrying down by Mabel's left side, then crawled back into bed with her.

"I thought you might be a little hungry this morning."

"This smells good. I didn't know you could cook."

Mabel grabbed a strip of bacon and took a bite. She tore her eyes away from the painting to look at the woman next to her, watching her closely.

"When did you do that?" she asked, pointing at the wall with a piece of bacon.

"I started it two weeks after I bought this house. I never told my parents about the insurance settlement since they disowned me. I finished it last month. This way you would always be with me."

"I'm glad some good was able to come from the accident."

"I almost fainted when I saw all those zeroes on the check. Mabel, nothing but good has come to me since then." She reached out and touched Mabel's arm.

"You almost lost your leg and you could've died."

"But I didn't. *We* didn't."

She allowed herself to fall into Bonnie's arms, her own arms tightening around Bonnie of their own accord. In an instant she knew she'd loved her since the moment she waltzed through those gymnasium doors.

Despite everything her dad had done to try changing her, he had failed. His efforts to keep her from Bonnie only succeeded in making her love her more. She clung to Bonnie as if she were holding life itself in her arms. Bonnie ran her fingers through her hair, eliciting a shiver as Mabel felt the loving kiss land on her forehead.

Mabel turned to the mural one more time. This time she saw it with new eyes. She saw the love that was captured in the beautiful design. Bonnie had not forgotten her. She fought with everything she had to come back to her. Mabel had never felt more loved than she did in this moment and pulled Bonnie into a tender kiss.

The kiss quickly turned passionate as they let love heal the wounds of the past. Mabel broke off the kiss and wrapped her body around Bonnie. She let the memories of the last three years wash over her. Smiling as she felt Bonnie's strong fingers caress her skin, Mabel knew she'd found her way home. Whatever plans life had for the two of them no longer mattered. They had each other now, and that was all they would ever need.

Taking one last look at the painting, Mabel finally saw herself as Bonnie saw her. She was a beautiful woman. She was loveable. Mabel was the inspiration for Bonnie. Bonnie was the courage for Mabel. Snuggling deeper into her arms, Mabel said a prayer of thanks for Bonnie as she fell back asleep, dreaming of dancing on the clouds with the woman in her arms.

Acknowledgments

I like to thank all the people who made this dream come true. Michelle thank you for loving and supporting me through all the ups and downs of this journey. I want to thank all the little people who were sure I would forget them. How could I forget you? Without you this book wouldn't be a reality.

About the Author

Frances McCoy is a new author who loves telling stories around paths not taken. She draws from her experience growing up in the heartland during a time when the paths for women were limited. She keeps busy training project managers in accelerated learning techniques so they can obtain their professional certification. When she isn't busy writing or working, she spends time by the pool hanging out with her dogs or exploring new paths to take.

Connect with Frances

www.francesmccoy.com

9 781732 480841